SINCE *we're here*

CHRISSY HOPEWELL

ALSO BY CHRISSY HOPEWELL

If We Pretend

Unless It's You

One Hundred Lights (novella)

Sign up to Chrissy's newsletter for extra content, including free novella *One Hundred Lights* and bonus scenes for every book.

www.ChrissyHopewell.com

Content Note: *Since We're Here* is a contemporary romance novel meant for mature readers. It includes swearing and explicit sexual encounters between enthusiastically consenting adults.

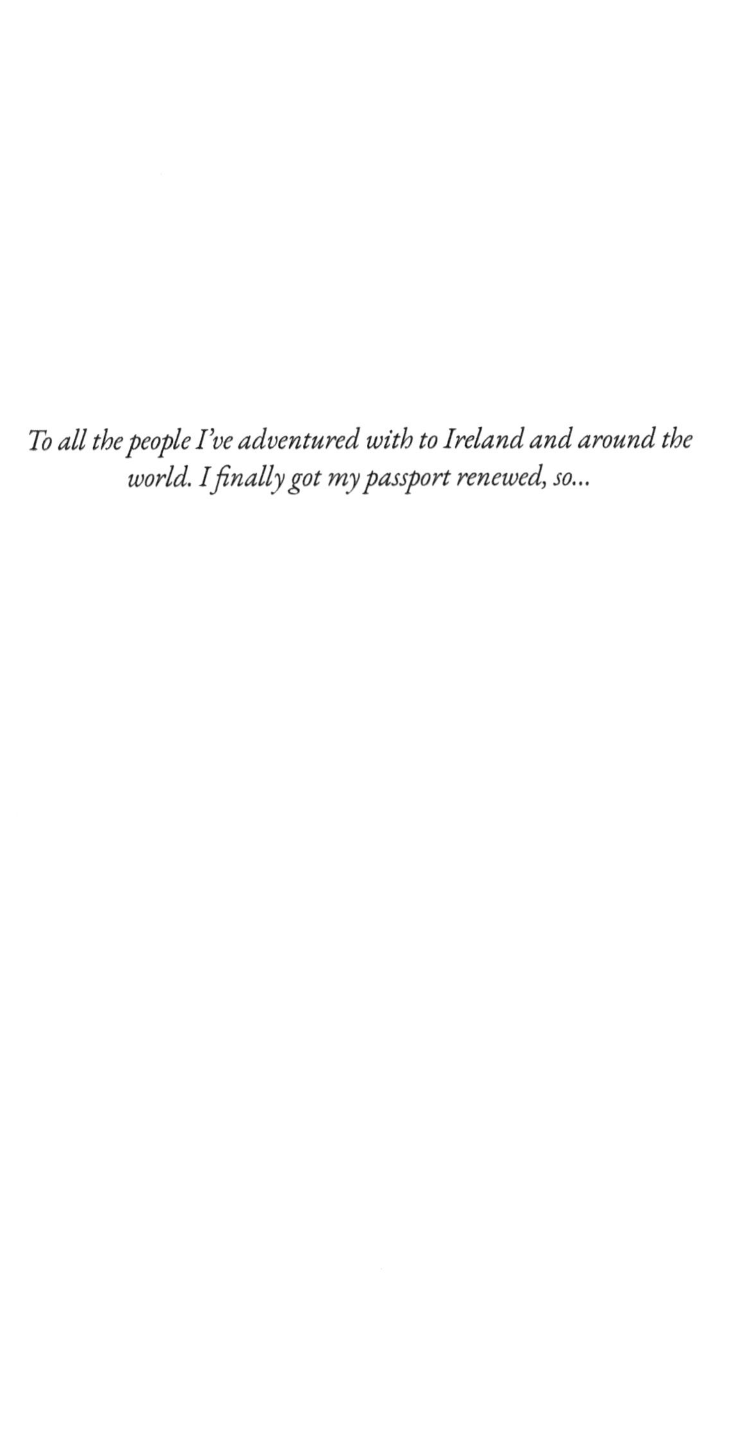

To all the people I've adventured with to Ireland and around the world. I finally got my passport renewed, so...

1

MADDIE

Friday, February 28

Ten jobs. Ten men who—together with my own dreadful decision-making—have led me to this depressing moment in rainy Ireland.

Boyfriend Disaster #1: Jonathan the Sketchy Line Cook
Job Location & Length: Chili's, 1 year
My Age: 20

After dropping out of college, I decided to waitress while I figured my life out. Jonathan was a line cook. He wore t-shirts that declared edgy bands like The Killers and Snow Patrol. He was thirty, an entire decade older than me, and I thought it was so cool that I could attract a real man.
In hindsight, it was a big fucking red flag.
He groped my ass in the dingy breakroom that crunched with chip crumbs on every surface, and after having extremely fast (on his part) and extremely lackluster (on

mine) sex with him in a car that smelled like fajitas, I quit with no notice.

Breakup Reason: bad sex, inappropriate age gap
My Distress Level (*on a scale of 1-10*): 1
Lesson Learned: There's absolutely no reason for a thirty-year-old man to be hitting on a woman barely in her twenties.

———

MY OVERSIZED SUITCASE bounces along the narrow cobblestone sidewalk in Dingle, and I shiver in my rose-pink puffy jacket and mid-thigh sundress amidst the darkening gray winter sky. Severely underdressed and underprepared.

I blame Aunt Evelyn for my situation, at least partially. Our late great-aunt used her twisted sense of humor to send me and my sisters each on a crazy bucket list journey last year, which is part of the reason I'm in Ireland now. In a very roundabout way.

Go on a vacation. Volunteer. Help your sisters. Change your life. Aunt Evelyn said all these things in her will.

My sisters seemed to have no problem with their lists—everything's worked out perfectly for both of them. Stella fell in love with her ex-boyfriend's best friend in London. Reese started her own website design business in New Jersey after fake dating her daughter's Scottish soccer coach.

But me? I seemed to mess up my life even further, not make it better. And somehow in the process, I volunteered to plan Reese and her fiancé's combined bachelorette and bachelor party. A twelve-day-long Irish road trip.

There's a guy I need to find in Dingle—Reese's fiancé's Irish best friend—who is supposed to be helping me plan but hasn't returned my emails. I think it's reasonable that I now escalate the situation and show up at his doorstep.

In Ireland.

Not that I know where his doorstep is.

Or have his phone number.

This is probably not what my great-aunt had in mind.

I moan and shift the backpack on my shoulders. I'm achy and exhausted. And freaking freezing. Admittedly, the picture my brief research painted of Ireland at the end of February was about as far as possible from what I'd originally planned—a trip to visit my (now ex) boyfriend in Saint Lucia, disguised as an internship for my hospitality program.

I'm filled with rage at the thought of that cheating asshole, and the anger warms me just a tad. I should've left it as a holiday fling, like Reese had begged me to, instead of falling head over heels, like I always do.

I stop on the sidewalk to glance at my phone screen. There are no new texts from the estate agent who rented me an apartment— I guess I should say *flat*—for the month. I continue to follow her earlier directions from the bus station, wishing I had on jeans and a chunky sweatshirt.

But when I left New Jersey yesterday morning, dressing like that felt like giving up. So I shoved the pile of sundresses meant for an island vacation into my suitcase and slipped on a green flowy one for the flight over.

The estate agent seemed doubtful I'd make it to Dingle by evening, and after the journey I just took, I understand why. I flew overnight from Newark to Dublin, then lugged my giant suitcase onto a bus from the airport to Dublin Heuston train station. I thought maybe it'd be smooth sailing from there, as the four-hour train ride through the Irish countryside was delightful, showing off rolling green hills, small towns in the distance, and a whole lot of sheep peppered throughout.

But no. It wasn't smooth sailing.

I arrived in a tiny town called Killarney and had to wait around to catch the bus for a three-hour ride to Dingle. Including a transfer. My stalwart cheery facade crumbled somewhere in Tralee, the town where I switched buses.

Pausing before a bend in the road, I roll my neck. I need a bed, or a drink, or a massage. Ideally all three. But as miserable as the weather is, Dingle has a small-town charm, with colorful store-fronts, narrow cobblestone streets, and well-kept signs. If I was wearing pants, maybe I'd be enjoying myself. Or if a feeling akin to regret for making the choice to come to Ireland wasn't gripping my insides.

Spontaneous is the nice word for it. *Impulsive* is the negative one.

A scattering of people wanders up and down the street. It's a Friday night, after all.

My phone finally vibrates in my hand.

NOREEN

I'm here, just outside the pub. Flat is next door.
Follow the sound of music!

Thank god. I turn the corner and she's about ten doors down, waiting under a red, well-lit awning with upbeat Irish music drifting onto the sidewalk from inside.

She walks a few steps toward me, and within a minute I've stopped in front of a broadly smiling woman who is probably around my age, so early thirties. She's got her curly brown hair in a messy bun and is dressed in warm-looking jeans, a v-neck sweater, an unzipped lined jacket, and a wool hat clutched in her hand. She looks worlds warmer than me.

"You must be Madison."

I nod. "Maddie, please."

"I'm Noreen. Lord almighty, you must be freezing!" She looks me up and down, her eyes lingering on my bare knees showing between knee-high black boots and the hem of my dress.

"I'm okay. I'm happy to finally be here." I shrug and smile. So what if I can't feel my thighs?

Even frigid and wet, this remote Irish town is the perfect place for me to hide out and get my shit together. During this little life interlude, I'll show my sisters that I can plan an epic road trip. Then I'll go home and start over.

"The flat is right here." Noreen gestures next door to the pub entrance.

The Irish skies open and dump buckets of cold rain on us. I groan and a violent shiver shakes my body. Noreen pulls her hood up and waves for me to follow her.

"Jaysus. Let's get inside the flat and warm up." She unlocks the door that opens to a small entry area, just big enough for a bike, leading to a steep set of stairs. Noreen doesn't hesitate before trotting up in her sensible lined boots, and I struggle to follow, dragging my suitcase behind me.

There's another door at the top of the stairway. Noreen unlocks it with a different key and pushes it open to a dark room, which illuminates when she flicks a switch.

"You're the first tenant since the owner moved out. It's a wonderful flat. Two bedrooms, although one is quite tiny. Just store your suitcase there. I made up the bigger room for you."

I slowly spin around the flat. It's warm and cozy.

"There's another locked entrance over there." Noreen gestures to a door off the living room. A wooden carving in the shape of Ireland is on the wall next to it. "That door goes to the pub, but it's locked. Just use the main entrance."

I nod.

Could I have just kept the airline credit when I canceled my flight to Saint Lucia? Yup, sure could've. But I was desperate to get out of New Jersey. Out of my sister's house. Away from reminders of my bad decision-making. Planning the Irish road trip will be far easier to do while in Ireland. I'm gonna make it special, not just use some cut-and-paste itinerary.

But I need more than a quick break. More than to plan a road trip. I need to reprogram myself. Learn from all my failures.

Impulsively flying to Ireland is just like me—the old me. I didn't tell Reese that it ended with my ex, Blue. She tried so hard to convince me that what happened with him in Saint Lucia was a holiday fling and that I should move on. We had literal screaming matches about it.

She was right.

I've been disappointing Reese since I was twelve years old. Another item for the list: dropping out of my hospitality program before coming to Ireland. I only started it because Aunt Evelyn told me in the bucket list to go change my life, and that's what I came up with. Getting away from restaurants and into something else.

But turns out, I hated the program.

Stella, my other sister, wouldn't be as judgmental about it . . . but she is so successful and bold and confident, I feel like a meek little mouse compared to her.

"What are you up to in town this month?" Noreen tilts her head.

"Oh, ah . . ." I consider what to admit. Because telling her I'm here to find the random Irish guy who's supposed to be helping me plan a road trip sounds unhinged.

Patrick McNulty is Reese's fiancé's best friend and former professional soccer teammate. He was a goalkeeper, apparently, not that it's important what position he played. Reese promised he'd help me but, save a curt answer from my first email in January, he hasn't responded.

"I'm meeting an old friend."

"An old friend?" Noreen raises her eyebrows. "Here in Dingle? Who?"

"I mean, it's a friend of a friend. I need to look up their name." I glance at the door to try to dismiss her before she can ask any follow-up questions.

"Lovely," she says, but looks confused. "Anyway, I bought you some bread and butter so you don't starve. If you need coffee in the morning, Dingle Brew is just a few doors down." She turns to leave, then looks back at me. "If you're up for it, come on down to O'Brien's. Tourists aren't around yet, so it's not so crowded. You could get a pint and listen to some live music."

"Thanks. That, uh, sounds great." I nod and she drops the keys on the coffee table before disappearing down the stairs.

"Okay," I say to the empty apartment when the door clicks shut. Apartment, flat, whatever. I collapse on the couch, jacket still on, and lean forward, elbows on my knees.

What do I do now? Go to sleep? Get that drink? Cry into a pillow?

I fish out my phone and slide it next to the keys. The sturdy, thick wooden coffee table is really nice—a nonsymmetrical oval shape with dark swirls of wood under the finished surface. I glance around the room. The kitchen wall showcases three artsy sheep photos. They all have varied solid color backgrounds, like the old elementary school pictures I have a stack of somewhere. One sheep is against a gray background, posing with its head tilted. Another is a sideview of a sheep looking over its shoulder —yup that's possible—against a bright green background. The third is against blue and is a sheep butt. Seriously. The butt of a sheep.

Above the couch behind me, there's a striking photograph of an entire flock of sheep blocking a narrow road between two rolling hills. Looks dangerous.

A sheep-themed flat? Not sure the description I read offered that detail, but it's charming.

I drag my suitcase down the hall to the bigger of the two bedrooms. I pause in the doorway. Unsurprisingly, there's a large, framed watercolor of a sheep above the bed. I snort.

The bed has a proper fluffy duvet, and I consider diving into the soft comforter and dealing with everything else tomorrow. But I'm not going to sleep at seven o'clock in the evening on my first night in Ireland. Besides, I can hear the music from the pub drifting up through the floorboards. This room must be directly on top of the bar.

I unzip my suitcase and strip off the clothes and boots I traveled in, choosing another short dress (this one with long sleeves, at least) and my favorite gray thigh-high boots. Much warmer. After running a brush through my too-long, tangled hair and slapping on some fresh eyeliner and a generous amount of blush, I don't look awful.

I shove the keys to the flat—there's a sheep keychain that says *I KNOW YOU HERD ME* so I'm sure not to lose it—my wallet, and my phone in a small purse and practically bound down the stairs with a second wind, finally not weighed down by luggage. Or my jacket, given the pub is literally a twenty-second walk away.

I hesitate for just a second under the bright red awning, O'Brien's written in swooping Celtic letters on the matching red building. I'm freezing my ass off, not to mention my legs, and cheeks (both sets), and neck, and entire body.

Jumping nerves flit around in my belly like tiny green grasshoppers. I'm starving, but I could've eaten buttered bread upstairs. And honestly, I'm so exhausted, I probably should've cranked up my white noise app and collapsed on that cozy bed.

"Alright, love?" An older gentleman is standing behind me. "Go on. I'm freezing my arse out here."

"Same. Sorry." I pull the heavy wooden door open, and my senses are overwhelmed by the scene in front of me.

To the right of the door there's a band playing upbeat Irish folk music on a small stage. A man with a fiddle, another with a guitar, an accordion player, and a woman with a flute are bouncing up and down as they play. Luckily, the music drowns out the small talk the older man is trying to make with me, and after a few seconds, he gives up and heads to the bar.

Round tables are scattered throughout the room, filled with people drinking and talking. Where should I sit? What am I doing here? Where is Noreen?

But then I meet the gaze of the bartender.

And he is smoking hot.

Tall, broad shoulders, thick dark hair a striking contrast to his pale skin, a shadow of a beard, and intense eyes which lock on mine like a vice. He's wearing a black t-shirt that's tight around his thick biceps, O'Brien's in large white writing across the front. Heat floods my cheeks and I know I should look away, but just cannot.

With no acknowledgment, the bartender turns his attention to the older man in front of him, the one who practically pushed me through the doorway. The doorway, where I'm still standing, probably looking like a lost puppy.

A newly familiar voice shouts my name.

Noreen waves me over to where she's sitting with a pair of guys. She gestures to the empty chair across from her, and I head her way, relief washing over me.

"You made it!" Noreen smiles broadly. "Sit! I got you a pint, just in case."

"Thank you. I think I fell asleep on my feet for a second by the door." It had nothing to do with the incredibly hot bartender, who I sneak another look at now. I was hoping he'd be staring longingly at me, but he's doing his job serving drinks. I slide into the seat and take a deep swig of the amber beer. The liquid warms me from my mouth to my belly and I sigh contentedly.

"I'm Gray," one guy says. He has red hair and green eyes, but only briefly glances at me, then returns his gaze to Noreen, linking his hand with hers on the table.

"And I'm Liam," the other man says. "What do you think of the beer?"

Noreen rolls her eyes. "Yeah, yeah, that's his family's brewery, so please act impressed."

I chuckle and smile at the good-looking brown-haired, blue-eyed man fake scowling at her.

"It's delicious."

He makes an exaggerated victory pump with his fist.

"What is it?"

"New Dingle Brewing Amber Ale." Liam runs a hand through his floppy hair, pushing it off his forehead.

"I'm not sure why you're so surprised she likes it. Everyone drinks New Dingle." Noreen presses her lips together, a smile hiding behind them.

"Did you know the brewery is now on a tour bus stop?" Liam asks earnestly, looking between me and Noreen.

Noreen groans and Gray laughs.

"Yes, everyone knows that, too. Mostly because you tell anyone who will listen," Gray says.

"I'm gonna go get a flight so she can try the rest." Liam grins widely and stands.

"That's unnecessary, really." But I'm smiling, because his enthusiasm is contagious.

"My god, you're obsessed with yourself." Noreen shakes her head.

"I'm committed to my business, you mean?"

The table laughs, but Noreen nods to me. "Are you hungry after your long journey? Do you want a cheese toastie?"

"Oh, no, well, I mean, I am ravenous, actually. But I can get something myself."

"I'll get it. I insist." Liam's gaze remains on my face a beat longer than necessary.

Maybe this impulsive trip to Ireland was one of the best ideas I've ever had.

Maybe it's just the thing to allow me to escape the judgmental voices of my sisters.

I don't want to get involved with anyone. Not for real, anyway. No more falling in love, getting in over my head, and ruining my life.

The Blue drama was the final straw.

But a little fun in Ireland might be just what I need.

2

PATRICK

The gorgeous woman in an inappropriate sundress goes to sit at Liam Smith's table. That fecking eejit. In my pub, ordering his own family's beer. Isn't that tacky? Come on. Sure, New Dingle is one of my biggest selling beers, which annoys the hell out of me. As does my parents' positive relationship with the Smith family, who run New Dingle. In my opinion, Mam and Dad shouldn't fraternize with the local rival to Slea Head Brewery, the business they started over three decades ago.

There are other reasons to stay away from the Smiths, but I won't think about *her* right now.

Dad's stroke last autumn was terrifying, and we're lucky he's doing well these days. It was the motivation my parents needed to let me take over our family's brewery—in addition to running my pub—so they can slow down.

Unlike New Dingle Brewing under Liam's leadership, Slea Head Brewery hasn't kept up with the trends in brewing. That's going to change now that I'm in charge. But it might take a while, especially with a head brewer stuck in the way we did things thirty years ago.

I was there back then, too.

I spent my childhood on the brew floor, tagging along with my father on sales visits to local pubs, curled up in a corner of the brewery office with toys or eventually a book or homework. Summer meant helping with the brewing process from end-to-end until soccer took over my life.

Slea Head Brewery is part of who I am. So is Dingle.

And that woman is definitely not from around here. I pull the tap handle and let Guinness flow into a pint glass, careful to keep the foam low until I get to the top. It's before tourist season, so I know ninety percent of the people who walk in that door. I slide the full pint next to another one and accept a credit card from the patron.

That new woman's wearing a short dress. In Ireland. In February. With no jacket, no hat, and tall boots that revealed a strip of her thighs when the wind from the chilly evening blew in with her.

I swipe the customer's card on the iPad and half listen to the next person order a pair of New Dingle Amber Ale pints.

She has to be a tourist, which means she might be my perfect next one-night stand. It's been six long months since the last one. Tourists are my best option: no commitment, no second date, no awkward conversations in the light of day. They have a quick night with an Irishman and then move on with their lives. I don't have to worry about saying the wrong thing or see that bewildered look on their faces as they try to figure out if I'm being sarcastic, or an arsehole, or both.

Relationships just don't work for me. I tried with Cara, Liam's older sister and my fiancée. For seven years. *Feck. I'm thinking about her.* That ended after I retired from soccer and followed Cara to Dublin. It was a disaster.

As soon as Cara and I broke up, Liam became my nemesis instead of a mate.

Because even though she's the one who cheated on me, I know it was my fault. I ruin all my relationships.

Which is probably why my parents never seem to take my side against that family.

I have three goals: get Slea Head beers distributed in behemoth Irish pub chain Wellington Pubs, help my sister Saoirse with my nieces, and be there for Mam and Dad. That's it.

Women who aren't my sister or my mother or my nieces don't fit in those priorities. At least, not for more than a night.

Liam leans in and says something to make the woman laugh, then he stands and heads this way. Maybe she's not a tourist. Walking in alone and sitting with locals doesn't exactly point in that direction.

"Two flights of New Dingle. And a cheese toastie." Liam frowns, waiting for me to serve him.

I don't respond verbally, just prepare the popular flights. Not only do I carry New Dingle's five-brew lineup, I've got them all on tap. I've been carefully watching which beers sell the best since I returned to Dingle and bought O'Brien's—and the flat above it—five years ago. I'd always wanted to take over Slea Head. And now that the brewery is mine, I want our own five-beer flight by autumn. That means adding two more: an IPA and an autumn brew.

"Playing tomorrow?" I ask as I fill the final small flight glass.

"Yeah. You know I am."

"Good luck." Is it fair that, as an ex-professional goalkeeper, I'm on one of the town's soccer teams? Probably not. But it feels damn good when we play against Liam and he fails miserably at scoring against me.

Liam examines my face. He used to be able to tell if I was being sarcastic, serious, or just plain awkward, but not anymore.

"Piss off." Liam walks back toward the table.

"Don't forget the toastie," I call, satisfied that I annoyed him.

But the feeling disappears when I watch the tourist smile at his approach.

O'BRIEN'S GETS CROWDED, and I'm not able to keep an eye on the cute woman, not until she shows up right in front of me at the bar, arms crossed loosely, a relaxed look on her face.

She's even more gorgeous close up. Her dark hair is long and wild, her cheeks pink from the alcohol, and her eyes a deep chocolate brown, like the color of a fresh Guinness.

"What can I get you?" I lean my hands on the bar.

"A water would be best at this point." She gives me an easy smile.

"You're American." I state the most obvious thing ever. It's amazing I get women, given how bad I am at flirting.

"Yes. I arrived in Ireland today." Her hair falls in a long curtain next to her cheek.

I curse myself for letting Noreen talk me into renting out the flat. I've had my cottage for almost a year now, but I've been fixing it up, and it's been useful to also have the flat for nights I work late or have a few drinks. Or have someone to take back there. But I'm in my cottage full-time now, so it didn't make sense to leave it empty.

I've never taken a woman back to my cottage. It's too personal. Not with the room decorated for my nieces when they come for a sleepover, my work-in-progress furniture that's been on hold since taking over the brewery, and my pet sheep. It doesn't feel right for a one-night stand.

"What are you in town for?" I fill a small glass with water.

She blinks at me and accepts the water, chugging the entire glass and keeping her eyes locked with mine. She breathes out deeply when she's done.

"Actually, can I also get a pint?"

"What would you like?" I expect she'll ask for a pint of New Dingle, maybe the IPA that even I admit is excellent.

"What do you recommend?" She leans forward over the bar,

resting her elbows on the counter and unintentionally giving me a generous view of the valley between her breasts.

"Do you like dark beer?"

She shakes her head. "Amber ales are my favorite. And IPAs."

I lean closer to her again and there's a stirring inside of me at the sight of her plump pink lips and the smooth skin of her neck, leading to the swooping neckline of her dress. I impulsively reach out and tuck a thick strand of hair behind her ear, sparks shooting up my fingers when I make contact with her skin.

She breathes in sharply, her nostrils flaring. But she doesn't pull away.

What is wrong with me? Who reaches out to touch someone like that? Me. Awkward-as-feck me.

I clear my throat and lean back. "How about a Golden Amber, Slea Head's amber ale? It's similar to the New Dingle Amber Ale that was in the flight, but better, in my opinion." I leave out the part that I'm the one who runs Slea Head Brewery, because that would sound like I'm trying to impress her. I've weirded her out enough for one night.

"If you recommend it, sure."

There are a few regulars waiting patiently behind her, but I take my time pouring the ale from the tap.

"You passing through town? Backpacking around Ireland?"

She laughs. "Definitely not a backpacker. You won't catch me at a hostel."

"Where are you staying?" The question slips out before I can stop it. I've definitely moved into creepy territory, but I'm just trying to make small talk.

"So many questions." She tilts her head and I'm surprised she doesn't turn around and run.

I push the full pint over and hold her gaze as she sips the top two inches from the glass.

"This *is* good. Thanks for the recommendation."

I take an order from another customer, but when I turn back

from the refrigerator with two bottles, she's gone, and there's some cash left on the bar. She's not back at the table with Liam, either.

"We need a bottle of Merlot," calls the other bartender, Declan.

"I'll get it."

"And a Chardonnay."

"On it." I wipe my hands on my jeans and head down the dim hallway next to the bar which leads to the small pub office, restrooms, and two other doors. One goes to the basement storage room, and one to my old flat, a locked door here and at the top of the stairs leading into the living area. It used to be super convenient.

And right next to that door stands the American tourist, leaning against the wall and staring down at her mobile. She doesn't see me but runs her hand around the back of her neck, rolling her head around and pulling a heap of hair over her shoulder.

I approach her, because how can I not?

"Lost?"

She glances up, and for a second I catch a sad expression on her face.

"Oh, hey." It's replaced with a bright smile. "The bartender."

I stop about a meter from her. "You okay?"

"If you must know, I'm jet-lagged, exhausted, and kinda tipsy." She pushes back from the wall, sliding her mobile into a hidden pocket in her dress.

"And kinda cold, maybe?" My eyes flick to her bare thighs, lingering for a second too long.

She huffs a laugh, and when I meet her gaze again, her cheeks are pink.

Feck. Don't be creepy.

"A bit. I was supposed to be on a warm island, not Ireland. Also an island. But not the same."

"Is that why you're wearing . . . that?" I gesture to her sundress.

She blinks at me. *Uh-oh.* I play back what I said and yeah, even I hear that it sounds offensive.

"That came out wrong. It's a nice dress, but not for winter."

She breathes out. "Yeah. I have some regrets on the wardrobe I packed. And . . ." She rubs the back of her neck again. "Since you're a total stranger, I can be honest. I'm kinda wondering what the hell I'm doing here."

"In this pub? Or in Dingle?"

"Yes, all of that, but also in Ireland."

"Well, if you thought you were heading to an island with sunshine and warm beaches, I can see your confusion."

The bright smile on her face fades.

"What *are* you doing here?" I take a step closer, towering over her. My height was key in my successful goalkeeper career.

She tilts her head up to mine and swallows. I follow the length of her throat.

"You're, like, incredibly hot," she says.

I laugh, which is not something I do all the time. Her eyes widen.

"Did I say that out loud?" She bites her bottom lip.

"You did."

"Fuck. I told you I'm drunk."

"If it makes you feel better, I say inappropriate things out loud all the time."

And sometimes I can't even tell until people give me offended looks. But why am I saying that to this girl? She'll have figured it out on her own by now, even though she's smiling at me.

"I'm also getting over someone, so struggling a little with that."

I raise my eyebrows and wait for her to continue. She bites her lip and takes a deep breath.

"What would really help, like, distract me, is to kiss someone else."

Like the traitor it is, my cock twitches. I know in the head on my shoulders I shouldn't play along with this, but the head pushing against my jeans highly disagrees.

"The Irish are a hospitable people." My voice is low and my hands tingle with the need to touch her.

"How hospitable?"

"If it'd help you . . . how can I say no?"

"It would." She licks her lips, and with that movement of her tongue, I lose the battle to be good.

I slide my hands on either side of her jaw and lower my lips to hers. They are soft and sweet, and she tastes like peppermint gum. Desire shoots through my whole body and I can't help but gently press myself against her.

She moans softly and slides her hands around my waist, leaning into our touch. She flicks her tongue against my bottom lip. My heart's pounding so hard in my chest, I might have a cardiac event. I must be losing my fecking mind.

Footsteps sound in the hallway but instead of pulling back, I lean in even more and press the tourist against the wall. She intakes a breath sharply through her nose but pulls me harder against her.

I should stop. This is wildly inappropriate. And yet . . .

I push her arms up and around my neck so I can slide my hands between the wall and the back of her dress, low enough that I can feel the curve of her, the bump of the top line of her underwear, which makes my already hard cock freak the fuck out. I lower my hands ever-so-slightly, and she makes a hot squeak.

What I would give to pull up her dress and feel her arse in my hands. Have her wrap her legs around my waist so I could press against her center.

Two women enter the hallway on the way to the restroom chatting and laughing, then go silent. I pull back when they are gone, their fresh giggles fading.

"Feck," I say, my voice husky with need. "Did that help?"

My hands are still on the top curve of her behind, my body

pressed against hers. She's breathing hard and staring up at me with hooded eyes.

"Yeah. Yeah, it did, actually." She sucks in her top lip and doesn't move her gaze from mine.

I reluctantly remove my hands from her body and step back, releasing her from where she's pinned against the wall. The tourist stands up straight and attempts to smooth her dress. She's still close enough that I feel the heat radiating off her.

"Thanks for your, uh, hospitality."

"Anytime." I reach out to stroke her bottom lip just once with my thumb. "I need to get back to work." I dash down the basement stairs to get the wine, the whole reason I was even in that dark hallway.

Anytime? I'm a dick.

Maybe I'll see if we can meet up when my shift is over. Maybe she'd wait for me, and we can go back to her lodgings together. Or we can just hang out. Why couldn't I have just kissed her like she asked? Why did I have to make it so fecking horny?

Maybe I should apologize to her instead.

But when I get back up with the bottles of wine, the American tourist is nowhere to be found.

3

MADDIE

Saturday, March 1

My head is pounding, and I roll over in the unfamiliar bed. Weak mid-morning light comes in from the large window, and a wooden sheep figurine that I hadn't noticed last night casts a menacing shadow on the dresser. My exhaustion from the journey and jet lag made the few pints I had hit me so much harder than normal.

I wait for my brain to clear, and then I remember—my sisters think I'm in Saint Lucia for a month-long internship at an island resort near the man who's supposed to be my boyfriend.

Not in Ireland doing whatever this is.

I groan and pull the heavy duvet over my head, but just for a second, as it's hot as hell in this flat. I push it off my head.

Last night . . . oh, shit.

I asked the tall, dark, and smolderingly handsome bartender to kiss me in the hallway of the pub.

And it wasn't just a kiss. It was an event. A party. Novellas could be written about how it felt to have that man pressed up against me, his hands almost on my ass and his tongue halfway down my throat.

But that was a kiss that should have been saved for a place where I'd leave forever the next day. The pub is literally downstairs from where I slept, and now, I'm going to have to avoid it for the entire month I'm in Dingle. *Fuuuuck.*

Or, maybe not avoid it? Look for a repeat kiss? Tough call.

I grab my phone, which has a full battery, thanks to an Irish charger left for me by Noreen, and see missed texts from my sisters—who think I'm on Saint Lucia time—from last night. I do a quick Google search before I open the text chain. During daylight savings time, Saint Lucia is the same time as New Jersey, but after the clocks change in the US in the fall, Saint Lucia is an hour ahead until spring. And right now, Ireland is five hours ahead of New Jersey, but apparently the clocks move in Ireland three weeks later than they do in New Jersey, so that'll make Ireland four hours ahead.

At least Stella in London is in the same time zone as I am.

Can't wait till I mess this up.

> **REESE**
>
> Did you get to Saint Lucia okay? Let us know you're safe and sound!
>
> **REESE**
>
> And send pictures immediately! We're supposed to get eight to twelve inches of snow overnight in Jersey
>
> **STELLA**
>
> Explain in great detail how delightful the weather is. It's cold and gray in London
>
> **REESE**
>
> I just looked it up—it's eighty-five and sunny on Saint Lucia. I hate you!

Reese fakes it really well. I know she's still upset from our last fight, when I told her I picked an internship in the Caribbean so I can see Blue. The joke's on her, though—I'm not doing an internship *or* seeing Blue.

I notice she didn't ask about him in her texts.

Blue was an American who had traded his days in a corporate cubicle farm to teach surf lessons in the turquoise waters of the Caribbean. I fell for him almost instantly. It was the island air, the nights listening to the waves with our toes in warm sand, and the sheer lack of clothing. Absolute bliss.

After heading back from a hot and romantic month together, Blue and I talked daily through texts and FaceTime until we met up for a long weekend in December in Miami. It was a little awkward at first since I hadn't seen him in six weeks, but after a few hours, everything seemed great.

Until after New Year's.

He was busy all the time. I told myself it was fine, that we didn't have to talk every day. I didn't let myself complain to Reese, and I didn't want to bother Stella, who was busy with her life in London. So, when the opportunity came up, I decided to surprise him by grabbing the resort internship located on Saint Lucia.

Thank god I logged onto Instagram and found his new girl's account before leaving. She'd tagged him multiple times while always in a bikini with a surfboard, at first posing innocently next to him, then progressing to biceps pressed together, then his arm around her shoulders, then, in the last one, they were kissing on the beach, the sunrise in the background. I was sure they'd been there all night.

We broke up over text. He called us a holiday fling.

Aunt Evelyn wanted me to change my life for the better with her bucket list and inheritance. She wanted me to volunteer for something—so I volunteered to build houses for a month. She wanted me to take a vacation—so I went to Saint Lucia, combining the volunteer work with a beach holiday. And she wanted me to use her money to build my future—so I quit my job and registered for a one-year hospitality program.

But I think I missed the point. I fell right back into my old bad habits with Blue. My great-aunt would be so disappointed.

A quick glance at the window shows gray skies outside the flat. I squeeze my eyes shut. The weather is not delightful in Dingle. It is not eighty-five degrees.

Well, maybe in this flat it is. I kick the duvet completely off my body.

Is it even safe that my sisters don't know which continent I'm on right now? In Jersey, I'm always telling Reese where I am. I even share my location with her on the regular. What if I get kidnapped, or hospitalized, or something while I'm across the Atlantic?

And how am I going to send them proof-of-life photos that should have a white, sandy background when I'm in this awful country where it's freaking freezing and I haven't seen evidence of the sun?

I tap out a text as I assume at some point Reese will panic about me not responding.

ME

Sorry, passed out early last night! Safe and sound at the resort. About to go explore

Then I do the time zone math: it's ten o'clock in the morning here and in London. Take away five hours for Jersey and six hours for Saint Lucia, so it's five o'clock and four o'clock in the morning. Well, shit. I've already messed it up just by texting them.

I do a quick search for Saint Lucia sunrise photos, then another search for sunrise time and realize it's hours away. Oops! I switch to a Saint Lucia sunset search and screenshot a few that don't look too professional. I have some great pictures from when I was there in the fall, but my sisters have seen all of those.

> I'll explore after coffee, of course! These are sunset pictures from last night

I hate that I'm lying to them. But I'm in way too deep.

I take a long, hot shower and draft Oliver's friend an email as I eat some buttered bread and drink a gallon of water. I appreciate Noreen leaving some things for me . . . but good lord, I need coffee. And as soon as I send this email, I'll venture out and find some.

To: Patrick McNulty
From: Madison Elizabeth Hart
Date: Saturday, March 1
Subject: Here in Dingle!

Hello Patrick, I'm in Dingle—surprise! I had some time free up on my calendar and thought I'd come right to the source to plan the Best Road Trip Ever (trademark pending) for all of us. Reese and Oliver deserve an amazing pre-wedding vacation, don't you think? Anyway, it's a secret that I'm here in Ireland, so please don't tell Oliver or my sister.

Do you have time to meet up to talk potential itineraries? Everyone's booked their flights to and from Ireland, so I need to fill the twelve nights they're here with something amazing. They arrive in Dublin on Friday, April 18! Let's do this!

Can we meet up for coffee? A drink? Maybe you can show me around Dingle?

Thanks a bunch,
Maddie

After adding a dozen emojis, I press send. There. That's done.

I'm honestly not sure what I'm going to do with the time between now and the road trip. A month here in Dingle . . . then what?

I need caffeine. And headache meds.

The flat is on Main Street, and as I head down the stairs to street level, I open my map app to see what else is around besides the pub and the coffee shop Noreen mentioned. I need to buy myself a hat and some gloves, and I suppose I should've dressed in something other than a long dress and light puffy jacket. Like a full-body snowsuit.

I shade my face from O'Brien's as I pass, as if the hot bartender will be peering out the pub at this very moment.

He's not.

Dingle Brew is a cozy little café, with only a few tables pressed up against the front window. The smell of coffee beans and baked goods is delightful, and I order the largest size coffee they have and a buttery chocolate croissant.

"You a tourist? A little early in the season?" The barista is a pretty, middle-aged woman with shoulder-length brown hair, shallow wrinkles on her forehead, and well-established laugh lines around her mouth.

"I'm not really a tourist. Well, kinda. I'm here for a month."

"Are you now?" She raises her eyebrows. "Welcome then."

"My name's Maddie."

"I'm Maria. I'll see you around then, Maddie."

Another friend! Hooray! But I don't want to linger, as she might do what Noreen did and ask questions about the quest I'm on in Dingle.

A man behind me steps forward and I smile at Maria before leaving the coffee shop, alternating ripping off pieces of the delicious chocolate croissant with chugging the hot drink.

Down another side street, a giant park sprawls in front of me. I glance down at my map app. Dingle Town Park. There's a soccer game happening, and I absolutely shiver just thinking of how cold they must be in their athletic shorts and jerseys.

I pop the last bite of croissant in my mouth and wander closer. What else do I have to do? Patrick hasn't responded to my email—it's only been fifteen minutes—and I have literally no plans for the next, oh, two months.

For the hundredth time since boarding the plane to Dublin, I wonder what I'm doing here.

There's a small crowd of people watching the men play, and I pause far enough away from the sideline so as not to be weird. It's mostly women—probably all wives and girlfriends—and a couple of children. They're all bundled up.

And me, some random tourist, in a dress and insufficiently warm jacket.

Reese's fiancé used to play professional soccer in the UK, and actually, Patrick McNulty did, too. They were on the same team, and before Reese met Oliver in Scotland, he'd spent a year here in Dingle with his old teammate. That's why we're doing an Irish road trip, and that's why it has to include Dingle and Oliver's best friend. Patrick.

No one looks cold as they run around the field. My eyes land on the goalkeeper. He's incredibly tall and dark and muscular, a shadow of a beard on his face. He's standing in the goal with his arms crossed, watching the game, calm, calculating. Not sweaty. Goalie gloves cover his hands, and he starts pacing back and forth in front of the net, and OH MY GOD.

It's the bartender from last night.

Fuck, this is a small town!

My body physically reacts to seeing him again, my knees softening like putty, heartbeat accelerating, and my hand rising to touch my lips where he kissed me.

Damn, he's even hotter in a soccer jersey and shorts, his muscular, thick thighs straining against the fabric. That moment last night when he pushed my hair behind my ear at the bar . . . It was surprising, but I thought I was going to melt into a puddle on the pub floor. So when I saw him in the hallway, I said fuck it. Why am I here, if not to kiss a few hot men with accents?

Sound reasoning last night. But not as much this morning. What have I done?

I've had so many disasters with men. So many times, I was impulsive and let myself fall too hard, too fast. I'd get too involved, and always end up unemployed and with a broken heart.

A player from the other team breaks through the bartender's team's defenses and races toward the goal. The hot bartender is completely unperturbed, and when the player takes a shot, the bartender easily plucks the ball from the air.

And, *oh shit*, the striker is Liam, the New Dingle Brewing guy from last night. He also looks extra hot in soccer gear.

I giggle and sip my coffee. This morning just got a lot more interesting. And ridiculous. Maybe I shouldn't spend a whole month here, considering what a mess I've already made. I just need to get Patrick to respond to my emails first.

But . . . wait. My brain whirls and makes a distant connection.

Then a closer connection.

Reese told me Patrick was a goalkeeper when he was playing professionally.

And . . . didn't she also tell me he worked in a pub or at a brewery or something? I only vaguely paid attention because it didn't matter. Patrick was my sister's fiancé's friend who lived in Ireland, so he was so distant to anything that mattered to me, there was no need to keep facts about him in my brain.

But I have a sinking suspicion that the bartender from last night is the same person as this goalkeeper who is the same person I emailed this morning about meeting up to plan an Irish road trip.

Fuck. Me.

The referee blows a whistle, and the bartender's team—*Patrick McNulty's* team—lets out a cheer.

So it's not just that I made out with a man who bartends below the place I'm staying. It's that I made out with my *sister's fiancé's best friend.*

Someone I don't have the luxury of never seeing again.

Someone who I sent an email to this very morning.

I hold back a hysterical laugh, covering my mouth and backing away from the field before spinning around toward Main Street.

Patrick McNulty is the hot bartender I demanded a kiss from in the dark hallway. I wanted more from him. So much more. But now?

Out of sight of the field, my phone buzzes in my pocket.

REESE

Beautiful picture! Have the best time!

Oh, I am, sister, I am.

I'm going to have to face Patrick, and he's going to realize who I am. That's definitely happening.

A grunt sounds in my throat, and I finish the rest of the coffee, now cold and bitter. Have I already fucked up my sister's pre-wedding road trip by kissing her fiancé's best friend?

No. I can't mess this up. It isn't a job I can quit and run away from. Getting this right is the most important thing in my life right now.

Eventually, Reese and Stella will find out about me breaking up with Blue and dropping out of the hospitality program and lying about where I am.

So I need to distract them with The Road Trip To End All Road Trips. That means facing Patrick and what we did last night, and most importantly, behaving myself around him from now on.

When I'm at the door to the flat fumbling with my keys, my phone pings with an email notification.

It's from Patrick.

To: Madison Elizabeth Hart
From: Patrick McNulty

Date: Saturday, 01 March
Subject: Re: Here in Dingle

You're here? In Dingle? Why?

*I've just finished with a soccer game and will be at O'Brien's
—my pub—to do some brewery paperwork later this afternoon. I'll be there after three if you'd like to stop by. I can
then refer you to approximately one thousand websites that
have easy Irish road trip itineraries already prepared.*

Patrick

I continue inside and collapse on the comfortable couch, wiggling my legs out of my boots. Is he fucking with me? He's totally fucking with me. He's not going to just send me to some website, is he? We need to make this trip extraordinary. Super special. Something that will make my family forget how much I suck.

I am *not* looking forward to seeing the look on his face when he realizes who I am.

I scoot into a horizontal position and pull down the soft fleece blanket from the back of the couch. My phone buzzes with texts from my sisters, but I turn it on silent and close my eyes. Exhaustion from the jet lag takes over and I drift away.

I'll face Patrick McNulty—sexy bartender, soccer player, and hot-as-hell kisser—after I've had a solid nap.

4

PATRICK

The day manager at the pub is still new, so I'm trying to be around in case she needs help.

"Any questions, Beth?"

"No." She gives me a look I can't read. "Sorry again about forgetting to mark the inventory yesterday. I did it, but I just forgot to make a note. My daughter was up sick all night."

Beth is a single mom who my sister knows from the kids' school, and she's nice enough, but I'm not sure I made the right call hiring her. Honestly, she just looks exhausted, which made sense once I learned she also has an evening part-time job.

"I hope she's feeling better." My attempt at sounding sympathetic—which I am—comes out sounding harsh. Honestly, single mothers have all my sympathy. It's why I try so hard to help Saoirse with my nieces when I can.

Beth furrows her brow and returns behind the bar, while I head to a table and open my laptop back up. I might be micromanaging. But good help is so hard to get. I've spent most of the five years since buying the pub hiring and training people, just to have them quit and force me to do it all over again. It's exhausting.

Back then, I was happy to have a distraction from the end of my relationship with Cara.

After leaving Winchester Football Club in England, I was so bone-deeply happy to be going home to Dingle and Cara. But she was already packing for Dublin, looking for adventure outside of the sleepy Dingle Peninsula.

I should've let her go and stayed in Dingle, but that's not how I was raised. My parents had some marital issues when Saoirse and I were growing up, but they worked through it. And since then, they've been the happiest couple you could ever find. So I was sure Cara and I would end up like that, too.

But I didn't do anything right. I didn't say the right things, ask the right questions, call her the right amount, text her just enough. None of it. We were finally in the same place, and nothing felt right. Cara said half the time I didn't say anything at all, and the other half I asked aggressive questions like *where do you go all the time?* or *do you like hanging out with them more than me?* or *are you seeing someone else?*

Turns out I was spot-on with those questions, even though she denied it right up until I walked in on her with him.

I don't think I'll ever get that image out of my head.

There's been plenty to fill my time in the past five years. Saoirse's girls are now eleven and seven, and I've tried to be the best uncle possible. And Saoirse and I help our parents now that they're older.

But since I took over Slea Head two months ago, it's been less about staffing issues there and more about coming up with a good plan and convincing Sean—the head brewer who's been around for thirty years—to embrace change. He and my dad have been good friends for all of that time. I've known him since I was a kid. And while he's great at his job, he's highly resistant to change and outright hostile to anyone under the age of forty, including me and Cormac, the twenty-five-year-old assistant brewer.

Unfortunately for Sean, change is exactly what I'm going for.

I minimize my email, including a message from Oliver's fiancée's sister, and click through to the brewery management software I recently implemented. Sean hates it, but it makes our process so much smoother. I'm trying to ditch the *bulletin board and pinned scraps of paper* system Dad and Sean had.

A text comes through. I glance down and see the first part of the message pop up in the preview screen.

> **NOREEN**
>
> Your new tenant arrived last night! She signed a one-month lease. Her name is—

And then it cuts off. I don't tap the text to read more. I'll deal with that later, as it doesn't seem like there will be anything for me to do. I note the time on my mobile before flipping it screen-down.

I need to head over to the brewery to do a second check on Cormac's job cleaning the fermenter yesterday. Monday's a brew day for our amber ale and there's a ton of prep work to do. I remind myself to swing by tomorrow and heat the water tank so it's ready to go Monday morning.

And most importantly, I need to chase the Wellington Pubs people about setting a date for me to pitch Slea Head Brewery for distribution in their network of Irish pubs. It's a huge victory that they're even responding to my emails. If I could get our brews in their twenty-five locations in Ireland, then maybe they'd consider carrying us in their five hundred UK pubs.

It would change everything for me.

What I *don't* have time for is Oliver's fiancée's little sister to show up in Dingle. To plan his stag do road trip? There are countless websites and travel agencies and random people on the street who could easily give her a list: Dublin, Belfast, Giant's Causeway, Donegal, Galway, Dingle (obviously), and a few other stops between here and there. This is not rocket science. I cannot believe she flew all the way to Ireland and came here, of all places, to do what could have been done in front of a laptop or a mobile phone. I don't have time to babysit. I'll have to think of some way to satisfy her with minimal effort.

She'll probably show up any second. I roll my shoulders back. I have to be nice to her. Cordial. I can't swing friendly on a good day, and definitely can't match the vibes of that annoying-as-shite sunshine-y email she'd sent.

The door to the pub swings open and I glance up, expecting the sister to walk in, or maybe one of our regulars.

But it's not. Certainly not.

It's the hot American tourist from last night, and my face heats at the memory of her pulling me in by my waist, tilting her head up to mine, asking me to make her forget her ex. Those pink, plump lips and the way they felt against mine. The top of her arse under my fingers, the line of her underwear begging me to slide lower.

I swallow hard. Those dark hallways are made for making out. I'd never realized it before.

She's wearing another dress today, long and covering up those sexy boots I fantasized about last night. She stops in the doorway and wiggles out of her puffy jacket, not yet looking at me, and the front neckline of her dress dips down to show a hint of the swell of her breasts.

Maybe this is a second chance. I can book a room at the hotel Saoirse works at down the road and see what this woman looks like without that dress.

I groan softly. *I'm an eejit.* And I'm committed to being single. I've got everything I need in life. I'm not looking to start anything with a woman, even and especially one who is just passing through Dingle, probably looking for a bit of adventure.

That word—adventure—makes my skin crawl. All because of Cara.

The American tourist finally looks up and meets my gaze, and I raise my eyebrows and lean back in the wooden chair, crossing my arms and cocking my head. Instead of heading to the bar and Beth, who looks confused counting the taps (*the feck, Beth?*), the woman walks slowly toward me, her long dress moving with each step. She's got a strained smile on her face. Her shoulders are raised and she's gnawing on her bottom lip. I pull the screen of my laptop halfway down.

"Patrick?" she says and stops a meter from me.

"Yes." But a beat later, I narrow my eyes. How does she know my name?

"Hey. Nice to, uh, meet you. Again. Sort of meet you." She breathes out loudly. "I guess we didn't actually meet, not officially. I was tired and probably not making the best life decisions, and you were working, so there wasn't much time for formal introductions . . ."

My eyes widen as she speaks, twisting her hands together. Nothing like the flirt she was last night. She's nervous? To be around me? I guess it might make sense after what we did in the hallway.

"I don't think I caught your name last night," I say. Did we introduce ourselves and I completely forgot?

But she had been the one drinking, not me, and I only remember some brief banter before we kissed.

"We didn't exchange names." She sighs and stands there, a tentative smile on her face.

I blink at her.

"How do you know my name?" Did she ask around about me? That'd be weird, but who am I to judge someone for being weird.

"You responded to my email this morning," she says slowly. "So technically, you should know my name as well."

"Email?" There's a low buzzing sound in my ears. Time seems to slow as realization dawns.

"Yup."

Ohhhhh. Oh no.

No fecking way.

"Oh, feck."

This woman—the hot American tourist from last night—is not a random woman passing through Dingle.

No. She wasn't. She *isn't.*

She's Oliver's fiancée's little sister, the one who arrived in Dingle to plan the simplest road trip ever.

"I'm Maddie Hart."

"Fuck."

"You said that already." Maddie lets out a huff of laughter and her face relaxes.

"I said feck before, not fuck." My face, on the other hand, is definitely not relaxed.

"Whatever. Either way, it's kinda how I felt when I figured it out."

I'm not sure what to even say. Oliver is going to kill me. No, forget that, I'm *never* going to tell him. Then I remember Maddie's email, where she asked me to keep it a secret from Oliver that she's here. *Done. Jaysus, so done.*

"You can, you know, pick your jaw off the table now." She makes an upward motion with her pointer finger.

"And when . . ." I gulp. "When did you figure this out?"

Maddie takes a few steps forward until she's only an arm's length away from the table. I wish she'd back away, instead of coming closer.

"This morning, when I walked through town and saw you playing soccer."

I cock a single eyebrow. "You watched the game?"

"Not intentionally." She glances at the empty chair across from me. "May I?"

"I'm very busy—"

"I feel so much better getting this all off my chest." She pulls out the chair and sinks down, facing me, using two hands to pull the thick, long chunks of her dark hair over her shoulders until the tips gather on the table.

"I can't say I agree." As a matter of fact, I feel a billion times worse than when she first walked in, when I was fantasizing about what the afternoon could bring with the woman I'd kissed.

Maddie presses her lips together, barely suppressing a smile. It's true, she looks far less tense now. What the hell is she thinking? I know what I'm trying *not* to think about, and it's the feel of her hips as I pressed her against the wall last night, the way her lips parted as we kissed, the way the entire pub fell away.

This is not good. I need to get rid of this woman.

"So, Madison Elizabeth Hart," I say, awkwardly stumbling over the sender name from her email. "What can I do to help you?" The unspoken second part of that sentence is *what can I do to get you out of my pub and out of my town?*

"Madison Elizabeth? What are you, my mother?"

"It was in your email."

"Hmm. I guess so." She bites her bottom lip and leans back in her chair, hair shifting in waves over the front of her dress, cascading around the curve of her breasts.

Her gorgeous fucking breasts.

No. Nope. Off-limits. No matter how cute she is, this woman is *definitely* off-limits now. Besides the fact that she's Oliver's fiancée's little sister, she's not just passing through, and that's way too complicated. I need her out of here.

I give her my best morning-after-get-out-of-my-flat glare. Which isn't hard, because that's generally my default expression. It scares off most women in the light of day. Actually, it scares off most people, especially the ones who don't know me well.

I'm good at scaring women away. After Cara, I tried to date a local woman in Dingle. But that experience only reinforced what Cara told me when we broke up: it's impossible to be in a relationship with me. Cara was right. I was trying so hard not to ruin that new relationship, but I broke it anyway. It's hopeless for me to try, so I stopped.

"First of all, call me Maddie, not Madison."

But I don't scare this person, apparently. She seems to settle in more with each second.

"I prefer Madison."

"Ohhh-kay." She tilts her head at me.

"What's second of all?"

"Huh?"

"You said *first* of all."

"Oh, right. Second of all, I need help planning the road trip."

"Jaysus. You mean to tell me you really flew across the Atlantic Ocean to do something that can easily be accomplished with a simple Google search?"

She blinks at me.

"You did, didn't you?"

Maddie nods. "I don't want it to be a normal Irish road trip. It has to be special. For example . . . what's the coolest thing you've ever done in Ireland?"

"What?" I chuckle, and she waits for me to answer. "Kiss the Blarney Stone."

"See, there we go!"

"I was being sarcastic. That's a disgusting tourist trap."

"Still, I'm adding it to the list."

I groan. "Please don't."

"Even though there might be other reasons I'm here, planning the trip is definitely in the top, like, five."

"You have *five* reasons to be here?" What other possible reasons can this woman have to be in Dingle?

"Dingle's one of the top tourist spots in Ireland, don't you know that?"

"Yes, which is a great reason why it should be a stop on the road trip. Just like all the websites recommend."

"Are you always this grumpy?" Maddie stretches her arms over her head and yawns.

"Yes."

"Well, you weren't last night." She rolls her shoulders back and grins at me.

"My god, woman, that never happened, okay? If I'd known you were Reese's sister, I wouldn't have touched you, whether you asked me to or not." I stumble over the last words. The lady balls on her. Christ.

"I did ask you to, didn't I?"

"Yes. Who does that?"

A crooked grin comes across her mouth. "I'm really not that forward normally. I'm just in this awkward spot in my life."

I refuse to ask her to elaborate, even though I'm kind of dying to know more.

"Anyway, you didn't fight me on it."

I make a rumbling noise in the back of my throat.

"Easy, Patrick, no need to growl at me." She leans back and crosses her legs to the side of the table, within my line of sight. I find myself wishing she'd worn a short dress where I could get a peek at her thighs. "Hello?"

"Sorry." Feck. I was staring at her covered legs. The side of her mouth twitches.

"Okay, well, we have time to figure this all out because I'm in town for a month."

"I'm sorry, what did you say? Surely it's not that you're in Dingle for a whole month?"

"Yes. That's what I said."

I can't help but laugh, and it attracts Beth's attention from behind the bar.

"Why? Where are you staying?"

"Above the pub, actually. There's a flat right there." She points at the ceiling.

Oh, feck.

"You're not serious."

She nods and crinkles her forehead. "The owner is absolutely obsessed with sheep. It's kinda weird."

I grab my mobile and click through to read Noreen's full text.

NOREEN

Your new tenant arrived last night! She signed a one-month lease. Her name is Maddie Hart and she's a delight. She was at the pub last night, actually, but I didn't get a chance to introduce you two. Be nice if you see her around town!

"I counted at least half a dozen framed pictures and paintings of sheep. And when I woke up this morning, there was a sheep figurine glaring menacingly at me. I swear it wasn't there last night."

Bollocks. I'm absolutely not telling her that I carved that sheep figurine, and I also made the coffee table in the living room.

"Oh my god," I whisper.

"What? You look . . . disturbed." She reaches out and touches my hand, an exaggerated look of concern on her face.

I almost yank it away at the jolt her touch gives me. Sure, we touched last night, but this is different. We're sober. I resist the urge to turn my hand over and press our palms together.

Should I tell her that she's sleeping in my old bed, since I left it there when I built myself a bigger one for the cottage?

"Seriously, are you okay? It's not like you have to hang out with me every day. Or at all." The smile falls off her face, and she pulls her hand away slowly. It's like a live wire being dragged away from the back of my hand, leaving a trail of crackling electricity. Then she leans back and licks her lips, this time more as an anxious movement. I can't watch her do things like that for a whole freaking month.

I also hate that her mood seems to have shifted back to the anxious one she had when she walked in.

"That's my flat."

"Huh?"

"The one you rented. Look." I flash her my mobile screen. "Noreen texted me this morning that I have a new renter—although she said you were a delight and I'm not yet convinced on that part."

"No way." She laughs so loudly that I let myself crack a smile.

No. No smiling at the tourist. No. I wipe the pleasant look off my face and let my resting arsehole face take back over.

"Well, Patrick McNulty, we are meant to be, I think."

"Meant to be?" My eyes widen.

"Friends, obviously. Jesus, don't freak out."

"I wasn't freaking out."

"You were." She presses an elbow onto the table and leans her head in her hand. "I'll mostly stay out of your way, I promise. And we can, like, pretend last night never happened." She rakes her eyes down my face and stares at my lips, eyes heating.

"Stop that," I snap. "Please don't talk about it ever again."

She grins. "But I won't stay out of this pub, because it's delightful, just like Noreen said I am. The music was amazing, and I enjoyed that pint you poured me."

I warm slightly to her. "The Slea Head Golden Amber? That's my family's brewery."

"You didn't say that last night!" She lifts her head from her palm.

"I know." I shrug.

Maddie pauses for a beat. "Since I'm here—since *we're* here—do you want to get one together sometime? A Golden Amber? I could use a friend in this town."

"No. Definitely not."

"Just a friend."

"I don't have time for friends."

"We don't have to make out."

"God, no." If I was a nice, normal human being, I'd offer to take her around town. As a friend.

She sighs deeply. "Don't hide your real feelings on my account."

"I'm very busy. I don't have time for fun."

At least not with this hot ball of energy across the table from me. This off-limits woman.

Something tells me spending time with her would be the worst idea ever.

5

———

MADDIE

Tuesday, March 4

Boyfriend Disaster #2: Brent the Traitorous Waiter
Job Location & Length: Maya Mexicana, 3 months
My Age: 21

Brent was an age-appropriate server at the Mexican restaurant where I worked for just three months after fleeing
Jonathan's terrible sex. We laughed about mean customers
and our annoying manager, our eyes would meet in the
kitchen when we picked up food, and we'd whisper
together during breaks about the other servers. He was so
cute and a huge flirt, but he made me feel special.
For just a moment, it turned out.
We'd go for drinks at the local bar around the corner
after our shift and order a pitcher of beer. I took it
slower with him, insisting we were just friends until he
gently kissed me by the Pac-Man arcade game in a quiet
corner. It was only when we'd been sleeping together for
three weeks—at his apartment, not the back of a car—

that I realized he was also sleeping with another server named Heather.

I hated that job. My hair smelled like tacos all the time.

Breakup Reason: He had another girl on the side. Or maybe I was the side girl? Hard to tell.
My Distress Level: 2
Lesson Learned: Don't trust the restaurant flirt . . . you're never the special one. Also? No more waiting tables in restaurants that serve tacos.

I'm down by the harbor in Dingle, standing next to my wobbly rented bike, drenched and frozen from the persistent rain that's fallen for five of the five days I've been in Ireland. According to the sign taped on the front window of the rental shop, biking is the best way to see the area. Overlooking the beautiful harbor, it feels like that might be true. But I'm not yet brave enough to ride out of Dingle and bike along Slea Head Drive, the famously beautiful circular route along the Atlantic Ocean. Maybe another time.

Every day since arriving, I scour the internet and send my sisters a new borrowed photo of Saint Lucia. I've been on social media, stock photo sites, blogs, and travel websites, taking screenshots and editing away watermarks. Luckily there's a ton of idyllic photos online of the white-sand island. Reese and Stella have seemed satisfied so far, although last night Reese directly asked if I'd seen Blue. I haven't responded to that question yet.

Reese and I had our last huge fight two weeks ago—shortly before I found Blue's new girlfriend's Insta. Reese had accused me of looking sad after he hadn't picked up a FaceTime call for the fifth day in a row (accurate) and suggested maybe it was time to move on (unhelpful). I shouted something sarcastic like *Stay out of my business, Mom,* and stomped down the hall, slamming the guest bedroom door.

But Reese was right.

Blue and I broke up over text, but not until after I called him multiple times. Called. Him. On the phone. He didn't answer, so I left a voicemail. A *voicemail.* Maybe even more than one; I've blocked it out. I haven't left a voicemail in a decade. Or . . . ever, maybe. I might've screamed in one of them. Did I cry? I dunno.

I'm not sure if it was the reality of losing Blue, or the realization that I'd done it again. I'd let myself fall too hard, too fast. Obviously, I'm still a terrible judge of character.

But I've closed that chapter of my life. Things will be different from now on.

The rain drips down my face, coming down harder than it has all day, and I stare out at the colorful ships with tall masts tied up along the water. The skies are gray, the wind is whipping around, and I basically want to die, despite the beautiful scenery. I might, actually, because I didn't get a helmet when I rented this contraption, and my biking muscle memory hasn't quite kicked in. Plus, my eyes were bothering me this morning so I'm wearing glasses instead of contacts, which means my visibility while riding the bike sucks.

Yup. Gonna die.

I'm probably the first human being to ever visit Ireland and absolutely hate it. And I hardly ever hate anything.

My phone buzzes and I fish it out of my pocket, hunched over it like a cave goblin to keep it dry.

REESE

How's it going in Saint Lucia, Mads? I'm so envious. It's freezing today, and all the snow that fell the other day is still on the ground

STELLA

Send more pictures, please! It's actually sunny
in London, but still cold. I would kill for a
Caribbean beach right now. You guys have
no idea

I half-scream into the harbor. *Oh, but I do have an idea, Stella.*

AFTER RETURNING THE DODGY BIKE, I trudge back up Main Street and duck into O'Brien's. I need something to warm my belly, but more so, I need to see a familiar—if not friendly—face. Even if it's the man who is avoiding me with every bit of his soul. Yesterday, I spotted him from five storefronts away and he ran from me. Literally ran.

The pub is warm and dry and I'm so happy I could cry. It's a Tuesday at two o'clock in the afternoon, so there's no one here, just Patrick perched at the end of the bar staring at his laptop.

He glances up and appears to sigh deeply at my very existence.

"Christ. What happened to you?" His eyes rake over my dripping hair, spotted glasses, soaked hoodie, soggy leggings, and squelchy sneakers.

"I went for a bike ride." I blow a breath up my face and water droplets scatter.

"You're dripping wet. Onto my floor." He nods toward the little puddle at my feet and grimaces with distaste, but I swear one corner of his mouth twitches up. "You're a mess."

"Those are facts." This man does not pretend to be friendly at all, but I kinda like that about him. I get the impression he just says what's on his mind. He comes off as standoffish and grumpy. Maybe it's just a front.

I'm gonna assume that's right and not let him scare me away.

"Can you even see out of those glasses?"

"No. I cannot." I get distracted by a giant drop of water dripping from the end of my nose and go cross-eyed watching it slide down.

"Jaysus. Come here, then." He slides off his stool and reaches behind the bar for a dry towel, seems to consider approaching me, then holds it out. "It's clean. Dry off and try to stop flooding my pub."

That accent. I'm not one to swoon over accents—wait, that's a lie, yes I am, as my ninth boyfriend, who I desperately try not to think about, is proof of that—but the way he says *Jay-sus* causes a flutter in my belly.

Or maybe I'm just hungry.

I reach for the towel, drying my face first, then attempt to clear my glasses. It does not work. He sighs again and holds his hand out. I hesitate for just a second before passing the glasses over.

"To summarize: you went for a bike ride, in the pouring rain . . ." He grabs a tissue from the box next to the stack of iPads. ". . . with glasses on and completely inappropriate clothing?"

"Affirmative."

"Were you wearing a helmet?"

I scrunch my face. ". . . at least I'm not wearing a dress?"

He scoffs and hands me clear, dry glasses. "At least. You need to wear a helmet when riding a bike."

"Next time." My eyes flicker longingly to the beer taps. "Can I have a pint, please?"

"Yes." Patrick slips behind the bar and expertly pours a pint of Slea Head Golden Amber.

I pull out a moist credit card and hand it to him.

"No," he simply says, watching as I reach for the pint. A tiny fluttering disturbs my chest.

"Thanks." Friends let friends drink for free, don't they? Maybe there's hope for us yet.

I lean against the bar and take a giant gulp of the ale, sighing with pleasure. "So good. Do you have an IPA?"

"Not yet." He walks back around and pauses next to the

barstool he occupied when I walked in. "We have three—Golden Amber, Slea Head Stout, and a dark brew called Devil's Dark." Patrick gestures to the Slea Head taps lining the bar, next to handles of Guinness, Smithwick's, Kilkenny, and New Dingle.

"What brewery doesn't have an IPA these days?"

He glares at me. "It's coming. Soon."

"IPAs are my favorite."

"Wonderful. But I don't want to talk about it."

"Hmm." I drop it for now, although I'm very tempted to find out why his jaw is suddenly clenched. "Where's everyone else?" I look around the quiet pub. No one is behind the bar, and there are no customers.

"Beth—one of my managers—just quit to go work for New Dingle Brewing." His face darkens. "So now I'm short-staffed." He leans one elbow on the bar and watches me drink. "You need to take that soaking wet sweatshirt off. You're going to get sick."

"You don't actually get sick from being cold. That's an old wives' tale. Are you an old wife?"

"Are you always such a pain in the arse?"

"Yes." It's so easy to get him to roll his eyes at me, I kind of love it. I slide the beer on the bar and struggle to strip the wet hoodie from my body, leaving me wearing a thin t-shirt, my dark sports bra clearly visible through the moist fabric. But it's a sports bra and a plain t-shirt. There's nothing less sexy.

I hop up on the barstool, some warmth returning to my frozen fingers. I don't miss the way Patrick's eyes dart down to my soaking shirt.

"Keeping staff is hard. I was a restaurant manager in my old life."

He doesn't respond, but keeps his eyes locked on me. My cheeks burn under his assessment. I let myself check him out in return.

He's still hot as hell. Even with (especially with) that grumpy-ass look on his face. He must only own tight black t-shirts. I would, too, if I were him, because the way the current one hugs his muscular shoulders and fits snugly along his waist, the same waist I got to grab last Friday night . . . I'm much warmer than I was when I walked in. I can only imagine what his abs look like. No! I can't. Shouldn't. I drag my gaze up to his face, where he's watching me with a hint of amusement in his golden hazel eyes. He's got the same five o'clock shadow he had the other night. I bet it's impossible to keep it away. And now I get why our kiss was so disarming. His lips are plump and red and *oh my god, I need to stop.*

Patrick's the only person I know in this town—besides Noreen, and I hardly think the real estate agent counts—and we have connections. I'm not some random. I can appreciate his attractiveness without turning it into something more. Even if he's just the kind of guy I would fall for and then have to get a new job to avoid. Each time it happens, I think I've learned some important lesson, but then the next time I think I'm in love or some other bullshit, I make the same kind of mistakes.

I'm done with that part of my life. Kissing him won't happen again, now that we kind of know each other.

"Madison."

His deep voice snaps me back to reality, and I realize he's looking at me like I'm nuts. Got it. Probably am.

"Sorry, zoned out there." Not thinking about how hot he is. Of course not. "And it's Maddie, not Madison, which I know I've told you before. Can we talk about the road trip? Or are you too busy?" I look pointedly around the empty bar.

"This again? I'll send you a link and it'll be done, okay?"

I sigh. "I really want to make this special. I'll do it with or without you." As soon as the words are out of my mouth, I regret them.

"Without me. I choose that option," he says.

"I take it back."

"Does this have to do with why you're hiding out in Dingle and I'm not allowed to tell Oliver you're here?"

"Yes."

Patrick narrows his eyes.

"Oh, no, you didn't tell him, did you?" My heart pounds faster in my chest.

"No, no, of course not."

"Phew." I'm guessing I'd already know if he had. Reese doesn't exactly hold her opinions to herself.

"Not yet, anyway. I don't really appreciate having to lie to one of my oldest friends."

"Oh, come on. It's not like you're actively lying to him. I bet he's not asked you anything like *do you ken where Maddie is these days?*" I attempt Oliver's Scottish accent and fail miserably.

But Patrick chuckles and I almost fall off the barstool. I chug my beer and warmth prickles my skin under his gaze.

"Aye. He has not asked me that specific question. Why all the secrecy, though?"

There's no way I'm telling him my whole sob story. I shrug it off.

I want to get my shit together without my big sister watching. I recognize that as a thirty-three-year-old, maybe I shouldn't worry about her judgment, especially as she's only been kind to me since our dad died. I was nine, and Reese stepped in as the mini-mom. Weighed down by grief, our mother withdrew into herself for a time, and Reese, who was six years older than me and four years older than Stella, took care of us. Aunt Evelyn helped, too. It worked until Reese left for college and I started partying, drinking, getting bad grades, dating shitty boys. I pulled it together enough to get into college but dropped out sophomore year.

And Reese's never stopped being my mini-mom.

"Reasons. My turn: why the super serious face all the time? You work in a pub."

"I *own* a pub."

"Right. And a brewery."

He nods.

"Sounds like a dream."

"It is." His face clouds over. "My parents wanted to sell the brewery, but I convinced them to let me take over. I've only been in charge a few months, and I'm trying to change some things to grow Slea Head into something bigger." He sighs and runs his hand over his chin, making a scratchy sound. "But O'Brien's requires so much micromanaging that it's hard to find the time to focus on the brewery. Especially when people seem to quit every other day."

People like me. I'm basically the exact opposite of the kind of person Patrick would want, in his personal life or in his pub. I'm flighty, undependable, and quit jobs at the drop of a hat, just like his day manager had.

"It's hard to find people really committed to the job." And it went the other way, too. There were always people waiting to take the jobs I quit. I know I'm incredibly replaceable.

He nods, staring at my face in an intense way that makes me want to make him laugh again.

"Well. I'm just in town for an adventure, but I can see how much you care about this place."

I don't tell him that the last thing I want is an adventure. I'm tired of quitting things and falling for the wrong people. This is my life interlude, my time to reflect. For example, Patrick and I would be a train wreck if we dated. He's got his feet firmly on the ground. I'd be a nightmare to him. Not that I'm thinking of dating him. Or that he'd ever date someone like me.

And anything that happened in Ireland wouldn't be serious anyway.

I finish my pint with one last huge gulp. Patrick's watching me with narrowed hazel eyes as I gently place the empty glass on the bar.

"I feel so much better, thanks."

"Another?" He grabs my empty glass.

"Nah, I'm good. I don't want to get trashed on a Tuesday

afternoon." I shake my head, although that doesn't sound like a half-bad idea.

Patrick starts wiping the perfectly clean bar. I pull my wet shirt away from my stomach and squeeze it out, dripping water onto the floor. He sighs at me and stares at the small puddle. I bite back a grin.

"What are you trying to change about the brewery?"

Patrick meets my gaze, seeming to consider his response.

6

PATRICK

Of *course* she wants adventure. That would have to be the word Maddie uses. What a nightmare.

Cara found her adventure, all right. She found it with her lips wrapped around an American banker's cock on the couch in our flat in Dublin, which I witnessed firsthand after getting off a bartending shift early. She jumped away from him but didn't even try to say something like *it's not what it looks like*.

It was exactly what it looked like.

And now Maddie's perched on a barstool in my pub, all wet and gorgeous, and telling me she's here for an adventure. But she's also my best friend's fiancée's little sister. These days, I know better than to feck with that kind of connection. I learned my lesson long ago when I dated a mate's sister.

But Maddie might need some protection. Clearly, she doesn't make logical decisions. What if she'd fallen off that rental bike and gotten hurt? I'd have to be the one to call Oliver and Reese.

"My parents haven't changed a thing in the thirty years they've run Slea Head Brewery. Same three beers. Same equipment. Same processes. Same head brewer. Everything."

Her eyes follow my movements as I mindlessly wipe the clean bar.

"New Dingle has dominated. That family has grown their business tenfold over the past decade. And now with Liam in charge, it's doing even better. He's aggressive with innovation."

Even I hear the bitterness in my voice.

I got together with Cara after I started seeing her regularly when I was back during breaks from soccer. Liam would meet me at the pub and bring his sister along. Eventually, I asked her out, and he was supportive of me dating her.

To this day, I'm not entirely sure I understand Liam's intense dislike for me. Before I found her cheating, Cara told me Liam hated that I left her in Dingle while playing soccer in the UK. But I was already a professional soccer player when we got together. That was my life. Everyone knew it. He thought it was my fault that Cara cheated, I guess. I don't disagree. She even said it during our last fight: I was too distant and closed off, which basically shoved her into the arms of another man.

Liam and I never discussed it. When I returned to Dingle, his hatred for me was obvious.

"Well, what do you want to add to your lineup?"

"An IPA to start with—I'll call it In Your Face IPA—and we're so close to getting it right. My assistant brewer said the batch is ready to try." I pause in my endless wiping. "I'm also hoping to have an autumn brew ready for this year called Irish Oktoberfest. Then we'll have a five-beer flight like New Dingle. And farther in the future, a white beer like a hefeweizen, and a high ABV IPA."

She nods and is quiet for a beat. "When did Liam take over New Dingle?"

I hate hearing his name come out of Maddie's mouth so casually, as if they're old acquaintances, and I glance briefly at her before turning and squatting down to check out the inventory of bottles in the fridges. I lose count immediately.

"Right when I got back to town five years ago. I wanted the

brewery then, but Dad wasn't ready to retire. Then O'Brien's went up for sale and I jumped on it."

"So it's just a business rivalry? Between you and Liam?"

"Well—" I start, but stop. I give up counting bottles and stand slowly, careful to wipe any emotion off my face before I look at her.

"Ohhh, come on. Spill. There's definitely more to this story than beer."

"No. That's all." Why am I telling her so much, and why do I feel a pang of regret for lying? Maddie's a stranger, and I was this close to telling her about Cara's connection to this all.

About Cara in general.

Jaysus.

That's none of her business, and not something I ever want to talk about. Only to Saoirse. My little sister is always firmly on my side when it comes to the Smith family, even though my parents have seemingly forgiven them for the nasty end to my engagement to Cara.

My mobile pings and I glance at the screen, a reminder popping up for the interview with a potential new product development manager in thirty minutes at the brewery. *Dammit.*

"For feck's sake," I mumble as I type out a message to the candidate. I can make it a phone interview and take it from here. If anyone comes in, I'll put her on hold.

"What?" Maddie presses, and when I look up, her wide eyes are locked on me.

I shake my head. "I have an interview with someone for the brewery, so regrettably, this conversation will have to come to an end." Which is good, because the tourist is making me want to confess way too much.

"Is anyone coming in to work?" She looks around the empty room.

"No. It's no problem. I'll do it via mobile. I just need to send the woman this message."

"Don't do that." She shakes her head and slides down from the barstool. Maddie runs her fingers through her drying hair, and I'm transfixed by the motion.

"Why not?"

"Do you really want to interview them over the phone?"

"No, I'd rather do it in person at the brewery."

This would be my first important hire. I want someone to help me do market research and develop a five-year innovation plan so we don't ever fall behind New Dingle again. And then I can focus on the Wellington Pubs pitch.

Maddie walks around the edge of the bar until she's standing next to me. She surveys the stacks of glasses, the iPads, the bottles of liquor lined up along the wall.

"I can run this pub in my sleep."

I laugh, because it's the last thing I expected her to say.

She steps toward me and puts her hand on my forearm, wrapping her fingers around my muscle and gently tugging.

"This is what I've been doing for the past decade. My last job was managing an Italian restaurant with a thriving bar."

I furrow my brow and process what she's saying, but it's hard with her standing so close and touching me. The connection between my skin and hers is sending daggers of lightning up my arm.

"Madison."

"Maddie," she corrects.

"Madison. You are here for an adventure. Working at a pub is not an adventure."

"Who are you to tell me what qualifies as an adventure?"

"You're delusional." I cringe after the words come out, sure I've offended her.

"Sure, no arguments there." She grins brightly at me. "But I can do this." Maddie slides her hand down to grab my fingers and reaches out and takes my other arm, and now we're in some kind of awkward pose like middle school kids at a dance. "Come on. Let me. Please. I need this."

"What are you hiding from, little tourist?"

She huffs with offense. "I am not a tourist."

I cock my head to the side and narrow my eyes.

"Okay. I'm planning a trip during which I'll be a tourist. But right now? I'm basically a local." She bites her lip and smiles up at me.

This girl is flirting with me, which never happens when women are sober in the light of day. Usually, they're scared off by . . . well, me. The things I say. The natural look of my face.

"You're not going to work at this pub."

"How long until that interview you have scheduled?"

"Feck. Probably about twenty minutes, now that you've distracted me."

"I bet that woman is already there waiting for you. You're going to force her to take the interview from her car. In the parking lot."

She's right, and it annoys the shite out of me.

"You're still all wet."

Maddie glances down at her shirt, still clinging to her stomach, then back up at me.

"There are O'Brien's t-shirts for sale right behind the bar. I'll wear one of those." She nods her head to the unorganized stack of shirts behind me. "By the way, you are missing out on a huge merchandising opportunity. Why don't you have long-sleeved t-shirts? Hoodies? Pint glasses? Key chains, bar mats, pens . . . you could pick anything and put an O'Brien's logo on it. Tourists would love it."

I ignore the last comments. I've got about one minute to make this decision.

She could cover for an hour or two, then I'd take back over. And deal with the rest of Beth's scheduled shifts later.

"And I can cover whatever shifts you have open tomorrow. And the next day. The rest of this week, even."

"This is the worst idea ever."

"Says the guy who now has fifteen minutes until a very important interview."

"It'll be a disaster."

"No, it won't." She squeezes my hand. "I'm here anyway; just let me help. I have nothing else to do."

I narrow my eyes and study her eager face, still flushed from her poorly planned bike ride.

"I suppose it would be helpful."

"Great, I accept! Only if you give me one unique thing you've done in . . . Dublin."

"For the road trip?" I pull away from her.

"Yup."

I sigh loudly and she grins.

"Guinness Brewery."

"Nope, try again. I don't need you to tell me that one."

"Temple Bar." I turn toward the stack of t-shirts. "What size are you?"

"Do you even want my help? I'm a medium."

"Fine. There's a spot in Dublin where a giant tree is eating a park bench." I pull a medium black O'Brien's shirt from the stack, replaying her interesting merchandising idea. I turn back around.

Feck. Me.

Maddie's in the process of peeling off her wet top, and I watch with my jaw dropped as she lifts it over her head and tosses it on the bar, left only in a black sports bra.

The sports bra has a deep neckline that clearly shows the tops of her breasts, and I swallow as my eyes travel down to trace the smooth curve of her waist. An unexpected wave of desire washes over me.

Unexpected and seriously inappropriate.

She blinks at me. ". . . eating a bench?"

"Very slowly." I swallow and hope she doesn't notice. "Over time. But yes. It's consumed half of it."

"Well. That's perfect. I'll put it on the itinerary."

Maddie tilts her head and reaches for the O'Brien's shirt, a slight blush crossing her cheeks.

"I'll skip that day of the road trip."

"No skipping allowed." She pulls the shirt over her head and lets it settle on her torso.

"Let me give you a quick tutorial on the iPads." I beg my eyes to stay on her face. Her bare skin caught me off guard. That's all.

"See how easy it is to help me with the road trip? Maybe we can do it again sometime, as it's why I'm actually here."

Thank feck she's covered up now. Maybe I can think straight.

"That's funny, because I get the distinct impression you're hiding from something. Or someone. Like your sisters."

She shrugs. "Are you going to help me plan the road trip or not?"

"Yeah, fine, I'll send you a Tripadvisor link."

"Patrick!"

I almost grin and vaguely note that I enjoy hearing my name on her lips.

I can hire her. Just temporarily. There's no risk. I need the help, and she's here, and she's offering. And now that I know who she is, I can keep this completely professional and platonic.

As long as she keeps her clothes on and her hands off me. Which *shouldn't* be a problem . . . except she just violated both those rules in the past five minutes.

One thing's for sure: no more kissing in dark corners.

7

————————

MADDIE

Wednesday, March 5

I push open the door to the pub with a big smile on my face.

Working at O'Brien's for a few hours yesterday afternoon wasn't just to help Patrick. I've been thinking about something since I hopped a plane to Dublin.

I really like working in restaurants.

I've missed it since I quit the Italian place last summer to volunteer in Saint Lucia before starting the hospitality program. Working in restaurants keeps me moving, serving, talking to people, doing all the things that are good for my extroverted soul.

The reason I applied to the hospitality program was to finish up Aunt Evelyn's bucket list. But the way Reese's eyes lit up when I said I was going for a certification? And maybe get a different kind of job, one with a more traditional life than the grueling restaurant schedule? It's obvious that's what she wants for me. And I crave her approval.

But on the other side of all that now, I'm not sure school is for me. It wasn't back when I dropped out of college during my sophomore year. Back then my family assumed I was too flighty and unfocused and that maybe I'd go back later. But I got a full-time job serving tables (and met Jonathan and his tragically fajita-scented car), and while I wasn't pulling in tons of cash, I was happy and could support myself.

I never really regretted dropping out of college.

Patrick sits at a table in the back of the pub, staring at his laptop like when I walked in last weekend. He looks up and before he can put on his grumpy mask, there's a look of pleasant surprise on his face.

"Good morning." I smile as I approach him, giddy and giggly at the prospect of working at a pub in Ireland. Job number eleven, which I will *not* ruin by dating someone I work with. Besides, it's not even a real job, so how can I ruin something that doesn't even really exist?

He looks me up and down, his eyes lingering at the bare skin showing between my boots and the loose bottom hem of my black dress.

"What are you wearing?"

I make a face at him. "That's actually rude to say to a woman."

He has the courtesy to flinch. "Sorry. I didn't mean it in a bad way. You look . . . nice. What I meant was that's not what my employees usually wear to work. Especially managers."

I thoroughly enjoy the slight pink tinge to his cheeks.

"The O'Brien's t-shirt is in the laundry, and this was the only other black piece of clothing I have."

He swallows, his throat moving in a wave.

"Right. It's fine." Patrick's voice cracks and I suppress a grin.

I'm making him uncomfortable, and that sends a mini jolt of victory through my body. I shrug off my jean jacket and reveal my bare shoulders. Maybe the dress isn't appropriate for March in Ireland. None of my clothes are, save a hoodie, a single sweater, and a few pairs of leggings.

Besides, I don't hear him offering another O'Brien's shirt.

"You okay?" I tilt my head and step closer.

"Yes. Why wouldn't I be?" Patrick looks away and appears to gather himself. "How was yesterday afternoon?"

"It was great. Ready to do it again."

He stands and stretches his arms high above his head in an exaggerated and possibly fake yawn, revealing a panel of his incredibly chiseled abs. How am I not surprised to see that he's ripped under another one of his tight black t-shirts?

Not that I was thinking about his stomach. Or what he might look like shirtless.

Crap. Of course I am. How could I not?

"I thought you might have changed your mind."

"Nope."

Now towering above me, he looks down, assessing, his eyes flitting over my face and darting so briefly down to the hint of cleavage on display.

A stutter of desire bats its wings in my center.

No. Nuh-uh. No desire! I'm a changed woman. A *changing* woman. A better one.

"Here's the list of opening tasks." He reaches down and grabs a paper from next to his laptop, handing it to me. "Why don't you get started, and I'll check back in half hour or so to see if you have questions."

Patrick grabs his laptop and walks past me, maneuvering his body so he doesn't brush against any part of me.

"Are you leaving? Do you actually trust me to do this on my own?" I follow him to the bar, but he continues walking down the hallway and I screech to a halt.

The hallway.

"No, not really, but I've got work to do."

"Down . . . there?" To the dark corner where he had his tongue down my throat while I was pressed up against the wall?

Patrick stops and turns. "Pub office. Down here." He nods his head to the cracked open door, across from . . . Then he glances to the spot on the wall.

He's totally thinking about last Friday night. I sure as hell am. His tongue wrapping around mine. The way I ached when his hands inched onto the top of my ass. Him pressing his hips against mine . . . *Nooo!*

"Right." I press my lips together and back away. "Okay. See you in a bit."

Patrick breathes in through his nose noisily and disappears into the office, muttering something to himself.

"Pull it together," I whisper and slip behind the bar to study the list of opening tasks. I start with checking the inventory levels in the cases behind the bar. There's a solid selection of beers like Heineken, Budweiser, Harp, and ciders, amongst others. A few are missing, and I make a mental note to go down to the basement to see if there's any extra stock.

I'm logging onto the payment iPad and feeling victorious for completing most of Patrick's list when the door to the pub swings wide open. I check my phone for the time.

"We don't open for another ten minutes," I say to the woman who walks in with two children holding iPads of their own.

"Where's Patrick?" the woman asks, stopping in the middle of the room and planting her hands on her hips.

Uh-oh. I blink at her. Wife and children? That shouldn't be surprising, given my history with men, but for some reason I *would* be surprised. Reese hadn't told me that Patrick was married. And he doesn't seem like the type of guy to kiss a woman in a dark hallway while he has a family waiting at home.

There I go again. Trusting too soon.

I go through an entire debate in my head, reminding myself of why I should not be thinking about whether or not he's married or that strip of ab muscles.

Why am I like this?

The woman is still staring at me. Shit.

"Uh, he's back in the office. Want me to get him?"

The two girls plop down at one of the tables, immediately swiping at the screens.

"Oh no, definitely not. I'd rather talk to you." She strides toward me and rests her forearms on the bar.

"Me?"

"When he texted me this morning that he'd found an American woman to be a temporary day manager for the pub, I knew we needed to stop by and make sure he wasn't lying and trying to do everything himself."

I grunt. "I haven't known him very long, but that sounds exactly like something he'd do."

She studies me, now smiling, and it reminds me of Patrick's assessing face from yesterday when I was convincing him to let me cover the shift. But friendlier.

"Mam?" the older girl, around middle school age, calls. "Where's Uncle Patrick?"

Uncle. Makes perfect sense now.

"He'll be around in a few, Erin. Just watch YouTube for a bit." She hops up on a stool. "They're always watching absolute rubbish on that app. I'm helpless to stop it."

"I used to hear that from my sister," I say with a laugh.

"I'm Saoirse, Patrick's sister."

"Hi . . ." I blink at the unfamiliar name.

"Saoirse." She spells it out for me. "But it's pronounced Sur-shuh."

"I wouldn't have guessed that spelling at all. So nice to meet you." I grin at the pretty woman with dark hair, just like her brother's, and hazel eyes to match. "I'm Maddie."

"Mam? Can we ask him about my doll?" the younger girl chimes in.

"Yes, Niamh, when Uncle Patrick comes out of the office, we'll ask him if you left it at his cottage."

So many interesting bits of information here.

Saoirse turns to me. "And while her name sounds like Neev, it's spelled N-I-A-M-H."

"Good lord."

Saoirse chuckles. "We came to see you and also to hunt down Niamh's doll. She must've left it at Patrick's last weekend."

I give her an inquisitive look. "Last weekend?"

I remember last Friday night. Yup. Sure do.

"Last Saturday, when they slept at his cottage. My brother keeps the girls for a night most weekends, to give me a bit of a break. He's been a godsend, especially since their dad and I divorced. Actually . . ." She leans forward and lowers her voice. "He's been amazing since he came back to Dingle five years ago. After he and Cara split."

"We can hear you, Ma," Erin says with an eye roll in her voice.

"Has he told you about her?" Saoirse ignores her daughter. "They were engaged. She was the worst."

Something moves in my chest. Cara. A key to understanding who he is. Not that I care, obviously.

I shake my head. "We haven't been having many heart-to-hearts, you know?"

Saoirse chuckles. "I'm not surprised. He'd be pissed I shared anything about her with you." She glances back over her shoulder at the girls.

"I won't tell." I make a zipping motion on my lips.

"He's so good with them. And he always makes it to biweekly family dinners with our parents. Not that he has anything else going on. No girlfriend or anything."

"Uncle Patrick *never* brings girls around," Niamh moans, not looking up from her iPad.

I stifle a giggle.

"Hush, dears. Want some crisps?"

"Yes!" both girls yell.

"Will you hand me two?" Patrick's sister nods her head to the bin of chips behind the bar. "You're American?"

"Yup." I nod, handing her the bags.

"Are you single?"

I practically choke on my own spit. "Yeah."

"Excellent. And what are you doing here working at this pub? In the winter? Not the best time for a vacation in Dingle."

"Yeah, I noticed. But I'm here to plan a bachelorette-slash-bachelor party road trip for my sister and her fiancé."

She raises her eyebrows and I explain Reese and Oliver's role in all this.

"Lovely. I know Oliver from when he spent time here in Dingle."

"Oh, I keep forgetting he lived here for a bit. We're not telling him I'm in Ireland, though."

"Sure, okay." Saoirse gives me a funny look. "Spring's a wonderful time of year for a road trip. There are many tourists, but less than in the summer. Loads of them come from the US. Patrick has a thing for American accents." She winks.

"Why do I feel like you're having a secret conversation with me?"

She shrugs. "It's my goal in life to get Patrick to date someone again. He's done so much for everyone else but hasn't had a girlfriend in years. So many years."

"I'm not sure what to do with that information." I swallow. "But I'm not looking to date anyone." Patrick's sister is oversharing, and I kind of love it.

"Of course, of course." She nods, but I have a feeling she's not interested in my protests. "Anyway, you'll not have a problem planning your road trip. There is so much to see."

"Patrick's coming on the road trip as well, and he's supposed to help me plan."

"Is he being helpful?"

I blink and press my lips together. She laughs.

"Didn't think so."

"I'm trying to make the itinerary unique. What's a weird or quirky thing to do in Dingle?"

"Hmm." She appears to think, tapping her lip with her pointer finger. "Ah. Along Slea Head Drive, there are these tiny stone houses called beehive huts. Apparently, hermit monks used to live in them when they were built over fourteen hundred years ago."

"Wow."

"Are you a Star Wars fan?"

"Nope."

She chuckles. "Well, if you were, you'd recognize them from the movies."

"That's definitely going on the itinerary. Anything else? Doesn't have to be Dingle."

"Got it." Saoirse holds up a finger. "It's a little dark, but there's a giant hole in the ground up in Donegal at St Patrick's Purgatory. It's supposed to be a gateway to hell."

I stare at her with wide eyes. "Well. Okay. That's definitely unique. And super creepy." I pull out my phone and make a note of both of those ideas, right below Patrick's suggestion of the bench-eating tree in Dublin.

I like this woman.

"How's it going out here?" Patrick's voice booms from the hallway. "Oh, Jaysus. You lot are here."

"Uncle Patrick!" Niamh jumps up from her chair and sprints across the room, throwing herself at her uncle. He easily lifts her up in the air and spins her in a circle before setting her gently back down.

"Hello, love." Warmth infuses his voice, and his face relaxes in a way I've not seen before.

"Did I leave Margaret at your cottage last weekend?" The little girl looks up at him, eyes wide and worried.

"As a matter of fact, you did. And I brought her here. Run back to the office and fetch her."

"Hooray!" Niamh dashes down the hallway.

"Saoirse." Patrick nods at his sister. "Hello, Erin," he calls, and his other niece waves without looking up from the screen.

"So I heard you need to help this woman plan a road trip? Sounds right up your alley."

Patrick groans. "Shouldn't the girls be at school? And you be at the hotel working?"

"No school for some reason and I'm off today. Thought we'd swing by and meet your new manager. She's delightful. You didn't mention that in your text."

"Why do people keep calling her that?"

I choke back a laugh, and Patrick gives me a glare. I roll my eyes in response.

"Well, since you're both here, try this for me." Patrick pulls a growler out of the refrigerator.

"What is it?" I ask.

"The new IPA. I don't think it's quite right." He pours three small servings of the cloudy liquid and pushes one to Saoirse, then one to me.

I sip the liquid. It's good, but it has a hell of a bite.

"Damn, that's bitter, Pat." Saoirse's face is far less masked than mine.

"That's what I thought. We have the right hops, finally, but the timing of when we add them to the mash isn't right for this batch." He sips his own glass.

"Mash?" I lean against the bar and watch him clear the three glasses.

"It's the crushed grains and water at the start of the boil, before fermenting." He slides the growler back in the refrigerator. "There will be another IPA batch ready in a few weeks. I'm hoping we crack it with that one."

"You'll get there," Saoirse says.

"Have you finished all the opening tasks?" he asks me, his tone a bit short.

"Patrick." Saoirse shakes her head at him.

"What?"

She turns to me. "My brother often sounds like he's being an arse, but he's really not. It's his . . ." She waves her hand at Patrick. "His face? Voice? How he looks at people?"

I bite back a giggle as Patrick turns his glare to his sister.

"Yes. Just like that." Saoirse winks at me and gathers up her children—including Margaret the doll—and heads out of the pub.

O'Brien's opens a few minutes later.

"See how easy it is to be helpful?" I call to Patrick, who's established himself at the table in the back corner. "She gave me two ideas."

"Good. Ask her about the road trip from now on." He doesn't even look up.

A pair of locals trickle in, greeting Patrick with a lift of their hands. They both order pints, then quietly chat at one end of the bar while I pour. The door swings open again to reveal a heavily tattooed red-headed man.

"Hello, mate." He looks from Patrick to me, smiling.

"Jaysus. Did my sister text you?"

"Aye. She did." The man strides over to me and holds out his hand. "I'm Ian. I needed to check out the pretty American woman Patrick hired."

Patrick groans and stands, walking over to join Ian at the bar. I pretend I didn't hear him call me pretty, but heat crawls up my neck.

"My sister needs to keep her mouth shut." Patrick claps Ian on the back and shakes his hand.

"I own the tattoo parlor down the road." Ian nods his head to the street. "I'm also dating Patrick's sister."

"Unfortunately," Patrick says, but he's got a hint of a grin on his face.

Ian's a good-looking man, with tattoos covering almost every bit of exposed skin—the back of his hands, peeking out from his wrists, his neck, and stopping at his jawline. His red hair goes perfectly with the freckles that cover his nose and cheeks.

"I'm Maddie."

"Oliver's fiancée's sister?"

Good lord, this is a small town.

"Yes. Nice to meet you. But we're not telling Oliver or my sisters where I am, okay?"

"No worries. Did you know that Oliver worked at the tattoo parlor for a bit while he was here? He also tended bar in this very pub."

"I didn't realize he'd worked for you, too." This secret is hopeless. I definitely didn't think through the connections Oliver has in this town when I jumped on that plane.

"He'll not hear that you're here from me." Ian nods solemnly.

"Don't worry, Madison, I'll get these customers." Patrick stares me down as he pours pints for a pair of women waiting at the bar.

"Thanks." I ignore his obvious sarcasm.

"He's not exactly an easy man to work for." Ian nods his head to Patrick. "Not sure if you've realized that yet. Which is probably why the other manager ran to New Dingle." Ian fake-whispers the last part.

"Ian, shut it," Patrick growls.

Ian ignores him.

"I can handle a tough boss." I slide my eyes to Patrick.

Ian scoffs, but it's good-natured. "What have you been up to since you arrived? Seeing the sights?"

"Just wandering around town so far, but I think in the morning I'm going to try to bike on Slea Head Drive before my afternoon shift."

Ian raises his eyebrows. "A gorgeous ride for sure."

"Like hell you are."

Ian and I swivel our heads to Patrick, who is glowering at me as he hands a credit card back to the customer.

"Excuse me?" I cross my arms.

"You came in last time looking like a drowned rat. You rented from that shite place down the road—those bikes are about ready to fall apart—and didn't wear a helmet."

"He's right about that bike shop." Ian nods.

"Are you going by yourself?" Patrick ignores another customer waiting to be served. So do I.

"Well, I'm not going with my friends, if that's what you're asking."

Patrick throws his head back and groans, and I let my eyes drift to his exposed neck and the dark stubble on his chin. "You're going to kill yourself."

I shrug. "I'll be fine." I probably won't be.

He shuts his eyes and appears to pray, moving his lips wordlessly. Ian looks back and forth between us, but I stare at Patrick.

"I'll go with you." Patrick opens his eyes and drags them in my direction, as if it requires great effort.

"What?" Ian and I say at the same time. Ian's voice is full of amusement and matched by a grin, and mine is truly shocked, given Patrick's previous response to my request to hang out.

"Let's get an early start. I'll bring an extra bike and helmet. I can show you the best views. Safely."

I narrow my eyes at him.

"Oliver would murder me if something bad happened to Reese's little sister. And I also don't want my new employee—even a temporary one—falling off a cliff."

"Falling off a cliff? I don't love the sound of that."

"Do you want me to have to call Oliver and tell him you ran off the road and plunged into the sea?" Patrick levels his gaze at me.

"No! No plunging into the sea. No calling Oliver." I hold my hands up. "Fine."

"Well, that's my cue." Ian turns to me. "Nice to meet you. Come stop by sometime, alright?"

I lift a hand to Ian, promising I'll do so.

When he's gone, I pour a customer a pint and stick a cheese toastie in the oven, struggling to figure out how to work the contraption. Patrick sighs and presses the big square *start* button, then strides back across the pub to his table.

I don't even try to hide my grin. Like it or not, he's finally agreed to hang out with me.

8

PATRICK

Thursday, 06 March

I glance over to my passenger seat, still shocked that Maddie Hart is there. At least she's wearing leggings and a hoodie instead of one of her endless supply of infuriatingly sexy dresses.

I can't believe I offered to cycle Slea Head Drive with this woman. I had to though, didn't I? Oliver would want me to. Reese, too.

I should be at the brewery working on the final recipe for the first autumn brew batches we're due to start this weekend. Sean attacks me for any mistake I make, so I need to be top of my game when it comes to him and Slea Head. And I should be working on that pitch for Wellington Pubs, who finally got back to me with a meeting date less than two weeks from now. I need to have a complete proposal and timeline ready for them. I want to be able to offer them all five of our brews—two of which aren't even ready yet.

But if I keep Maddie safe, I'll be doing Oliver and Reese a favor and also ensuring someone is around to help hold things down at the pub while I focus on the brewery.

Oliver texted me last night to catch up. He brought up the road trip, and while I didn't outright lie to him, it felt like I did. It made me very uncomfortable.

"Why are we driving to bike Slea Head Drive?"

"Because the entire route is about fifty-five kilometers." I look over at her briefly and she stares back, eyebrows raised.

"Sounds doable."

"That's thirty-five miles."

"That sounds much less doable."

"How much cycling have you done?"

Maddie shrugs and crosses her legs. She might not be wearing a dress, but I can practically see her skin through those black leggings. She'll freeze her arse off.

"Loads."

"Yeah?" I sneak another look at her.

"Well. I mean, it's been a while."

"Like how long?"

"I owned an amazing pink bike when I was in elementary school. It had pom-poms on the handles and a basket with flowers in the front."

"Madison, that sounds like a very long time ago."

"Are you calling me old? Because I'd hardly call twenty years a long time." She pauses. "Twenty-three years. Twenty-five, tops."

I snort. "Hear yourself?"

"Yeah, I do, and I hate it."

I peek at her and she's staring at me, smiling. *Christ.*

"Basically, we're cheating a bit and starting halfway. It's cold and windy out today, but at least it's dry. And we need to be back to the pub by early afternoon so you can relieve Saoirse, who's opening today."

"Good, she was fun. Maybe she'll hang out for a while."

I let out an exaggerated sigh.

"I thought she worked at a hotel?" Maddie asks.

"She does. She also helps out at the pub sometimes." Just as the gorgeous views of the ocean are close enough to gawk at, I pull off onto a dirt driveway.

"What's this place?"

"My dad's friend lives here. A regular at the pub." I gesture down the dusty drive. "Starting from here saves us a bunch of miles." I park far from the old farmhouse, which is barely visible from the road.

"That feels like cheating. Can I even say I biked Slea Head Drive?"

"Who would you say that to?" I open the driver's side door and turn to her.

"You know. People." Maddie shrugs and exits the car.

"What people?" I scrunch my forehead and stand, slamming the door behind me.

"People who care, Patrick." She plants her hands on her hips and watches me head to the boot of the car.

"Who? Give me a specific example."

"Like . . . people on Instagram."

"That's not specific. And why do you care about people on Instagram?"

"I don't! I've sworn off social media. And no one knows I'm here anyway, so I won't be posting."

I let it go, but I've never quite taken to social media. Swearing off it sounds like a good idea for Maddie. For anyone.

While I'm unhooking the first bike, she starts to pepper me with questions.

"Where did you grow up?"

"Dingle."

"Do you see your parents a lot?"

"Yes."

"What's your favorite part about living here?"

"My sheep."

"You have sheep?" She gasps and splays her hand on her chest.

"I do."

"Do you shear their wool and make sweaters?"

"No. Not if I can help it." I wrestle the second bike off the rack.

"No to which part?"

"Both."

"Why not?"

"Sheep generally don't like being sheared. And they're my pets, not a source of clothing or rugs."

She giggles and I hate how the sound makes me grin.

"Wait a minute." Maddie gasps and presses her palms to her cheeks.

"What?" I pause with a helmet in each hand.

"The flat. Your flat. It's decorated entirely in sheep decor. That was your doing. You love sheep."

"Love is a strong word." I do my best to keep my face expressionless, but a corner of my mouth twitches.

"There's a sheep shower curtain."

"So?"

"And dish towels."

"Your point?"

"The salt and pepper shakers, Patrick. They're sheep heads."

"Fine. I like sheep."

"That's . . . more than I can process right now. Can I meet your sheep?"

"No." I toss her a helmet—an extra I have—and she catches it. "Put that on."

"Please?" She wriggles the helmet on her head, and damn, she looks fecking adorable. But it's a wee bit big on her.

"Absolutely not."

"Do they have names? They must, if they're your pets."

"They do, and it's none of your business. Check your bike. It's a spare I had lying around. Is the seat the right height?" I asked my big cyclist neighbor if she had a bike I could borrow, and she offered to sell me this one. So . . . I bought it. Not for Maddie only, obviously, but it'll be good to have an extra. Erin is in the middle of a huge growth spurt, and she'll probably need a new bike soon, anyway.

"It's perfect." She throws a leg over the bike and settles on the seat with one foot firmly on the ground, then loses her balance and almost falls over. While standing still.

"Jaysus."

"What? I'm fine. No worries." Maddie adjusts the helmet on her head. "Do you have other farm animals?"

"No. But my neighbor has a goat with newborn babies." Why am I telling her this?

"Awww. Baby goats are so cute."

"Are they? Whatever."

"Can I meet the baby goats, if I can't meet your sheep?"

"Let's go." I don't answer her ridiculous question and instead swing onto my bike and push off toward the road, cycling slowly and speaking to her over my shoulder. "Stay on the left side of the road, close to the edge. The cars will go around you and you'll be grand as long as you ride steady."

"It can't be worse than the other day. At least I'm not wearing my glasses in the pouring rain."

I ignore her quip, and a vision of her dripping wet in a sports bra flashes in my head.

"This is about ten kilometers each way. We'll stop halfway at the best viewpoint in Slea Head. Then we'll continue to Dunquin, take another quick break, and head back. Should take us about one hour and a quarter, maybe an hour and a half."

"Sounds better than fifty-five kilometers."

"Sure does."

The elevation climbs and falls, and the views of Dingle Bay and the Atlantic Ocean are truly spectacular. Mossy piles of rocks line the roadway, changing eventually to old stone walls and fencing, keeping livestock from wandering into the road. We ascend, the ocean sprawled out on our left. It's been six months since I biked this way, probably since the end of last summer. The views do wonders for my stress levels.

We cycle in silence. I remain at a slower pace than usual to make sure Maddie's keeping up. Finally, I spot the paved pull-off at the high point.

I turn in and stop my bike in the small lot, leaving my helmet hanging off the handle. Maddie pushes out the kickstand of her bike behind me and drops her helmet gently to the ground before stepping next to me.

One glance at her face tells me she's as impressed as I still am each time I come here, even though I grew up a stone's throw away.

"It's breathtaking." Her body full-on shivers, and she slips her hand around my forearm and pulls herself close to me. "But freezing."

I don't move my arm for fear she'll remove her hand. Her eyes lock on the vast ocean in front of us, the waves crashing against the rocky shore far below.

"Should've worn more clothing."

"Is that your personal motto?" I lift my free arm in the air and wave it in front of us, as if I'm presenting her to a group. "Madison Hart: should've worn more clothing."

"Shut up and keep me warm."

A lump forms in my throat as she lifts my arm and wraps it around her shoulders, burrowing into the smooth side of my windbreaker while drinking in the scenery.

This I didn't sign up for.

She rotates us slowly, absorbing the whole view, taking in the white crucifix and statues behind us, the grassy, rocky cliff rising up against the clear sky, all the while staying snug against me, one arm wrapped around my waist. Her hair whips around her head and my own breath gets stuck in my throat as I can't pull my eyes away from her, not the view.

What is she thinking right now? I'm so . . . confused. I finally follow her gaze out to the ocean.

"This is the westernmost point of mainland Ireland. It's clear today, so you can see the Blasket Islands."

Maddie looks up at me, her eyes wide and wild.

"I can't believe you grew up here. I grew up in *New Jersey*." She laughs and shakes her head. "So unfair."

Something warm glows inside me.

"I mean, Jersey does have actual sunshine, and warm beaches in the summer, and pretty mountains. I guess it's not all bad. But it's definitely not this."

Whoever gets this woman will be lucky as hell. Who was she getting over when she asked me to kiss her? That person is an arsehole for losing her.

No.

I need to stop that train of thought right now. If I had Maddie —if she let me be with her—I'd ruin it. Maybe I haven't scared her away yet, but I would. I'd say something she'd misunderstand. I'd not be the person she needs me to be. I'd break it. I'd break us. It's what I do.

I'll never be part of an *us* again.

The only people who truly get me are my family. I can't say anything to scare them away. They know me. They accept me.

Any warm feelings I have toward this woman are ill-fated, so it'd be best if I squashed them right now.

"What are you really doing here, Madison?" I say, but the wind is whooshing around us and I'm not sure she even hears me. She gasps softly, then turns her whole body to me, pressing her face against my chest, her hair whipping around.

"I told you. I'm planning a road trip." Then she slips her arms inside my open jacket and wraps them around my waist. "So much warmer."

She looks up at me with a pure, genuine smile, and I can't help but notice that this feels right. Good. The most natural place in the world to be. When's the last time I was locked in an embrace with a woman like this? Not any of the one-night stands I've had in recent years, that's for sure.

I give in to the feeling and wrap my arms around her, covering as much of her body as possible.

"Oh, that feels so nice." Maddie's voice is muffled against my chest, and I look out over the wild Atlantic Ocean.

"Madison." I move my hands slowly on her back, with the excuse that I'm getting her blood flowing, keeping her warm so her muscles don't freeze up before we get back on the bikes. "Answer the question."

She breathes in deeply. "A series of things happened."

"Starting with?"

"I got dumped."

I look down at her, and she turns her face up to mine.

"Tell me."

"His name was Blue."

"Blue?" I snort. "You got dumped by a man named Blue?"

She presses her lips together and nods, a hint of amusement raising a blush.

"I met him in Saint Lucia in the fall. I was there for a month volunteering, and I thought we fell for each other. I fell for him, at least. I always fall too fast." Maddie says those last words mostly to herself. "I went back to Jersey to start my hospitality program."

"How's that going for you?"

"I'll get to that part."

"So what happened with Blue?" It takes a lot for me to say the man's ridiculous name.

"We talked a lot, video chatted, texted, everything. I saw him in December. After the holidays, he got quiet. I doubted everything. So I booked an internship at a resort in Saint Lucia."

"And then?"

"And then I found his new girlfriend's Instagram. She'd tagged him, and it popped up on my feed. He'd completely moved on and hadn't even told me."

"Hence your social media ban."

"Yup."

"Well. Feck Blue, right?"

Maddie steps back from me and crosses her arms on her chest, turning to face the gorgeous view once again. In every way, my arms feel immediately empty without her in them.

"Yeah, fuck Blue."

She's so far away, with that longing look in her eyes. I clench my fists at my sides, my hands itching to touch her again. To comfort her.

"But now you're in Dingle."

"Mmm, I am."

"I think I'm missing a connection between the two."

She glances at me. "I was too chicken to tell Reese. I didn't want her to know about my latest fuckup. When I couldn't get a refund for my flight, I thought about this road trip, and how I just needed a minute to regroup and restart my life . . ."

"So you changed your flight to Dublin."

"That I did."

"You might be the dictionary definition of impulsive."

"I also dropped out of the hospitality program."

I pause and examine her face. Close up, she's got freckles dotting her nose and under her eyes. It's fecking adorable.

"Why'd you do that?"

"I hated it." She shakes her head, helping the wind to lift the long strands of hair wrapping around her neck like a scarf. "And I didn't need it. I don't want to work at a hotel, and I know how to manage a restaurant, a bar, a pub, whatever. Even though I don't have a fancy college degree."

"Neither do I."

"I also didn't play professional soccer." She reaches out and pokes me in the arm.

I can't help but let my face soften. "You don't need to have done either of those things, you know." She's so vulnerable on this cliffside, and the most beautiful thing I've ever seen against the backdrop of the ocean and Blasket Islands.

"Thanks."

We stare at each other for a few seconds until she breaks our silence.

"You know what the stupidest thing is?"

"What?" I ask.

"His name's not even really Blue." She snorts. "It's Brian. He changed it to Blue when he started working on the island. He's actually from Ohio. Brian from Ohio. Can you get more boring than that?"

I throw my head back and laugh, and when I look at her again, she's smiling widely. It's like I'd made her entire day just by laughing. There might not be sun in the sky right now, but she's like a ray of light warming my soul.

"Madison, I can tell you for sure, Blue-Brian from Ohio is a total loser."

"Agreed. Okay, I've told you way too much. It's your turn. Tell me something super personal."

Well, feck me. This turned fast.

"I have nothing personal."

"Come on. I'm freezing my ass out here on the edge of the world. Throw me a bone."

I can't just offer up a part of myself. It's not who I am. I couldn't even do it with Cara. Or with the other local girl I dated.

"Ask me a question." But maybe I can try. She's starting her life over, maybe I can try to change parts of myself as well.

"I want to ask two."

"Go on."

"Have you always wanted to run the brewery?"

"Yes. But until Dad's stroke last fall—"

"I'm so sorry." She interrupts me and entwines her fingers together. "I didn't know that happened."

"He's doing well now. But it was time for him to step back, and he finally let me take over. So yes, I've wanted to run the brewery since I left soccer." I swallow. That wasn't so hard. "Next question."

Maddie narrows her eyes at me, her gaze darting quickly down to my lips in a fast movement I almost miss. "Have you ever been in love?"

"*Jaysus*. Not easing into personal questions, are we?" I run my hand from the back of my neck through my hair and down my face.

"Too scary for you? Do you want a different question?"

"Yes. That's my answer."

"With who?"

"That's a third question."

She blinks at me and raises her eyebrows, waiting for my response.

"Fine. Her name was Cara. We were engaged. After I left soccer, I followed her to Dublin. It was a disaster, and five years ago, I came back here—alone—and bought O'Brien's. And the flat."

I leave out the fact that she's Liam's little sister. That Liam used to be my mate. That I lost both of them in one fell swoop.

Maddie stares, waiting, her hair flowing around her like a sweet halo, but then she nods.

"Well, fuck Cara then, right? She can fuck off to Saint fucking Lucia and hang out with Blue-Brian from Ohio."

I offer her half a grin. "She's still in Dublin, I think with a different man than the one she cheated on me with."

"Well, we hate him, too. She's a stupid twit for leaving a hot ex-pro soccer player bartender behind who probably has awesome hobbies like crossword puzzles and knitting."

I bite back a laugh. "I don't knit. Or do crossword puzzles. And I don't do relationships anymore."

She cocks her head at me. "Like, never? Your sister told me you'd been single for years, but she made it sound like it wasn't by choice."

"Saoirse," I grumble under my breath. "It's by choice. I don't date."

"Hmm." She studies my face until it makes me uncomfortable. "What are you doing?"

"Trying to figure you out."

I sigh and shake my head. "Come on then, love, let's go to Dunquin." The term of endearment slips out, but she doesn't seem to notice.

We climb back on the bikes, and I lead the way along the winding road toward Dunquin Pier, which is only a ten-minute cycle. It strikes me how normal I feel chatting with Maddie.

I haven't said Cara's name out loud in years. It's basically forbidden in my presence.

Yet I just offered it up to Maddie Hart.

I glance back to make sure Maddie's keeping up, and she is, her hair flying out behind her from under the crooked helmet, a smile on her face.

This is fine. This is normal. She's my best friend's fiancée's little sister.

Basically, she's nothing to me. But I can still feel protective of her, right?

Nothing will happen between us. We've already established that. We're just friends.

Cycling one of the most beautiful, romantic roads in the world.

This is fine.

9

MADDIE

Saturday, March 8

Boyfriend Disaster #3: Vinny the Mama's Boy
Job Location & Length: Kinnley's Pizza, 1.5 years
My Age: 22

Vinny was the kind of Jersey guy who said he was Italian, but was *Jersey* Italian, not *Italian* Italian. He spent months dedicatedly making me laugh while he danced, twirled pizza dough in the air, and tossed individual pieces of shredded cheese into my mouth from across the kitchen. He talked about his mom all the time. He used too much gel in his dark hair.
But he was a truly nice guy, and eventually I said yes to his repeated attempts to get me to go out with him.
Vinny kissed me at the end of the first date and I knew immediately he and I were not a fit. There was nothing there. No zing, no passion, not even the smallest spark. I tried to tell him calmly, but he begged, cried, and then called his mom while I was still in his car.

Ending things with Vinny was extra painful because he really liked me, but I wasn't into it. It was all about me that time.

I couldn't face him. RIP job number three.

Breakup Reason: no spark
My Distress Level: 3, not because I was so into him, but because I wished I was
Lesson Learned: Don't agree to go out with someone just because they're nice.

I wake up in the flat absolutely boiling. This place is about a million degrees, and nothing I do to the thermostat changes how hot it gets. Last night I slept in my underwear and a tank, like the previous nights.

But as I lie on top of the soft duvet, staring at the ceiling, I think about who I could complain to.

Patrick.

It'd been one breathtaking view after another on the bike ride the other day, but my favorite part was when he let me snuggle into him. He wrapped his arms around me, protecting me from the wind. And the world.

He even made me laugh about Blue (Brian from Ohio). I hadn't found any part of that relationship amusing until yesterday.

And that feeling when he rubbed my back? My cheek against his hard chest? I need to be careful.

My phone buzzes.

PATRICK

I left something for you at the bottom of the stairs. I used my key to get in to the first door— I hope you don't mind

My eyes widen. Sure, there was a second door between us, but my heart speeds up a bit to think Patrick had been only twenty feet away while I was sleeping in my underwear.

I jump up and walk to the entrance, cracking it open and sliding out to peer down the stairway, phone clutched in my hand. A dark shadow leans against the wall. I blink and let out a surprised huff when I realize what it is.

ME

A bike?

PATRICK

Yes. For you to use while you're here. And the helmet. Let me know if you can adjust it to fit better or we can grab you a new one

ME

Thank you

PATRICK

No problem. I don't want you hurting yourself on some shite rental bike before I can hire your replacement

I bite my bottom lip, then press my phone to my chest and grin.

No matter his protests, I think I'm growing on that man.

PATRICK

Also, there's a soccer game at the park if you're interested in watching. We're about to start. My sister's here and suggested I invite you. She said something about you being sad and lonely, so . . .

ME

There's no way your sweet sister said that about me. I'm a social butterfly, happy and outgoing, and I have thirty-six thousand friends. Never sad or lonely

PATRICK

Sweet sister? Not sure who you're talking about

ME

I'll see if I can fit you in my schedule today. I'm very busy

He texts an eye roll emoji and I snort a laugh.

Patrick's inviting me to watch him play soccer? I dart back into the flat and get dressed as fast as I can, sweating my ass off and choosing another dress before grabbing my new rain jacket on the way out. At the bottom of the stairs, I pause to touch the bike before sliding out the door of the flat to street level, a grin on my face.

Friends. I'm making friends. See? I'm already starting over here, even though it's more like a practice run. I stride down Main Street and turn toward the park in the middle of town.

The players are all already on the field as I approach Saoirse, who is standing on the sideline. Her daughters are on a picnic blanket behind her, wrapped in warm jackets and winter hats, Niamh playing with a pair of Barbies, Erin staring down at her iPad and probably rubbish YouTube.

"Morning, Saoirse." I slide next to her, adjusting my hood to block the lightly falling rain.

"Maddie, hey!" She turns to me with those hazel eyes, her hair pulled back in a low ponytail beneath a colorful winter hat. "Did my brother actually text you?"

I nod.

"I told him to. I'm shocked he listened. I would've, but I don't have your number."

"We can fix that." I pull out my phone and text the number she gives me right away. The ref blows the whistle to start the game. I turn to watch.

Specifically, the smoking hot goalkeeper.

Patrick towers in front of the net. His thighs are thick in athletic shorts, and his biceps push against the sleeves of his tight, long-sleeved green jersey. He stands in the middle of the goal, arms hanging by his sides, padded goalkeeper gloves making him look like some kind of fighter. As I watch, he pulls the hem of his jersey up to wipe moisture from his eyes, revealing the bottom half of his chiseled abdomen—much more than I caught a glimpse of during his yawn the other day. The muscles in my lower belly clench and all my blood seems to rush between my legs. I reach in my hood and scratch my neck roughly to feel something somewhere else.

The rain falls harder. Saoirse pulls her hood over her winter hat. Her girls open an umbrella and huddle together.

I groan. "Does it always rain in Ireland?"

"Yes, it does. It's cold enough to need a hat and gloves, but usually not enough to snow. Lovely, huh?" She glances back at her daughters. "We won't last long. Probably just another few minutes."

The men are already slipping all over the place, the ball slick on their feet. Water is dripping off Patrick's face, and he shakes his head to clear the moisture as Liam dribbles up and takes a shot at goal. Patrick easily catches it and throws the ball three-quarters of the way down the field. Liam curses and chases the ball. He's cute, too, and really would be a better choice for me to fawn over, not the man I'm renting a flat from, working for, and planning a road trip with.

Patrick turns toward us and raises a hand, not smiling, but keeping his eyes trained in our direction while the ball's on the other half of the field. I wave back, although certainly he's waving to his sister or his nieces.

Next to me, Saoirse huffs a laugh, and I turn to her watching me with her eyes crinkled at the corners.

"What?"

"It's just that I haven't seen my brother acknowledge another woman in public in a long time."

"I'm sure he was waving to you." My cheeks burn. And even if the wave was for me, we're friends. I'm absolutely not thinking of that hot hallway kiss, the one that definitely doesn't haunt my days and nights. Thankfully, there's zero percent chance he told his sister about *that* incident.

"He already said hi to us."

I look back on the field, where Patrick's standing with crossed arms watching the game. Someone scores and his team celebrates, Patrick pumping his fist in the air once.

Again, he looks over to us. My chest squeezes.

"I heard you went on a bike ride?" Saoirse asks, more a statement than a question.

Shit, she's still watching me, which means she's observing me drooling over her brother. I force myself to look away from him.

"Yeah, I think he was worried I'd ride on the wrong side of the road or fall off a cliff."

"Hmm." Her eyes flit over my face.

"Hmm what?"

"Many women would be happy to throw themselves off a cliff if it'd get his attention. But he never gives it to them. At least not for more than one night."

I get it. He's not a relationship guy. He doesn't date. It doesn't matter to me, because that god on the soccer field over there? He's not mine. He'll never be mine. I can't even hold the attention of some drifter who renamed himself Blue, or nine other dudes, so I definitely can't snag Patrick McNulty.

"He's a really good man." Saoirse's voice is soft. "My brother's been hurt. He doesn't think he's capable of being in a relationship."

Who would cheat on *him*?

"I'm sure he'll find someone eventually." It won't be me. It can't be me. I'm not even supposed to be here.

"It doesn't help that my marriage fell apart, too, so he looks at it as another example that true love is unattainable. Except for our parents, of course."

"He said that?"

She laughs. "No. He didn't say that. But I know that's what he feels."

My heart grows two sizes in my chest. And it's my heart I have to be careful with here. It would be way too easy to let myself fall for Patrick, the same way I've done so many times before. I swallow hard as I think of jobs number eight and nine. The most painful ones.

I need to make sure I don't let that happen here.

Because apparently, I'm not a great judge of character. Or a person who makes good life decisions. I need someone to ground me, to keep me from losing sight of my goal.

I blink and keep my eyes trained on Patrick as he dives for the ball, easily capturing it in his gloved hands, mud and water spraying up as he slides. He reminds me of a wild lion in the African savanna, and we're just a bunch of tourists in a Jeep, gaping.

This time—here in Dingle—it will be different. I know what's going on. I understand who I am now. The mistakes I've made. I've learned so many lessons.

I know I'm going to quit O'Brien's, sooner rather than later. I know I'm going to leave Dingle, Patrick, all these people I've just met. This time, I'll get it right. I thought I was doing it right in Saint Lucia with Aunt Evelyn's voice in my head, telling me to create a better life for myself. But Blue distracted me.

This time, I won't forget what I'm here for.

For now, I might as well enjoy myself. My shoulders relax and I let out a deep breath.

Glad I got that all figured out.

Saoirse and the girls leave before halftime, her asking if I'll stay for drinks with her and Ian after my afternoon shift ends tonight. I agree.

I should leave the chilly, wet game as well, but I don't. And at the end, I'm the only person standing off to the side, under a tree fifty feet back from the field.

"Shit," I whisper as the teams start filing off the field. I should've escaped when I had the chance, instead of being the only spectator left. I slip behind the thick tree trunk, pressing my back against the bark and praying no one sees me.

I'll just hide till everyone's gone. That's reasonable, isn't it?

Players walk past and I try to look casual and stare at my phone. I don't see Patrick, but maybe he went another way. I'm about to dash off toward my flat when he rounds the tree.

"Madison Elizabeth Hart." Patrick stops in front of me. "Are you hiding?"

My eyes widen and I swallow.

"No."

He's drenched, dripping wet from head to cleats, his dark hair flopping over his forehead, raindrops sitting on his eyelashes. His long-sleeved jersey clings to his chest.

I want to throw back the hood of the rain jacket I bought in town this week and kiss him in the pouring rain, the way it might happen in a movie.

"No?" He tilts his head and twists his mouth.

"Not hiding. Just . . . sheltering." I peel myself off the tree and try to look casual, even though I'm clearly the most awkward human being in all of Ireland.

"Come on. I'll walk you home. I parked in front of the pub."

I nod and fall into step next to him, thankful he's not calling me out further.

"I wasn't coming to watch you, you know." But apparently, I can't keep my mouth shut.

"You weren't?" He cocks his head and touches my arm as we cross the road along the park. "You must look right first, love, or you'll get run over."

"Thanks. And no, I came to see your sister."

He snorts adorably. We step back onto the sidewalk in the direction of O'Brien's, his hand sliding off my arm, the touch lingering.

"Pub tonight? Are you working? Drinking?" I bite my lip and turn to watch him consider.

"I've got the girls."

Damn.

"Have any fun plans with them?" My disappointment is immense, but I picture Patrick picking up Niamh and spinning her around, and that makes me smile.

"We're going to paint wooden figurines," he answers without hesitating.

"That sounds amazing. I'd love to do that." I cringe when I realize it sounds like I'm fishing for an invitation. "I'm meeting up with your sister and Ian after my shift."

"Have fun." He slides a look in my direction. The man is impossible to read.

"You are getting drenched."

"I already was drenched." He meets my gaze, streams of water flowing off his face, and stops.

"What's wrong?"

"This is you." Patrick nods his head to the flat door.

"Oh. Right."

"See you later, Madison." Patrick's gaze lingers on me for a beat before he turns and walks three cars up, pausing at the passenger door and pulling a towel out from the car to wipe his face down.

Then he peels off his wet jersey.

"Sweet baby Jesus," I whisper and know I should unlock the door and go inside. Instead, I watch him rub his abdomen with the towel before sliding it up around his neck. When he's done, he quickly strides around to the driver's side, already wet again. But before he ducks into the car, he glances my way. A grin quirks his mouth before he lowers himself into the seat.

"Fuck!" I whisper-scream and spin to face the door. I was

standing in the rain getting all hot and bothered, water dripping down around my hood and into my jacket, gawking at him. What is wrong with me?

Despite the pep talk I gave myself at the soccer game, I'm not sure I can resist that man. It's a good thing we're just friends.

10

PATRICK

"**D**a? Mam?" I call out to my parents as I slip off my runners on the front mat. I'm a wet, muddy disaster from the soccer game and drove here shirtless in an attempt to dry off. My mobile buzzes and I fish it out of the bag with my dry clothes.

MADDIE

> Does the bike mean you'll go for another ride with me?

ME

> Unsure. I don't really have time for fun

MADDIE

> So you're saying I'm fun?

I bite back a grin. Maddie watched me strip off my wet jersey, which also makes me smile, something I seem to do a lot around the American tourist.

"In here," my father calls from the family room.

"I'm just going to grab a quick shower." In my parents' bathroom, I turn on the hot water and strip off the rest of my clothes, shoving them in a plastic bag. I'm in and out of the shower in five minutes, all the mud and rain washed away.

My parents live about a kilometer from me in the house Saoirse and I grew up in, which felt too small when we were kids, but is perfect for them now. Saoirse also lives close, so when I had the chance to buy my cottage . . . it's exactly where I wanted to be.

I peek my head in the family room. Dad's sitting on the couch with a newspaper—probably one of the last houses in Ireland to get an actual paper delivered—a blanket on his lap and a thick wool sweater on his body. His feet are resting on one of the last pieces of furniture I finished before taking over the brewery. I'm proud of that one, and the fact that they finally let me replace their decades-old coffee table.

It was only after Dad's stroke six months ago that I truly accepted that my parents were aging. Of course, I knew it all along. I'd be gone for long stretches while playing soccer, so each time I visited, I'd see differences in a marked way.

But until last year, it didn't feel as real.

"Hello, son. Your mam's in the kitchen." Dad smiles at me and nods his head in my mother's direction. Even the way he says her name showcases how much he loves her. It's soft and sweet and always said with a smile. It's hard to believe that they were separated for an entire year when I was young. They never told us what happened, or how they worked it all out. But they did and are blissfully happy to this day.

Letting go of the brewery was their passage into the next stage of their lives. I'm still furious that their first instinct was to sell it, not pass it to me. Apparently New Dingle—Liam—had approached them multiple times over the past few years with offers to buy. I had to practically beg to get them to give me a chance. I think they didn't want to burden me with a barely-profitable, complex business. They thought I was happy with just the pub.

I think they keep hoping I'll meet someone and settle down, start a family.

I'd been back in town for a year after breaking up with Cara when I started a new relationship with a local woman. She was sweet and open and so full of life. I tagged along with her for six months, trying to heal myself from the hurt from my broken engagement. I thought it was working . . . but she broke up with me. *I don't think you even like me,* she'd said, amongst other things. *It's like there's nothing there.* And *maybe you'd be better off alone.*

I tried to tell her I did like her, that sometimes I can't figure out how to say the right things, but the words came out all wrong. I knew then it was hopeless to try to find a woman who would understand me. I ruin any romantic relationship just by being myself.

And since the woman still lives in Dingle, I have to see her all the time. It's a small town. She's nice to me. Kind. Always has been. But having to see your ex regularly? Even one you weren't serious with? It's painful.

I decided I'd only do one-night stands. Brief encounters, and only with people passing through. No awkward conversations, no misunderstandings, no broken promises.

At almost forty years old, the desire for love, a relationship, or a family of my own is all gone.

"I'll get you tea." I reach down to hug my father from his spot on the couch.

I find my mother in the kitchen, cleaning up bowls from a meat-and-potatoes stew, the smell of which reminds me of my childhood.

"Hi, Mam." I kiss her on the cheek. She looks up at me and smiles, the lines etched in her seventy-year-old face another reminder of time passing.

"So tell me more about this American woman."

"What?" *Christ.*

"Saoirse told me some. She's quite lovely, according to your sister. Pretty, sweet, and apparently you took her on a cycle of Slea

Head Drive." Mam flips off the water and turns to me, a knowing look in her eyes. But also hopeful. Shite.

"She's Oliver's fiancée's little sister, Mam."

"Lovely, so she's not some random lass passing through, then."

I groan. An unwelcome—sort of—flash of kissing Maddie at O'Brien's goes through my mind.

"She's not random, but not someone I'm going to date." I don't even know her plans. She rented the flat for a month, but is she intending on going back home after that? Then coming back for the road trip, then the wedding in Scotland? Not that I care about her plans. Not one bit.

"Hmm." Mam opens the refrigerator. "Can I heat up some stew for you?"

"No, thank you." I need to make sure my mam has no expectations for Maddie. "We're just friends. And hardly that, even." I grab the kettle from the stove and fill it with water. "I'm watching out for her. Oliver would kill me if something happened to Reese's little sister."

"Okay." She clearly does not accept my assurances of a platonic relationship and turns back to the remaining dishes in the sink.

"Hello!" Saoirse's voice rings out from the front door, and my nieces chatter as they walk in. My sister pops into the kitchen, dark hair in a low ponytail.

I spin to her with crossed arms. "What have you been telling Mam about the American?"

"The American, huh?" She snickers, eyes shining. "I was filling her in on our lovely new friend."

I moan.

"Who I just saw going into O'Brien's," Saoirse adds.

"I'm surprised she keeps showing up." The kettle clicks off and I fill a mug with steaming water for my father, dropping in a fresh teabag. My parents like to reuse their teabags, which is disgusting, so when I'm around, I don't allow it.

Even though they claim they don't need it, Saoirse and I both help out as much as they'll put up with. I do small grocery runs for them, which Mam begrudgingly accepts. Saoirse cooks once a week, and we take turns with doctors' appointments.

"Maddie seems quite natural at running that place."

"She's opening the pub and working for a few hours. It's hardly rocket science."

"Whatever, Pat. She's a delight, and you know it."

"I knew there was something going on." Mam finishes washing a dish and adds it to the stack in the drying rack.

"Stop ganging up on me," I groan. "Why is everyone making a big deal out of Madison being here?"

"Madison?" Saoirse leans against the counter, watching me dip the tea bag in and out of the steaming mug. "Interesting that you can't just call her Maddie."

"Feck me." I sigh. "Mind your own business, woman."

"Language!" Saoirse calls out as I head back to my father, who is now surrounded by Erin and Niamh.

Saoirse seems to have it as her goal to get me to date someone. She's always introducing me to her single mom friends or women she works with at the hotel. I think that's one of the reasons why she pushed Beth my way.

Just because my sister's happy with Ian after her divorce, that doesn't mean I need to pair off as well.

"I like that you're spending time with a woman." Mam follows me to the family room, Saoirse right behind her.

"She's not a woman, she's just . . ."

Everyone looks up at me as I struggle to finish the sentence.

"She's just a tourist, really. Here for an *adventure*."

Saoirse's eyes widen. She knows all about what Cara said to me years ago.

"She said that?" my little sister asks.

"Her words." Were they exactly that? I forget. But the word adventure was definitely included.

Dad sips his tea and goes back to admiring the drawing Niamh handed him.

"Semantics," Saoirse says, but the look on her face is more serious than before.

"Well. I'm off. Need to feed Turtle and Kitty."

"That's a daft excuse to leave. They're sheep. They can just eat the grass."

"They like their afternoon treats. Besides, I need to swing by the brewery and do a few things." I glance longingly at the front door, a sweet exit from this interrogation.

"Pub tonight? Have some craic?"

"I thought I had the girls? I've got plans to paint with them."

"Ah, no, they're sleeping here. Mam pulled rank and wants them." Saoirse nods her head toward our mother, who is now sitting next to Erin on the couch, dutifully looking at the iPad with her. "Save it for next time?"

"We're going to bake blueberry scones," Mam says. "Then watch a film, then we're going to work on their birthday present lists."

"Aren't their birthdays not till summer?"

"Never too early," Mam says.

"How about tomorrow night?" The idea of a Saturday evening with nothing to do is both comforting—I could work on sanding down the bookshelves I've been ignoring—and depressing.

"A school night? Nah. Next weekend?"

"Fine."

"So, O'Brien's tonight, since you're now free?"

"Nothing like going to my place of work on my night off." My traitorous brain immediately thinks of the American.

"Great." Saoirse cocks her head at me. "Maddie said she's going to stay after her shift as well. We're at a texting-level relationship now."

"Why would I care if she's going to be there?" But my insides flip at the thought of seeing her tonight. Something about that woman makes me uncomfortable. Not bad uncomfortable. Good uncomfortable. Like I want to be around her.

Which means I should probably avoid her.

Saoirse laughs and rolls her eyes at me—again—and I slip my runners on and escape my parents' house.

My mind is scattered now that I have new plans for the evening. What was I supposed to do this afternoon? Feed the sheep, and go to the brewery, but I forget why. Admin? I can just deal with that from home.

I hate that I'm looking forward to seeing Maddie tonight at the pub. She's off-limits. I can't mess around with her.

But I'm really just looking out for her, right? Like with the Slea Head bike ride. I don't want her to get in trouble drinking in Dingle. What would I tell Oliver?

So I'll go and keep an eye on things.

11

MADDIE

Boyfriend Disaster #4*: Franco the Poet
Job Location & Length*: Starbucks, 6 months
My Age*: 23

As a break from serving tables, I tried working as a barista. Franco was one as well. And a poet. He'd stare at me longingly from across the coffee shop. He asked me out by writing a haiku on a napkin.

We had an epic first date that started at a (different) coffee shop and ended up at the Jersey Shore, an hour and a half drive away. He had a blanket and a bottle of wine in his trunk, and we sat on the beach passing the bottle back and forth, listening to the ocean and staring out at the moon-kissed waves. He read me poetry. We slept together that night and couldn't stay away from each other for the next two weeks.

Then I went to a poetry reading with him and a few other baristas. He took the microphone and read a piece he'd recently written. About me. And that night on the beach. In excruciating detail.

It was beyond humiliating.

I never showed my face at that Starbucks—or to him
—again.

Breakup Reason: He was using me as a muse.
My Distress Level: 4
Lesson Learned: Stay away from artistic types.

T he wet start to the day progresses into a cold, rainy Saturday afternoon. By the time six o'clock rolls around, the pub is more crowded than I've seen it since I started. It feels good to pour pints and talk to customers.

Declan is working next to me, and I'm waiting for Ronan, the night manager, to show up and relieve me. I honestly think Patrick could streamline his pub workforce more. He could promote Declan and hire a few more part-time bartenders. I also had an idea I want to share with him later about how to bring in more tourists this summer.

I've been here just a week, but it feels like much longer. I'm glad I have three more weeks to avoid my life back in New Jersey. I'm sure I'll be sick of the weather and this town and the walls of the pub by then. But somehow, Dingle already feels like home. A temporary home.

The door pushes open and a crowd of people arrives, including Ronan, who raises a hand to me then slips down the hallway to the pub office. Behind him, Saoirse and Ian walk in together. Patrick's sister smiles broadly as she approaches the bar, tapping her finger on her wrist and making a drinking gesture.

"Three pints of Golden Amber." Saoirse winks at me. "One's for you. It's time."

I laugh and retrieve three pint glasses, tucking one under the tap and pulling the lever. "As soon as Ronan's settled, I'll be there."

"Ronan's settled." The night manager takes the full pint from me, pushes it to Saoirse, then starts on the second. "I'm here, you're done, get out." The Irishman nods his head toward the crowd.

"Get out as in sit over there and drink?"

"Not a choice I would make, but whatever makes you happy."

I grab one of the full pints and follow Saoirse to the table Ian's claimed in the back corner.

"Is your brother joining us?" I slide into a seat across from Ian and Saoirse, noting a fourth empty chair next to me.

"I told him his presence is required. He was salty that the girls weren't sleeping over tonight. I convinced Mam to come up with a whole plan for them. Patrick needs a good night out."

"Aw, he was excited about painting wooden figurines with them."

Saoirse raises her eyebrows. "They can do it next time."

"My kids are with their mother," Ian says. "So this is a big night out for all of us." He rubs Saoirse's back with one hand, an obvious *us* between them. Envy sparks inside me. Not jealousy—because seeing the two of them happy together is wonderful—but a wish that I could ever have a relationship like that. Not one born from secrets or misunderstandings or sneaking around.

"Cheers." Saoirse lifts her pint glass to clink with mine. "Let's get drunk! Pleasantly drunk, and only drunk enough that I can still get up and function as a parent tomorrow."

"So maybe just buzzed?" Ian suggests.

"Stop trying to ruin my fun, baby."

Ian laughs and we all drink. I'm enjoying the moment until my phone buzzes. I pick it up as Ian whispers into Saoirse's ear.

STELLA

Hey girl, haven't seen any pretty Caribbean pics in the past few days. Why you holding out on us?

REESE

Everyone send a picture of what they're doing right now

Images pop up from both of them. Stella's at a pub with Ethan, her boyfriend, and Reese is at Target with her high school senior daughter, Chelsea.

Fuuuuck. Sometimes I forget that I'm not where I'm supposed to be. What if something happened and my family couldn't find me? What if it were really important and they tried to reach me in Saint Lucia?

Shit. I'm the worst.

"Hello." Patrick's deep voice cuts through my negative spiral as he settles in the chair next to me. "What's wrong?"

Saoirse and Ian are still whispering together, and she lifts a hand to her brother.

I lock my gaze with Patrick's. Those intense hazel eyes drill into me like he can see every bit of what's swirling around inside.

"What makes you think something's wrong?" My voice is slightly unsteady. The whole room fades away. He's a force of nature, impossible for me to resist. I don't understand why everyone around us isn't staring. He's like gravity, and I'm some dumb rock being sucked into his orbit. He's sitting close. So close. Close enough that if I reached my hand out, I could slide it up over the stubble of his cheek and to the back of his neck, then into his thick, dark hair.

"Madison."

I chug my pint and let the liquid warm my belly before taking a deep breath.

"You know, the usual. Just figuring out which lies to text to my sisters."

One side of Patrick's mouth turns up. "Just say you're busy. Or don't respond now, and later say you were napping. Or . . . cycling."

"Very funny. They want a proof-of-life picture. I've been googling beach images of the Caribbean."

"I've never been, but I can safely say that besides the ocean part, Dingle is about as far from the Caribbean as you can get."

"I know. They think I'm going to this made-up internship at a resort and hanging out on the beach. Damn, but the beach sounds amazing right now." I was still so frozen from this morning's wet soccer game, I'd even worn pants to work this afternoon. But it's always hot in here, just like it is in my flat, so I paired the leggings with a black tank top.

"Hmm." Patrick rubs his thumb and pointer finger over his chin, the five o'clock shadow on his face creating a sound like sandpaper on wood. "There must be Irish pubs in Saint Lucia. Just snap a picture in here and say you're out for drinks with the locals."

"I mean, it's not a terrible idea." I quirk an eyebrow at him.

"You're wearing a tank top, so you could be on a hot island." His eyes flick down to my torso and linger for a second longer than necessary to make his point.

Heat rises from my neck under his gaze. "That's because it's hot as hell in here. Just like in the flat."

Patrick chuckles. "Yes, sorry about that. The heating system is not well-controlled in this building." He pulls out his phone and types. "Let's take a look. Here." He holds it up to me and makes a face. "O'Grady's Irish Pub. They even sell margaritas, which means it's one hundred percent authentic Irish."

"It could work."

"But you are very much not tanned."

"Hey, look who's talking. You're the palest man I've ever met."

Patrick laughs, head back and neck exposed, drawing my attention to the muscles in his shoulders. Visible, naturally, through his tight black t-shirt.

Saoirse looks up from her conversation with Ian, watching her brother with wide eyes.

"Wait—" Patrick grabs my arm as I lift my hand to take a selfie. "Make sure it's a plain background." He gestures to the side wall, which only has a simple Irish flag secured to the wall. "Oliver knows this pub, but that wall is not identifiable."

"Good catch." I carefully take the selfie, show it to Patrick for approval, and send it to my sisters.

"Glad you could join us, Pat," Saoirse says.

"I didn't think it was optional." His voice is gruff, but he's got a smile hiding underneath.

"Right. It wasn't." Saoirse winks at me.

"Cheers to a night out," Ian says.

Saoirse and Ian clink pints, then turn to us, expecting the same.

After touching my glass, Patrick keeps his eyes on me.

"You've made quite the impression here."

"Have I?"

He shrugs. "On other people. Like Saoirse and Ian. And Ronan, and Declan. Not me."

I bite my lip. "Well, I'm glad I haven't totally fucked your pub up."

"You've slid into this job smoother than anyone I've hired in years. I have a hard time getting people to even show up. You flew into Ireland one day and grabbed yourself a job the next instead of hopping on a tour bus or lying around. I'm quite impressed."

"Thanks." A warm, cozy feeling fills my insides. It's probably the beer, but compliments don't hurt. "I had an idea, actually."

"What now?" Patrick sighs.

"Hear me out. Why don't you get together with some of the other businesses in town and create a Dingle Tourist Passport of sorts? Visitors can get a stamp or sticker or something for stopping by Dingle Brew, Ian's tattoo shop, the bike rental place, here, obviously . . . and then they get a free t-shirt, or sticker, or print of Dingle. Something like that."

As I talk, Patrick's words bounce around in my head. Quite impressed? I don't think I've ever been especially impressive at work. I do a good job managing restaurants. I'm a strong enough manager. But I'm super replaceable, as are most people in the restaurant industry. He's probably just buttering me up so I don't walk out on him like the last manager.

Ian slides two fresh pints in front of us. I didn't even realize he'd gone for more.

"I actually like that idea." Patrick raises his eyebrows thoughtfully.

"Yeah?" I grin at him. "Can you tell me more about how good I am at my job?" I stare into his eyes and drain my pint.

"I gave you enough compliments to last a lifetime. To balance them out, I can tell you what I find annoying about you. You're always fecking smiling."

"I can't help it if I'm a sunshine-y kind of person." I bite my lip and his eyes flick down to my mouth. In turn, I look at his. What would it be like to kiss him again?

"Even though your boss is kind of an arsehole."

I let out a laugh. "Nah. I think he's just misunderstood."

One side of his mouth turns up at that, and he starts to say something else, but stops abruptly with a glance at the entrance to the pub. I'm mid-gulp of my second pint and enjoying the warmth spreading throughout my body. The easy, relaxed look vanishes off his face and is replaced by a cold mask turned to the door.

"Patrick? You okay?"

He looks like he's turned into a different person. *What just happened here?*

"Oh, shite," Saoirse says.

I follow her and her brother's gaze to the door, where there's a new trio of people heading to the bar. Liam and another couple holding hands who I don't recognize.

"What? Is it Liam?" I glance from Saoirse to Patrick. His teeth are clenched so hard, I'm afraid he's going to crack them, and his mouth is turned down in a deep frown. Any light in his eyes has been completely extinguished.

"It's not about Liam." Saoirse's eyes narrow at the group as they shake off their jackets and look around.

"Who is with him?"

There's dark pain in Patrick's face. It's in the space between his eyes, where a worry line deepens. And the way his muscular shoulders are raised so much higher than they were while we were joking around a moment ago.

The group is now at the bar, and Liam turns and throws his arm around the unknown woman's shoulder. The woman laughs and pushes him away.

"Hello, hi, someone tell me what's going on?"

Ian sighs. "That's Cara. Liam's sister."

My jaw drops.

"Cara is Liam's sister?" I swing my head back to Patrick.

"You two have talked about Cara?" Saoirse was the one who originally told me Cara's name, but it was on our bike ride that Patrick had shared more.

"Y-yes. Just not the sibling part of the equation." I look back at the group, now getting served by Ronan. The other man walks up behind Cara and slides his hands on her waist.

I turn to watch Patrick's profile. He keeps his eyes trained on his ex-fiancée. So much makes sense. The soccer and brewery rivalry between Liam and Patrick. How they seem to despise each other. Why didn't he tell me this other connection?

"She's around town once in a while, but I haven't seen her at the pub in ages," Saoirse explains.

"I mean, why the hell would she come to her ex's pub with her boyfriend?"

I hate the way the life and energy seem to have drained from Patrick. I miss our flirty banter, the way he was making me feel, how my insides fluttered when I won a hard-earned laugh.

Saoirse's phone rings on the table and *MAM* pops up on her screen.

"I need to get this in case there's something with the girls. I'll be right back." She reaches over and touches Patrick's arm, but he doesn't react.

"I'm going to go check on my kids as well." Ian stands and follows Saoirse.

Now it's just the two of us at the table.

"Hey, this is shitty, I'm sorry she showed up."

He finally turns his head to me, and his eyes soften.

"It's not your problem."

"Fuck that, yeah it is. I hate that bitch."

He chuckles, and I get one of those fluttery feelings.

"It's bound to happen. This is a small town. I can't avoid her."

"In your pub? This is your territory."

He pauses, and I think he's done talking to me about Cara, but then he speaks.

"I hadn't been in love with her for a long time when we broke up, but I didn't realize that until much later." It's almost like he's talking to himself. "Her hooking up with that American banker . . . she did me a favor."

"A shitty ass favor, Patrick."

He's quiet for a beat. "It was difficult losing her and Liam at the same time."

I swallow, trying to absorb some of the pain radiating off him. He starts to turn back to the bar.

"Hey, look at me." I reach up and gently put my hand on his cheek, moving his face toward mine. Our connection is warm and tingly, and his eyes blink a bunch of times when they meet mine. "Fuck her. She messed up and lost you."

"But I don't do crossword puzzles or knit."

"Still a catch." My heart skips a beat.

A smile creeps over his face. My hand is still on his cheek, and his eyes dart down to my lips. Someone drops a glass by the bar, and I look over to see Cara staring at Patrick. Her ex-fiancé, who has another woman's hand on him. Her eyes are wide and her jaw drops open slightly.

Correction: Cara's staring at *us*.

There's a look on her face as she drinks him in, then me, then him again. It's curiosity, longing, maybe regret. That's what I think, anyway. She's ignoring everyone around her—including the man with an arm around her waist—and watching.

I turn back to Patrick, and he hasn't noticed her looking at us. Because he's looking at me.

I have the best idea ever.

"Hey, just go with this, okay?"

"Go with what?" The spot between his eyebrows crinkles.

I do the only thing I can think of. The thing that seems perfect for this moment. I put my other hand on his face and pull his mouth to meet mine.

I kiss him.

12

MADDIE

I kiss him because his ex-fiancée is watching, because she stomped all over his heart, and because, *damn*, I want to. Because he's hot, and he's been kind to me, and the way he looks at me sometimes melts my underwear right off.

He doesn't pull away. Has he been waiting for us to do this again, like I have? I've lived that hallway kiss over and over again, countless times a day. Has he, too?

Lordy, his lips are warm on mine, and I lean further into the kiss, sliding my hands from his cheeks onto the sides of his head, burying them in his hair like I've fantasized about.

He breathes into me and kisses me back, pressing our lips together while turning his head, as if he wants better access to my mouth. A hand slides on my thigh, already pressed up against his, and an electric current shoots up my leg into my hot center. A flick of his tongue between my lips and the breath leaves my body. My whole soul might be gone with it as well.

I let out a soft moan and I feel him pause and smile against me.

"What?" I whisper.

"Maddie. What are you doing?"

I can feel the words against my lips. And the answer is that I'm doing much less than I want to. I want to pull him into our dark hallway and let him do dirty things to me. I want to—

Shit. We're in the middle of the pub. *His* pub.

I pull back and catch my runaway breath. Patrick's eyes are hooded, and his lips remain parted, eyes locked on mine. Flames dance in his pupils.

"You kissed me."

"Mmm-hmm. I did." I suck in my lips, which are tingly. "You kissed me back." There's a slight edge of defensiveness in my voice.

"Trust me, I'm not complaining. But why?"

I sigh lightly. His Irish accent is more pronounced with a pint in him. And maybe, after kissing me. I could drown in his lilting words. I rip my gaze from his and glance back at the bar in time to see Cara swing her head away, face crumpled.

He looks over at Cara, then back at me, then snorts out a laugh. "You kissed me so she would see?"

My eyes widen. Is he mad? Offended? He might be. That was petty. Maybe he still has a thing for her. Exes are weird.

I should know, I have a lot of them.

But not an ex-fiancé. That might be different. What if he didn't want to kiss me in front of everyone at his place of employment? What if he didn't want to kiss me again at all?

But given his response, I'm pretty sure he did.

Still. I crossed a huge line.

"Yeah. I did. Is that okay?"

He's examining me, a weird look on his face that's a combination of a smirk and a grin and maybe a grimace, when both Ian and Saoirse come back at the same time.

"All is good!" Saoirse plops back down. "Just a question about how many books sneaky Niamh gets before bedtime. You know how she is."

Patrick nods, eyes on me. "She wants about ten."

"She gets three, though. But I bet you give in to her."

"Sure do."

Oh, sweet baby Jesus, the way this man is looking at me. I press my lips together.

"I brought shots," Ian states.

"Really, Ian?" Patrick finally turns his head toward Saoirse and Ian, who has a spread of filled shot glasses on a tray.

When I look away from Patrick, Saoirse is watching me with a twinkle in her eye. Did she see us kiss? Between this and her little speeches to me about her brother, I'm getting the feeling she's supportive of whatever just happened.

"Really." The tattooed redhead doesn't flinch from Patrick's glare.

"I'm not a big liquor person." I attempt a protest.

"Objection denied." Ian cheerfully slides a glass across the table to me.

"Aren't we too old for this?" I try again, pleading with my eyes to not have to drink the clear liquid.

"What does age have to do with shots?" Ian shakes his head.

Saoirse shrugs in agreement, and Patrick chuckles. The three of them knock the shots back and I follow suit, concentrating on not gagging at it burns its way down my throat.

An hour and another round of pints and shots later, everyone is trashed. Or at least I am, because three pints and two shots will do that.

"Anytime, lass, come on down and I'll get you sorted with a beautiful tattoo." Ian's face is lit up.

"Both my sisters have tattoos already, and I feel like I'm slacking. I mean, if responsible, perfect Reese did it, surely I can, too?" I concentrate on not slurring my words.

"Exactly."

"And your tattoos are just beautiful. What are those?"

"My kids' names." Ian holds out his right arm, pushing up the short sleeve on his biceps. "Eileen is seven, and Jack and James are both five."

Celtic swirls and knots surround the script names, masking the words beautifully.

"I love it."

"They are my everything. Well, them and Saoirse." He casts an intense glance at Patrick's sister, and she reaches over and touches his hand, even though she's in another conversation.

I bet they don't have a ton of messy complications. But another look at his tattoos contradicts that. Five children between the two of them, two ex-spouses . . . Maybe their love is strong enough to overcome?

"Hey, question for you," I say to Ian.

"Go ahead."

"What's a unique thing we can go see or do on our road trip? In Ireland or Northern Ireland?"

Ian twists his lips to one side and appears to think.

"Ah! There's a giant fish statue in Belfast."

I giggle. "Ohhhkay."

"It's called—wait for it—the Salmon of Knowledge."

"Perfect." I tap it into my phone.

Ian goes on to list other things for us to see in Belfast, but my mind wanders and my eyes flit to the striking goalkeeper standing a few feet away, talking to a man who might be from the soccer team. Patrick lifts his pint to his mouth and his arm muscles ripple. I wonder if he's got any tattoos under that tight black shirt? A sigh escapes my lips. I'm sure I won't find out.

Cara and Liam are no longer in view. I'm hoping they left, that Cara made the group go after seeing me kiss Patrick. I can't believe I did that. I can't believe Liam and Cara are siblings.

Patrick looks over at me, the other man still talking and waving a hand around, and he holds my gaze for a second longer than acceptable before turning away. The connection buzzes between us.

My heart squeezes and warmth floods my chest. How could anyone leave him? Cheat on him?

I'm in so much trouble.

I've known him for such a short time, but I'm feeling things I should not let myself feel. A kiss at a pub while on vacation is one thing. Even sex with a random Irishman would be okay. But letting myself feel anything for Patrick? That's a dangerous move.

I can't let myself make that mistake.

Ian excuses himself to follow Saoirse to the bar, but I hardly notice him go.

The room is hazy, and I decide the best thing I can do for myself is leave, before I do something stupid like make out with Patrick again. I stand and slide past him. He looks at me with questioning eyes and I gesture toward the bar, not telling him I'm leaving, suspecting he might not let me.

I slip out of the pub and into my front door twenty seconds later. My flat is a billion degrees—again. I strip down to my underwear and wiggle out of my bra, leaving on the tank top, before downing a tall glass of water and pain meds to fend off a hangover. I lie on the couch and scroll mindlessly on my phone until my eyes grow heavy.

Some amount of time later, I hear keys jangling in the lock. Not the front door, though.

I shoot up from the couch and spin to the other door. It's the door that I've never opened before, the one I don't have keys to.

The one that leads to the pub.

13

PATRICK

I haven't been this drunk in years.

I usually stop at two or three, max. I can't run a business, take care of my parents, and be there for my sister if I'm drunk or hungover all the time.

But between Saoirse—the sister I'm supposed to be helping—and Ian buying drinks, Cara showing up, and Maddie fecking kissing me . . . I'm a mess.

I stumble to the Jacks down the dark hallway—where I kissed Maddie the first time. After relieving myself, I trip back out into the hallway and my shoulder hits the doorframe, catching me from falling on my arse.

Where is she? I lean against the cool wood wall for a moment. I was half hoping to find her here, waiting for me.

I am so tempted to let myself go with her.

Logically, I know it would never work. Not only because she's leaving, but because of who I am.

I'm wrecked.

Time to go home and sleep this off. I run my hand down my face. Luckily, the door to my flat is right here, and the keys are in my pocket. Brilliant. I unlock the first door, which leads to the steep, dark staircase up to my flat. The door shuts behind me and the noise of the bar immediately dims. A sensor kicks off a low light, but I fumble with the torch on my mobile anyway and climb up the stairs. Aye—leaving the pub is the right thing to do. I need to sleep this off.

It takes me five tries to get the key into the lock.

And the moment the door swings wide to reveal the living space, I realize what I've done.

This is not my flat.

Well. It *is*, but I've rented it out.

To Maddie Hart.

She's standing a meter in front of me in the nearly pitch-dark, a beam of moonlight from the street side window gently illuminating her. She's in her fecking underwear and the tank top she was wearing earlier, but—*Christ save me*—without a bra, looking hot as hell, and aggressively holding what appears to be a butter knife.

"Patrick? What the actual fuck are you doing?" There's a slight shake to her hand, but her face relaxes.

"Shite, I'm so sorry, Maddie." I run a hand from the back of my head through my hair to my face, rubbing my eyes and then opening them to make sure she's still really there. Aye. I really did feck up this bad.

"Damn." She lowers the knife to her side and relaxes her shoulders, easing her fighting stance. "You scared me." Maddie puts her hand on her chest as if to feel her racing heart.

"I got confused. I forgot this isn't my flat to stumble home to . . . there were too many shots tonight. But I'll leave now." I go to turn but drop my mobile on the ground. "I just need to get my torch on again. It's dark as hell in that stairway."

"Wait." She steps forward. We're an arm's length apart now, the knife still in her hand at her side. "Where are you going? Because you're trashed."

"Back to the pub? Home?" I concentrate on making my words

clear and understandable. I concentrate on not looking down again—*shite!*—at her breasts, covered by the thin fabric of her tank top, the lack of bra and low moonlight showcasing her nipples through the thin black fabric.

"How are you getting home?"

I shrug, truly unsure of the answer. "Can you put the knife away? It's distracting."

As if *that's* what's screwing with me right now.

She glances down and huffs a laugh. "Yeah. I was protecting myself from whoever was breaking into the flat."

"You heard me coming in, jumped up from your bed, stopped by the kitchen for the bluntest knife you could find, and then had time to pose menacingly?"

"I fell asleep on the couch. And it took you a long time to get the door unlocked." Maddie cocks her head, then seems to remember she's wearing hardly anything at all. Her eyes widen as she quickly darts a look down at herself.

I lose the battle to keep my eyes on her face, and instead let them roam over her long legs, the curve of her thighs, and her high-waisted black underwear slightly askew and revealing a delicious curve of her arse. Her tank is bunched up on one side and exposes a line of skin between the top of her underwear and the bottom hem of the top. All the blood in my body rushes to my cock.

"Patrick." Her voice is a warning, although I'm not sure of what. "Just stay for a few minutes. You can hardly stand up straight." Even in the dark, Maddie's cheeks are tinted pink.

Jaysus. Does she know what I'm thinking? About cupping her arse with my hands, feeling her curves in my palms . . .

I should really get out of here.

"Not sure that's the best idea." It's a fecking awful idea. Stay here? In this flat, with her looking like that? With the memory of her kiss on my lips . . . again?

Yes. A dreadful idea.

She places a hand on her chest again. "My heart's still racing."

Wait. Maddie *wants* me to stay.

"I'll stay to make sure you don't have a heart attack." I shove the door shut behind me with a kick of my foot and step closer to her. Within touching distance.

"Did you call me Maddie earlier?" A slightly breathless question. "Just now and back at the pub, when I . . ." She trails off.

"Did I?" I lift my hand. "Are you okay? Maybe I should feel your heartbeat." I move my hand toward her chest, waiting for a protest, but she pulls it beneath hers and presses our linked hands just above her breasts. Her heart is pounding about as fast as mine is. There's something soothing about feeling that steady beat.

The softest sound squeaks from her throat.

I take another step until we're mere centimeters apart, and I slowly reach down for the knife, my fingers sliding down her hand, brushing hers. But instead of taking it, I leave my hand over hers and move my other one from her chest to the bare dip of her waist. She breathes heavily, her chest rising up and down, and I gently tug her closer until she's flush against me. Maddie gasps, and I get why. The feeling of our bodies pressed together is intoxicating.

"You kissed me tonight." I suddenly feel much more sober. Our bodies touching illuminates in my mind what I want.

Her. Christ, do I want her.

"Yeah, I did."

The knife slips from our fingers and clatters to the ground next to my mobile. Neither of us glance down. She entwines her now empty fingers with mine and fists a handful of my t-shirt with the other hand, as if making sure I don't flee.

"Are you mad about it? Me kissing you? You didn't answer the question before."

I shake my head, words lodged in my throat, and slide my hand over the top of her arse, down to where the hem has ridden up, giving access to her exposed cheek. Another quiet squeak emerges from deep in her throat. She feels perfect. I gently squeeze a handful of her arse.

"So you kissed me first in that dark hallway. I kissed you next in the pub. Now I think it's your turn." Maddie turns her head toward me, tugging on my shirt, pulling me down.

Those words are all that I need. I crash my mouth onto hers, bending so our height difference doesn't even matter. Our connection is an explosion on my lips and desire roaring from my groin. I thrust my tongue in her mouth, sweeping and searching and exploring. She throws her arms around my neck and jumps up, wrapping her legs around my waist. I easily catch her and hold her in place by her arse, pressing her against me so hard, I can feel her center against my cock.

This is exactly what I need. Her body against mine, her moans in my mouth.

Right now, it doesn't feel like I would break anything having to do with Maddie. How could this be wrong when it feels so good?

I back us over to the couch, dodging my homemade coffee table, and collapse so she's straddling me, wiggling on my hips as our lips remain locked. Fuck, I'm incredibly hard. I run my hands up her back under her tank top, the feel of her skin like smooth, warm water on my hands.

I pull back for a second to look at her, her wild dark hair scattered over her shoulders and back and chest, those dark eyes smoldering into mine, like she's a sparking firework about to explode and blow my head off.

"Hey." I push a chunk of hair out of her face.

She smiles at me, leans in for one kiss, and moves her body slowly against mine. I'm hyper aware of the thin fabric of her underwear. I bet she's soaked for me. I groan and savor the sensation, my mind craving the feel of her from the inside, but I focus on the curve of her face, her irises that seem almost black in the moonlight.

If only I could have her. Have this.

"You're wearing too much clothing." Her voice is husky and

filled with need, and the movement of her pelvis is making it hard to think about anything except that raging need to bury myself in her.

I'd do anything to feel it.

But I don't unbuckle my jeans. I don't strip my shirt off.

This woman isn't some random American tourist that I can sleep with and push out of my bed. She's not someone who will leave tomorrow to drive the Ring of Kerry or take a tour bus through Dublin or Galway or head up to Northern Ireland to check out the tourist sites.

She's not a one-night stand.

One-night stands are my rule. It protects me from the inevitable rejection once they get to know me. It protects them from deep disappointment.

Maddie's more important than all that.

Not just because she's Oliver's fiancée's little sister.

Not just because she's my current day manager.

Not just because she's renting my flat.

The room spins lazily as we stare into each other's eyes. She's waiting for my move, and I want to make it so badly, to strip off her remaining clothes and be with her completely.

A flicker of doubt crosses her face.

"Oh shit," she whispers. "You don't want this." Maddie practically leaps off my lap, throwing herself next to me on the couch, a chilly cloud settling between our warm bodies.

She thinks I don't want her? I swallow hard and lean my head back. Feck, it's hot in here.

"Maddie, if you think I don't want this . . ." She couldn't be more wrong. I shift my hips and obviously adjust my stiff, aching cock in my jeans, proof of my desire for this woman.

My cock is furious with me for what I just did.

I turn to Maddie, who has her legs bent up and tucked against her chest, forehead pressed to her knees. I can't see her face through her thick hair.

How I want to pull her into my arms and kiss the pain away. As if I want to reject her? That's the last thing I want.

"What are you doing here, Patrick?" Her voice is so hurt. It twists that blunt kitchen knife into my heart.

"I forgot. I just . . . forgot."

She laughs gently without humor. "It was really a mistake?"

But was it? Or was I coming to find Maddie? I was searching for her in the pub, in the hallway, and I must've remembered somewhere beyond the half dozen pints that she was up here. And that I had a key.

She groans. "And then I assaulted you. This time with a weapon." Her voice is choked with a tinge of humor.

"No." I grin in the dark. "That's not what that was." Against my better judgment, I grab her by her waist and pull her onto my lap. Instead of burying my face in her breasts, I wrap my arms around her in a giant hug. She hesitates for a second and then nestles into me, her cheek pressed against my chest. A glowing warmth fills me, and I kiss the top of her head.

"I'm pissed."

"Huh?" She jerks in my arms.

"Locked. Trollied. Plastered. I'm drunk, Maddie."

Her body settles again.

"Oh. Right. So am I. Which is why I left the pub." She turns her face up to me and our lips are so close, it takes just a slight movement to join them again.

This time, it's gentle, a pressing of our mouths together, just the slightest flicker of her tongue against mine.

I moan and pull away.

"This shouldn't happen, for so many reasons. You know that, right, Maddie?"

"You keep calling me Maddie." Her mouth turns up in a lazy grin.

"Do you prefer Madison?"

"You know I don't." She settles in the nook between my

shoulder and my neck. Her hot breath on my skin makes my heart race even faster.

My self-control is about ready to break, but then she nods against my chest.

"Because we're drunk."

"Yes."

"Because I work for you."

I hesitate. God knows I don't give a feck about that. Not with her.

"Because of a lot of things, love."

She pauses, then says in a voice so low I almost don't hear it as much as feel it, "Because I'm too much."

Feck.

"No. You're not too much."

She sighs, and I want to say more, but her body is warm and soft against mine, and I don't want to ruin the moment any more than I already have.

We sit that way until our hearts slow and her breathing steadies. Wish I could say the same for my raging hard-on.

"Lay down," I whisper. I adjust my body so we're in a horizontal position, and she stretches out on the couch, our bodies touching in every spot. Her eyes are shut.

I should carry her to her bed. I should untangle us before we are hopelessly entwined in every fecking way.

Before I shut my eyes and wait for sleep to come, I have a realization.

I really like this woman.

I like her sunny personality, her bright smile, the way she lights up any room she walks into. The way she's not afraid of me, not even a little. I like her laugh and her dark eyes and the layers of her, the top one a cheery facade and deeper ones etched with the pain of a past I know little about.

I press a kiss to her head and breathe her in. I haven't felt this way in a long time.

14

MADDIE

Sunday, March 9

It's still dark when I wake up, but there's the slightest hint of the approaching dawn coming in the window.

I'm not in my bed.

I'm not alone.

I'm in Patrick's arms on the couch, my back pressed against his chest, his warmth touching me from my head to my toes. His knees are tucked in to the back of mine, his arm heavy around my waist.

It takes a few seconds for everything to come crashing back to me.

Keys in the door after I'd passed out, then Patrick standing in front of me, looking like he wanted to eat me alive.

But he stopped himself.

I turn my head and he's wearing his t-shirt and boxers. He must have stripped out of his jeans after I passed out.

He didn't want to sleep with me? No, that's not right; he did. It was because we were drunk. And other reasons.

Patrick told me on the bike ride that he doesn't do relationships. He doesn't date. But why? Is he like me, with an ex who messed him up so much he doesn't want to let another person in?

He deserves to have someone close, someone who really knows and appreciates him.

I want to be that person. I want to be close to him, in any way possible.

My pulse quickens and I'm aware of every spot where his body is touching mine. The hair on his legs tickling me from behind. Sturdy chest pressed to my back. His pelvis lightly against my ass.

I snuggle back into him, and he stirs.

"Maddie." His breath is hot on my neck and his voice is filled with sleep.

"Yeah." God, he feels good against me. I shift my hips again and he inhales sharply, pressing his groin against me, sliding his hand along my side. There's proof he wants me in the form of a hardening cock.

"What are you doing?" he whispers.

I twist my body around so I'm facing him, our knees knocking together.

"I had a thought."

"That sounds dangerous." His hand drifts from my hip to the valley of my waist, then stops, so I move it up to my breast, which spills out of my tank top, my nipple barely covered. I wonder if he's going to say no again, but he moves his hand, squeezing and pressing and rubbing his thumb on the hardening peak of my nipple.

Fuck, that feels good, and the ache between my legs intensifies. I rub my thighs together, but that doesn't help at all. I look down and I can see his need for me, his cock fully hard and pushing up against his boxers.

"Madison, we can't." In one movement, he removes his hand from my chest and sits, pulling me to an upright position next to him and reaching for his phone. "It's five o'clock in the morning. I should get home."

I almost chicken out. But even though he's trying to push me away and staring at a spot on the floor, I know he wants me. He *needs* me.

"Maybe we should be friends who kiss sometimes."

He turns to me, and desire radiates off him like steam from a hot spring.

I press my lips to his and pull the phone from his hand, tossing it on the couch. Pulling back for a second, I meet his eyes, my pounding heart like a drumbeat.

Patrick lets out a shaky breath, and I can see the strength of his objections weakening as I press our foreheads together.

"Or more than kiss?"

I slide a leg over his lap and straddle him, hovering above his pelvis.

"Feck, Madison." He practically growls at me.

And so I drop down onto his waist, letting the weight of me settle slowly on his hard cock, separated only by my thin underwear and his boxers. "You said you don't want to."

"First of all, I didn't say that."

"Do you want me to stop? Because if you say so, I will." I shift my body against his and press down on the source of my ache. An involuntary moan escapes my mouth.

"I think I said I shouldn't. I definitely didn't say I don't want to." He looks into my eyes as he gently thrusts up. I whimper. As a response, Patrick slides his hands on my ass, pulling down my underwear until it's bunched at the top of my thighs and his hands are massaging bare skin, pressing me down against him, rocking me back and forth. I throw my head back and he buries his face in my chest, removing one hand from my ass to push down my tank so he can get his lips on my nipple, sucking and licking while his rock-hard cock pushes up against my soaking wet underwear.

I moan. "What's the second of all?"

"Huh?" He lets go of my nipple.

"You said first of all. What's second?"

"Feck if I know."

"Here's what I think." I sit up straight and try to stop moving for a second.

His eyes are closed.

"Look at me," I demand, and Patrick's eyes spring open.

"I'm looking. I'm listening."

"Why don't we do this just once. To get it out of our system."

"Sounds like an awful idea." But he continues to gently move under me, making it hard for me to form cohesive thoughts.

"But if we don't, all I'm going to do is think about it. I won't be able to concentrate. It'll be so distracting. I need to plan the road trip. You need to focus on the brewery."

"You can be quite convincing." Patrick leans forward and plants a series of small kisses on my neck.

"Great. So we're doing this." Before I can lose my nerve, I lift my hands and yank off my tank top.

Patrick's mouth gapes open, and he looks up at me.

"Christ, Maddie. You are perfect." He stares at my breasts and cups them with his hands, leaning forward to wrap his lips around a nipple again.

I tug at the hem of his shirt. "Sure, now take this off."

He pulls off his shirt and I shamelessly ogle him. His chest is incredible. He was a professional athlete. He doesn't sit around on a couch all day. But still, the man should pose shirtless for February of some calendar. His hands roam my sides and my breasts, and I can barely focus on what's in front of me. I touch his chest, at the artwork carved there, hidden completely when he wears a shirt.

There's an intricate dragon with outstretched wings, ending right under each pectoral muscle. It's fierce and angry. I look up at him questioningly.

"Ah, yeah, it was about me being a beast in goal. I got it fifteen years ago."

"It's huge. Did it hurt?" I trace the outline of the dragon and his flesh twitches under my touch.

"I hardly remember. I was young and stupid."

"It's beautiful."

"No." His voice is quiet. "You are."

His words wash over me. We're not drunk anymore, and the night's almost over. We've only got a couple of hours before the sun rises.

"Let's go to the bedroom," he says. "I'm not doing this on a couch."

"So romantic."

He chuckles before standing and pulling me up, shoving my underwear the rest of the way off my body. He then lifts me, and I instinctively wrap my legs around his body, my bare pussy pressed against his groin. I moan and we almost end up back on the couch.

"Stop that," he breathes out.

I still my body and let him walk us to my room.

"Just one time, Madison, right?" But his eyes are hungry for me. If I disagreed, would he still do it?

I nod. "One time."

"To get it out of our system."

"Yup."

"Promise?"

"You want me to promise to sleep with you just once?"

He nods, his eyes as serious as I've ever seen them.

"I guess I promise." I produce a huge eye roll. "Now take me to bed."

He drops my legs right inside the doorway and slides me down his body like it's a fireman's pole.

"Wait here." He disappears back down the hall and reappears holding a condom, swooping me back up before walking us backward into the bedroom.

Patrick gently tosses me on the soft bed. A second later he's naked, and he sinks between my legs, nudging them apart, only giving me the quickest view of his cock.

"What do you want, love?" he murmurs, his tongue flitting

out to play with one of my nipples, his hand sliding down between my thighs, stroking gently until I see stars.

What do I want? I want to play a part. I want to not be who I usually am—who is someone who likes to please, someone who is easily left behind, looked over. Someone who falls too hard and too fast.

I'm not doing that with Patrick. I'm not falling for him, I'm not dating him, and if I don't do any of those things, then I can't get hurt.

"I don't want you to make this some big romantic thing."

He stops sucking my nipple and looks up.

"I want you to lick my pussy, make me almost come, and then fuck me hard and fast until I can't see straight." I bite my lip. I have definitely never spoken that directly about what I want during sex.

It feels damn good.

His eyes burn and I watch his throat move as he swallows.

"We're not dating." I prop myself up on my elbows. "I just need someone to want me. To make me feel hot and desired. And no more questions."

"Feck, Maddie. If that's what you want, I'm down, but . . ."

"Just do it."

He snorts and follows directions, lowering himself between my legs and pulling me to his face by my ass.

I gasp as he licks me again and again, sucking on my clit at the end of each swipe of his tongue. I roll my hips into his face, and he buries himself in me. I'm almost there. There's an incredible building of pressure inside me.

Two seconds later, he stops and rips open the condom package, then his face is level with mine, his dick pressing into my entrance.

"And call me a good girl. I've always wanted to hear a man say that to me."

"Good fucking girl," Patrick says with a wicked smile before pushing himself inside me.

I giggle and pant as he completely fills me. It almost feels like too much. My eyes roll back in my head and I moan, wrapping my legs tightly around his waist. I can feel his eyes on my face, watching me, making sure I'm okay.

"More," I demand, thrusting up to meet him. "Tell me more."

"Take my cock like a good girl, Maddie." Patrick's words make my walls clench, and I almost come right away. He pushes one of my legs up against my body, hitting a spot that pushes me to the edge.

"Patrick," I gasp.

"Yes."

"Do it harder."

He doesn't need to be told again, and he pushes harder and faster until the whole world blurs around me.

I don't need love. I don't need a boyfriend. In this interlude of my life, I only need this. For once, I feel in control. I'm getting exactly what I want.

But he kisses me in between thrusts, and it's soft and sweet and gentle. There's a confusing contradiction to what's going on with the bottom half of our bodies and what's happening with our mouths.

"Maddie, I . . ." he whispers, but one second later, my muscles contract and I'm coming, wave after wave, and my own moans make it impossible for me to ask him to repeat himself.

I think he finishes it with *like you* or maybe it's *need you*.

I pretend I didn't hear it.

This is just the one time, anyway.

15

———————

PATRICK

I pull in the driveway of the cottage and dash inside. I need to feed the sheep and shower before heading over to Slea Head Brewery. It's brew day for our autumn batches. On Friday, Sean prepared the malt and Cormac cleaned the fermenter. He did a great job with the last batch of Golden Amber, so I didn't even check his work this time. I'd like to start giving him more responsibility. He's up for it, I think.

But thoughts of the brewery flit in and out around flashbacks to last night—and this morning—with Maddie. At the pub. On her couch. In her bed.

My head has not been on straight since that woman arrived in town.

Christ, leaving her this morning was the last thing I wanted to do. She was standing in the kitchen wearing pajama pants, a fresh tank top, and her adorable glasses, almost making her sexier than when she's in one of those sundresses or even wearing nothing at all.

I wanted to grab her and kiss her as I left, but once the sun came up, our *just one time* was over. A stab of regret slices through me at the deal. But it has to be over. That's what we agreed to.

I swing by the kitchen before striding out the sliding glass door to the backyard. Kitty is waiting for me right outside the house and baas loudly.

"Hey there, girl. Where's your brother?" I pet her rough head and she nudges into my other hand, where I have a handful of oats. I open my palm and she laps them up eagerly. When she's done, I walk through the backyard (also sheep pasture) to the small barn that I built last year after getting suckered into adopting these two giant cotton balls. It's also where I do the sawing and messier work for my furniture.

I need to find time to get back at the furniture. There's something about making big, heavy wooden pieces that is soothing to my soul. Not like the flimsy bookshelves and coffee tables you find at the big discount stores. I like the idea of something I create being unbreakable.

I quickly toss an armful of hay in the corner of the shelter and wait for Turtle to round the corner and acknowledge my presence. Rolling green hills crest and fall beyond my property and my eyes roam them.

There's a dark worm of negativity squirming in my gut. I see it. I feel it. But it's not regret. It's something else more dangerous.

I told her I liked her.

She might not have even heard it. But I said it. Worse, it feels like a lot more than liking her, and that's where the peril lies.

When we're together, there's something about the unrelenting way Maddie is simply *with* me.

Cara broke me, even though I know it's my fault, that I'm the one who did it by shutting her out and not communicating well and always saying the wrong damn thing, until she had enough and sought what she needed elsewhere. The hope that I'd be able to have the kind of marriage that my parents do—the commitment, resilience, everlasting love—disintegrated.

When Cara showed up last night, Maddie knew what I needed. She saw me going down that dark path. She came after me with a flamethrower to melt my icy walls. Those warm lips brought me back. And later, as I talked to other people at the pub, I could feel her, an electric wire connecting us even when we weren't looking at each other. That's why I drank so much, let myself go a little.

The way Maddie has slipped through to me is confusing.

It can't happen though. She's leaving. She's my best friend's fiancée's little sister. I'd mess it up anyway.

I feel naked. Vulnerable. Like now that Maddie's gotten through, I won't be able to push her out again, not until I ruin it, which is inevitable.

Turtle approaches and nudges my hand. I reach in my pocket for the cup of oats, pouring them into my palm and letting his rough, warm sheep lips scoop up the treat.

I scratch underneath his jaw, and he watches me and chews. Last year, I ended up with two sheep as pets, instead of a dog or a cat like a normal person. I'd gone with Saoirse and the girls to a farm visit, and when they heard that some of the sheep would be going to slaughter (who tells kids that? I left a terrible review for that place), those girls looked at me and absolutely begged. Saoirse laughed, thinking there was no way I'd agree, but I nodded and asked the farmer if I could buy a pair of sheep off him.

So here we are. My backyard is a sheep pasture. I have pet sheep.

Twenty minutes later, I'm showered and on my way out the door to meet Sean and Cormac.

I'm still in my driveway when I get a text.

CORMAC

Almost here?

ME

Be there in ten. All okay?

CORMAC

Sean says you were supposed to heat the
water yesterday?

Oh, feck. That was what I forgot to do yesterday afternoon.

ME

On my way

I'd planned to go to the brewery to do paperwork and turn on the heater in preparation for today, but instead I did some work at home, distracted by the new plan to see Maddie at O'Brien's. How could I forget to do that one task? Damn. That means today can't be a brew day.

A few minutes later, I walk into the brewing room and face Sean, who's standing with his arms crossed and jaw clenched.

"Morning." I try to sound casual and confident, but we all know what happened.

They both stare at me, Cormac with wide eyes, Sean with his lips pressed in a thin line.

"I thought you were supposed to turn on the heating systems yesterday?" Sean throws his hands in the air. "We did all the other prep on Friday."

"I know. It slipped my mind." This is my fault, I realize, but I hate how aggressive Sean is toward me.

"How could it possibly slip your mind?" Sean glares at me with narrowed eyes.

I glare back. He's never been supportive of me taking over the brewery. He's been waiting for me to mess up. As close as he was to my father, he's had no interest in my plans for innovation and the evolution of the brewery. We've both been around Slea Head since the beginning. Both of us want it to succeed. I don't know what his problem is.

"We'll have to delay the brew till tomorrow." Cormac's voice is steady, but I can sense a hint of annoyance, probably at having been dragged out of bed on a Sunday morning for no reason.

Sean growls at me. "This brewery only works if we all do the jobs we're supposed to."

I clench my jaw and stop myself from snapping back. Because, in reality, he's absolutely right. I told them I'd do it. And I didn't. I messed up. *Bollocks.*

Slea Head is behind breweries like New Dingle because Dad wasn't interested in product innovation. He doesn't disapprove of what I'm doing now, but he never wanted to change things. Sean has the same mindset. But I need to innovate if the brewery is going to survive. Saoirse agrees, although she's never been keen on running the brewery.

The interview I'd had with the product innovation candidate had gone really well, and I offered Lola the job later that same day. She's extroverted and friendly and I actually think her and Maddie would get along great.

Not that it matters.

Lola starts this Wednesday. I need to get a work plan together for her in the next two days so she can show up and make a difference right away. She's just in time—the Wellington Pubs meeting is a week from Tuesday, and I need to finalize my pitch and slide deck. I'd like to be able to tell them we have an IPA and an autumn brew that'll be ready soon.

It's finally coming together. And now I'm screwing it up because I'm distracted by Maddie Hart.

But this isn't a disastrous screwup. It's a one-day delay.

I have to keep more on top of things from now on. Getting trollied at the pub last night didn't help. And I should've gone right from Mam and Dad's house to the brewery yesterday afternoon.

"What's the look on your face?" Sean says sharply.

"We'll shift the brewing day by one, like Cormac said."

"We have a schedule. A plan. One that I don't always like, but we should stick with it." Sean runs his hand over a gray-and-white beard, making a grating scratching sound. "Brewing is a science, not an art. The process should be followed exactly."

I don't respond, because I don't agree. Brewing is an art, too. The different flavors and recipes we've been testing may not be

Sean's thing, but it's what people want. I love testing and learning and adjusting until we get it perfect. Golden Amber, Devil's Dark, and Slea Head Stout are the foundation of our brewery. But there's so much room to grow.

Sean still thinks I'm the same five-year-old kid he met over three decades ago. It's hard for him to accept I'm almost forty and now his boss.

"Sorry to make you both come out. Let me get the heating system turned on—"

"I already did," Sean says.

"Thank you. Go on home, then. I'll double check everything —" My mobile buzzes in my pocket and I fish it out under their watchful eyes.

> MADDIE
>
> I'm making you dinner tonight, all right, boss man?

I press my lips together, the pleasant surge in my center at the idea of seeing Maddie tonight smoothing over the discomfort from screwing up at the brewery.

Cormac clears his throat, and I pocket my mobile.

"What was I saying?"

"That you'll double check everything . . ." Cormac offers helpfully.

"Right. Exactly."

Sean huffs, but I lift a hand before he can say anything.

"See you in the morning." I turn and head to the tiny brewery office, happy to get away from Sean. I swear I hear him mutter something like *eejit*, but I ignore him and close the office door, settling into the chair to craft a response to Maddie. The three little dots dance around in our text chain.

> ME
>
> Don't call me boss man

MADDIE

Why not?

ME

Because it makes me feel like we shouldn't
have done what we did this morning

A pause, and the three dots disappear. Uh-oh. Are we not supposed to talk about it? Should I have pretended it didn't happen? But there's no way I could pretend such a thing.

MADDIE

Regrets?

ME

No

MADDIE

Are you sure?

She's doubting herself. There's not a bit of regret in me for what we did last night, but as usual, I'm saying the wrong thing.

ME

Positive. I promise

MADDIE

Glad we got it out of our system

Right. Just one time. We'll keep it professional from now on. No more getting drunk and showing up at the flat uninvited.

MADDIE

Be here at six. Bring beer. And get ready to
brainstorm ideas for the road trip. I need your
brilliant Irish brain to help me

What about showing up at her flat, invited, not drunk, but with beer? Is that keeping it professional?

Probably not.

I should say no. No more screwups at work. No more distractions.

But last night felt different. Different from every one-night stand I've had. Different from the local woman I dated. Even different from Cara.

Maddie makes me feel good. Like I shouldn't be ashamed about who I am. Not like I'm saying the wrong thing all the time. Not like she's waiting for me to screw things up.

I've not let myself entertain the thought of being with a woman for real in years. But what if I let myself go with Maddie, just a little bit? It would be a test run. She's leaving anyway, so there's no hope for a real future. It'll be only a slight detour from my one-night stand philosophy.

Since she's already here, I can try it out. Since we're already friends, it'll feel easy and natural.

But it feels dangerous for my heart.

I head into the brew room, double checking the temperature on the fermenter. It's correct, not that I ever doubted Sean would do it right. He's good at what he does.

I want to smile around Maddie. I want to listen to her tell me stories about her life and her family and . . .

The malt is ready for tomorrow, weighed and milled in preparation for brewing. I dig my hand into the container and let the pieces fall through my fingers. The grind is perfect, a combination of big chunks of husk and smaller ones.

I like to hear about her life because we're friends.

But I also know I'm the tiniest bit smitten.

If I'm going to spend time with her, I need to keep my shit together at the brewery and the pub.

And whatever I do, I need to protect myself from the inevitable end. Maddie will leave Dingle, I'll see her for the road trip and the wedding, and that'll be it.

I can't let myself forget that.

16

MADDIE

Boyfriend Disaster #5: Todd the Married Manager
Job Location & Length: Another Soulless Chain Restaurant, 2 years
My Age: 24

At my next job, I kept my head down and worked my ass off, and it finally paid off when I got promoted to assistant manager after a year. Finally, I was making progress. Maturing. Figuring life out.

So it caught me off guard when Todd kissed me.

He was my tall, blue-eyed manager who was hired six months after I got promoted. Todd was older—early thirties, but not really inappropriate like it was when I was twenty and Jonathan the line cook was thirty—and had a great, easy laugh.

One night, as was normal for us, we'd stayed after a shift to catch up on schedules for the upcoming week. No one else was around when he slid a hand on my thigh and leaned forward to bring our lips together, so tenderly. *Maddie,* he'd said, *I've wanted to do that for ages.*

And with that, I was right back to my old ways.
We'd kiss in the break room or sneak into the storage
closet. It was exciting, and fun, and I felt so wanted. Did I
know I was fucking things up, but worse this time since I
had more to lose with the promotion? Yup. Could I stop
the absolute garbage train wreck from happening? Nope,
sure couldn't.
A woman came in one day, double rings stuffed with
sparkling diamonds on her left ring finger, looking for
Todd with a clenched jaw and narrowed eyes.
He was married. That's why we never met up outside of
work. Cue my resignation, effective immediately.

Breakup Reason: He was a liar and a married cheat.
My Distress Level: 5
Lesson Learned: I am a horrible judge of character. This
one threw me. I swore to myself I was done messing
things up.

"I had the best idea ever for the road trip." I drink from the
bottle of Harp lager Patrick brought, feeling warm and
cozy in the hot flat, but also basking in the delicious scents
of pre-made lasagna and garlic bread in the oven.

I'm trying not to make it obvious I'm thinking about the last
time Patrick and I were on this couch twelve hours ago. My cheeks
heat at the memory of waking up to find him draped around me in
boxers and a t-shirt. The way he grabbed handfuls of my ass and
raked me over his . . .

Now I'm really sweating.

"Go on." Patrick swigs from his bottle, hazel eyes locked
on me.

"I'm going to give the road trip a theme. I'm already working on a list of weird things we can see on the trip—with very little help from you, I might add. What about if we put a few brewery stops on the itinerary? Won't Oliver like that?"

Patrick nods. "Aye, he and I went to quite a few breweries while he was here. As research, of course."

"Perfect. So is that something you can help me with without rolling your eyes?"

His mouth twists. "I suppose."

"And I was thinking of calling it Quirks, Brews, and Views." I wave a hand in front of me, as if I'm revealing something on the wall.

"Quirks?"

"Yeah, like quirky things. We're going to go see a giant salmon statue in Belfast, Patrick. Ian's suggestion."

He presses his lips together and raises his eyebrows.

"Where are we stopping again?"

"I have a list—no thanks to you." I pull out my phone and scroll to the notes app.

Patrick scoffs. "A simple internet search—"

"Hush. Here. This is what I got so far from my online research. Oh, and from your sister."

"Could've been done from New Jersey." He tilts his head and drinks, and I try not to stare at the way his lips wrap around the neck of the bottle.

"No, it definitely could not have. Just listen. We'll start in Dublin and do things like Temple Bar, Guinness Brewery, and go see your Hungry Tree—"

"It's not my tree." He groans. I ignore him.

"Then we'll head to Northern Ireland, first stopping in Belfast, where we'll see the giant fish statue. Then drive through the Dark Hedges, which look amazing. Giant's Causeway and the Carrick-a-Rede rope bridge to finish off Northern Ireland. Then we'll stop in Donegal, where your sister told me about some hole in the ground that's the gateway to hell, so that sounds delightful—"

"Christ."

"Shhh. Then to Galway, Cliffs of Moher, stay in Limerick for the night, then end up in Dingle. We'll find some tiny stone houses along Slea Head. Thank you, Saoirse."

"I could've pointed them out on our bike ride."

"But you didn't." I give him a withering look. "When we leave Dingle, we need to stop by your favorite: Blarney Castle, where we'll kiss the rock while hanging upside down for good luck."

"That is a disgusting, dirty stone that thousands of other people have put their mouths on."

"Yup."

"Don't expect me to participate. No self-respecting Irishman would do such a thing."

"You suggested it."

"I was joking."

"Noted. Then we'll head toward Dublin, and everyone will go their separate ways." I gulp at the idea of flying out of Dublin at the end of the road trip. "I need a few more ideas for quirky things."

Patrick doesn't answer right away, but there's a shadow of a grin on his tempting mouth.

"I think it's a good list, but we might have to adjust a few stops to make it work within our twelve-day timeframe," he says finally.

"Yes!" I pump a fist in the air. "I knew it was brilliant."

"Did I say brilliant? I don't think I said that."

"Shut up." I reach over to push his biceps and let my hand linger there for a second, scooting closer, tucking one leg beneath me so that my knee is touching his thigh. I love being this close to Patrick. There's an energy that radiates off him, and I want to be near it. A crackling between us. He's a magnet and my body is made of iron.

"I like it. Really." His voice is softer, and his arm hardens beneath my hand. He shifts his body so it's turned to me, our knees now touching. "In Limerick, we can take an easy hike to a beautiful waterfall in Clare Glens forest."

"Sounds lovely."

"And I know a brewery in Donegal."

"Perfect. And in Dingle we'll obviously go to . . . New Dingle Brewing. I hear they have a great tasting room." I remove my hand from his arm.

He shakes his head and closes his eyes. "Jaysus help me. Please, never step foot in that place."

His accent is intoxicating. How did I never realize the Irish accent is so hot? Reese is always going on about Oliver's Scottish accent, and Stella's boyfriend has a sexy English one . . . but I hadn't even had Irish on my radar.

Or maybe it's just Patrick.

"Fine, I promise. And see? This part definitely couldn't have been done from New Jersey. The inspiration is here." I throw a hand in the air. "In Dingle. Also, you wouldn't respond to my emails, so . . ."

"Whatever you say, Madison." He's opened his eyes and is fighting a smile. I know I got him. He's finally interested in the road trip.

"We're back to Madison again? Do you only call me Maddie when you kiss me?"

His eyes widen. "No comment."

"Why?" My eyes flit to his lips. "For some reason, we said last night was a one-time thing. That must have been your idea. Was it? If so, not your best one."

He studies my face, his expression serious again.

"You are not like most women I know."

"Not like the other American tourists?" I swallow.

His mouth twitches, but he doesn't deny it.

Is being here in Ireland on this couch with Patrick my one-third life crisis? Where I figure out what to do next, reflect on the past decade, and decide how I want to live the next one? Yeah, I think it is. And this time, I will really transform my life, like Aunt Evelyn told me to.

I promised myself I wouldn't immediately fall for someone the way I have before. So if I go for this thing with Patrick, I'll see it for exactly what it is. I'm in touch with my feelings about him. I know exactly where I stand. I'm his best friend's fiancée's little sister who's here bugging him about a road trip.

Who he might have had sex with just once to get it out of his system.

And I like him. Yup, sure do.

I won't let that get out of hand. He can't dump me for the next American tourist that comes along because there's nothing real going on between us.

Still, the way he's looking at me right now—his eyes hooded and dark—makes me wonder, but I shove that thought away.

I feel safe with him. That's what I want right now: to spend time with someone I can trust. I want to know they can handle all my over-the-top cheerfulness and non-mysteriousness and still want to hang out. I want to know they won't dump me or abandon me, even if it's only because there's nothing to dump me from.

A friend.

Perhaps a friend with benefits. Because the things he did to me this morning? My face flushes with heat at the thought of him yanking my hips to his face.

"Listen." I take his bottle and slide it with mine onto the coffee table. I grab both of his hands.

"Yes?" His eyes are questioning, but he doesn't pull away, not one inch.

"There's no hope for a future for us."

He chuckles. "Are you breaking up with me?"

I shake my head and laugh with him. "No. I'm just saying, we can't be together, even if we wanted to."

"I never said I wanted to."

"Good lord. I know! You don't have to rub it in."

"Sorry," he says, and looks like he means it. "But you're being weird. And for me to say that is a big deal."

"I am weird. So are you. And that's okay. Can I finish now?"

"Mmm-hmm." He stares at me with that assessing gaze and a smile just beneath the surface.

"We're friends, right?" I take a deep breath.

He nods and cocks his head.

"Friends and mature adults. We had sex and it was . . . kinda hot. Like, really hot." If possible, my face gets even warmer. I'm sure it's scarlet.

"It was your idea, by the way." He moves his thumbs ever-so-slightly on the backs of my hands and tingles shoot up my wrists.

"Whatever. I say tomato . . ." I bite my lower lip.

"What's your point, Madison?" But his voice is lower, and his gaze drifts down to my mouth, making me want to lick my lips.

"Can I trust you?" I'm not sure I have the nerve to say what I want to. I bite my tongue to distract myself.

"Yes." Patrick's eyebrows crease together.

I swallow the nerves dancing in my throat.

"I'm thinking . . ." I lean forward, placing his hands around my waist and sitting up on my knees just a bit so I can put my mouth within reach of his, pausing before our lips make contact, giving him every single chance to pull away or push me away. "Maybe what we did doesn't have to be just once?"

Patrick makes a guttural sound, and his fingers tighten around my waist.

"We probably shouldn't." But he closes the space between our mouths by half, and the warmth of his lips radiates onto mine. The opposite of pulling away. "You promised me."

"What a stupid promise. And I forget why. Can you remind me?"

He closes the gap between us and kisses me gently on the lips, then with a pretty impressive maneuver, gets me to straddle him.

"I actually don't remember, Maddie."

I wiggle on his lap, trying to ease some of the need coursing through my veins. He breathes out sharply and runs his hands over my ass, pressing me down onto him in a repeat of this morning.

"We're going to have to keep doing this so you keep calling me Maddie."

It's hard to figure out if I'm digging a deeper hole for myself, or if I'm digging out of the hole I was already in. But right now, as Patrick presses his lips against my neck, I'm not sure I care one way or the other. I breathe out and throw my head back to give him full access.

This place—Dingle—while cold and dreary and not exactly what I expected, is also kind of intoxicating.

Or maybe it's Patrick.

Either way, I feel safe here with him. And I'm desperate to trust someone again.

But no matter how I insist I won't, I can feel myself falling, and the only safe landing place is with Patrick.

17

PATRICK

Monday, 10 March

I sleep like the dead next to Maddie Hart, waking up in the flat with my arms wrapped around her for the second morning in a row. Christ, how I wish I didn't have to head to the brewery. But I do, leaving her warm and half-naked in bed.

When I arrive at Slea Head Brewery, Cormac's just finishing up giving the fermenter a hot rinse with the pressure washer to remove any remaining germs. It'll take about four hours to brew the actual beer, then four weeks to ferment the lager, then another few weeks to carbonate before it's ready to try. I rub my hands together and imagine what it could be like to release Slea Head's first autumn brew—Irish Oktoberfest—in September.

My mistake yesterday only puts us behind by one day. It hardly makes a difference, but still, I grind my teeth together. Half-naked American woman or not, I need to make sure I stay focused on what's important in the long run.

But I can't move Slea Head forward all on my own. Cormac needs to learn more about the process. Sean has the experience, but he makes my life difficult every damn step of the way. I'm determined to pull Saoirse into the business at some point. I know she's settled working at the hotel for now, but I need her here, and I think if I could show her there's growth potential and security, she'd feel more comfortable working with me.

For now, I have the new product innovation lead, Lola, starting Wednesday. We have an onboarding and brainstorming meeting all morning. I don't feel prepared. I meant to put all of my plans into some kind of formal document, but it's still only up in my head. Then again, that's why I hired her, isn't it? To put a plan together, think things through, make sure it all happens.

I've got my pitch almost ready for Wellington Pubs. The meeting is a week from tomorrow. Just have to finalize a few of the slides.

Sean's listing all the potential problems with this brew, and I nod my head. I'm new to managing the brewery but I grew up around it, so I'm familiar with what can go wrong. I nod and tap a few notes in my mobile.

There's something niggling at the corner of my mind. Something that tells me Maddie is distracting me too much. I'm ignoring O'Brien's more than I want to, leaning too heavily on Maddie to run the place with the other managers, and even now, as I half listen to Sean, all I can think about is her. A woman who won't even be here in a few weeks.

I don't want to ever feel like I did after things ended with Cara. It's interesting though, because the pain and regret I always feel when I see my ex wasn't exactly the same on Saturday night. And it wasn't just because Maddie kissed me. When she walked in with Liam and her boyfriend, I only felt empty. Annoyed. But then Maddie kissed me, and I felt something else. Something warm and sparking. The opposite of empty.

But if Maddie and I end badly, we'll have to suffer through a twelve-day road trip together, and then Oliver and Reese's wedding in Scotland. Disaster.

"Did you get that?" Sean says with a sharp edge to his voice.

Nope.

"Yes." I lift my mobile, as if this proves I've been taking notes and not daydreaming. "Nice work. I'm going to do some paperwork in the office."

I slip away from Sean and Cormac as they carry on with the list of brew day tasks.

***

MADDIE SITS NEXT to me at a back table in O'Brien's, perched on one of the old wooden chairs, telling me an animated story about a pair of locals who came in this afternoon. I lean on my elbow and watch her, a finger reaching over to trace circles on her bare knee.

"They were absolutely trashed, Patrick. It was two o'clock in the afternoon." She emphasizes each word.

"That'd be Conor and Colin. They're old blokes—brothers. They've been coming in for decades."

"I've had tons of regulars in my jobs, so I get it. But these guys were just so drunk. And so . . . happy? Like, I felt bad cutting them off, but they were super nice and just stumbled out. One smashed his shoulder on the door as he left, and I thought I was going to have to call an ambulance. But he didn't even react."

I chuckle. "Sounds about right."

The pub is getting crowded. It's a Monday night, and the Irish band is warming up. The town knows to come out.

Maddie's wearing one of those short dresses again—this is the black one she wore last weekend, sleeveless and showing off her collarbone and shoulders—and those gray boots. She shifts toward me and watches my finger move on her skin.

"I'm not sure how you're dressed in such little clothing in Dingle in March."

"Would you rather I wear a hoodie and leggings?"

"Nope, this is completely appropriate." I reach out and pull the leg of the chair to me in a swift motion, the stuttering of the wood on the floor causing a few heads to turn.

But I don't give a feck, even though some of the locals let their eyes linger on me sitting so close to Maddie.

"Well, hello," she whispers now that the chairs are touching. I move my hand up her inner thigh until it's just at the edge of inappropriate, creeping up past the hem of her dress, and lift my face toward hers. At this angle, we're only a beat apart, and my heart pounds in my chest. Maybe I can even hear hers.

"Hello." I move my fingers a few centimeters up, between her warm thighs, and she breathes in quietly.

"It's remarkable how much nicer you are to me now than when I first got here." She leans in and her lips tickle my earlobe. "Is it because I'm sleeping with you?"

"Do you think I'm that easy to manipulate?"

She laughs, her hot breath on my neck. "Maybe."

Christ, this woman. My cock hardens.

"Come with me. I want to show you something in the pub office."

"Now?" Maddie pulls back and blinks at me, her brow furrowing.

"Now." I stand and pull her behind me, and we dodge people standing around as the band begins their first song, starting with a fiddle and a violin.

There are so many things I should be doing and thinking about besides this woman, but right now, I don't care about any of them.

She follows me down the dark hallway and I stop in the spot where she asked me to kiss her that first night. She knows exactly what to do and presses her back against the wall, pulling me against her.

"Kiss me?" she says.

I crash my lips into hers and pull her hips roughly against mine for a beat, reaching down to slide my hand up her inner thigh, swiping between her legs just once, feeling how much she wants me.

"Anyone can see," she whispers.

"Let them."

"Patrick . . ."

"Office. Now."

We part for a second and I follow her into the pub office, shutting and locking the door behind us.

"What if Declan needs to get in here?"

"I don't want to hear another man's name out of your mouth while I'm doing this to you." I back her up until she bumps into the desk.

"Doing what?"

I pull her dress up and slide my finger back and forth over the thin, soaking fabric of her underwear.

"This. And you're already wet for me, Madison."

"Oh." She leans her head back and breathes hard, arching her back so her breasts spill out of the top of her dress.

I slide a finger over her, gliding it back and forth, feeling her move against my hand. I unzip my jeans and tug my boxers down until my cock is free. I slip a second finger into her and pump them slowly inside her, rubbing my thumb on her clit as she moans against me.

"Say my name, Maddie." I run a hand over myself. "Say it."

"Patrick," she manages and groans.

I tug her underwear down roughly and pick her up, sitting her bare arse on the desk and knocking over whatever's in the way. Papers go flying. A laptop slides across the table and a glass of water precariously shifts next to it.

"Open your legs." And she does. I rip a condom wrapper open with my teeth, sliding it onto my cock as fast as possible. "Come here." I use two hands to pull her hips toward me and bury myself inside her.

She opens her eyes and looks at me, and for a second, there's so much there. It's not just lust. It's more. So much more that my heart aches and I feel the most vulnerable I've ever felt in my life.

And in her eyes, there's hope. Trust. Vulnerability of her own.

This isn't just sex.

"Jaysus, Maddie." There's so much I want to say. "I love . . . the feel of you."

Her soft look blinks away, and the only thing left is raw need.

"Me too. Now do it harder," she gasps, wrapping her arms around my neck and crashing her lips on mine.

There is nowhere I'd rather be in the entire world than with Maddie Hart in the tiny, dark office of O'Brien's.

What is this spell this woman has cast over me? I'm overthinking this. I must be. Kissing her, our tongues are rough in each other's mouths. I feel like I'm drunk, but I'm not.

I'm overwhelmed. I want nothing but to be with her, but deep down I know it won't last—it can't last, and I need to focus. My family are the only people worth investing so much time and energy in. I know that. I know I'm not someone any woman can get close to. Not close enough to last, anyway.

But for now—feck it.

I close my eyes and wait until I can feel her muscles contracting around me, until she yells my name, too loud, but the Irish music covers up the sounds of what we're doing in here.

A climax as intense as any I've had in my life hits me, and with dread, I recognize that I'm falling for Maddie Hart.

18

MADDIE

Friday, March 14

Boyfriend Disaster #6: Jacob the Obsessed Customer
Job Location & Length: The Bank, 1 year
My Age: 25

Todd the Married Manager was such a disaster that I promised myself I wouldn't hook up with anyone I worked with at The Bank, a lively bar in Hoboken that was open from five in the evening to two in the morning. It was a much-needed change from the soulless chain restaurants. Enter Jacob, a hot hedge fund manager who would come in with his colleagues every Friday night. He'd plant himself at my end of the bar, allowing only me to pour him drinks and tipping five times the cost of his gin and tonics. I finally gave in and agreed to go out with him. Why would I not? He wasn't a boss or a coworker or even in the restaurant business. I was making progress. Maturing.
We slept together at his swanky Hoboken apartment after our third date, and then he started coming in on Thursday

nights. Then added Wednesdays. Eventually, it was every night I worked. My manager said I shouldn't date customers, and definitely shouldn't have a boyfriend sit at the bar for twenty hours a week.

I didn't like him doing that, either.

Jacob didn't take my suggestion that he spend less time at The Bank well. He only got more possessive, with constant texting and phone calls. He'd get angry when I served other men, which was a big problem.

When I broke up with him, he didn't stop showing up. It got so bad that I blocked his number.

And quit.

Breakup Reason: stalker-like obsession
My Distress Level: 3
Lesson Learned: Maybe it's me, not them. What am I doing wrong?

I t's a sunny day in Dingle, Ireland. I didn't think that was possible, but the rare warmth beams right into my heart, and I practically skip out of the flat. I pass the entrance to O'Brien's and pop into Dingle Brew.

"Morning to you, Maddie. Off to the pub?"

"Yup, opening today." I smile at Maria, the barista behind the counter who I met that first morning in Dingle.

"Lovely."

"Hey, Maria, can you tell me about something really unique you've done in Ireland? So I can add it to my road trip itinerary?"

She chuckles and fills a large to-go cup for me.

"I can do that," Maria continues. "The Butter Museum. In Cork." She adds cream and sugar to my coffee before securing the lid and handing it over.

"A butter museum?"

"Yes."

"Well. Okay, thanks!" I grin as I walk out the door up toward O'Brien's. A butter museum? Weird.

My phone buzzes as I unlock the heavy front door of the pub.

REESE

I'm so sorry about Blue, Mads

Last night, in a moment of stupidity, I accidentally told my sisters about Patrick—*I met someone*, I'd typed, with about a hundred heart emojis—which means I had to backtrack and tell them about breaking up with Blue.

REESE

But tell us everything about the new guy.
Where's he from?

I'm not in the country I'm supposed to be. I'm not doing what I said I was doing. I'm not even in the right time zone.

I can't tell them I'm in Dingle, on my way to my job at a pub after waking up this morning tangled up with Reese's fiancé's best friend.

What's the harm in telling them a little truth? Maybe it'll help me remember the details I'm making up.

ME

Actually . . . he's Irish

REESE

No shit! What's he doing there?

STELLA

I love the Irish accent

REESE

How would your English boyfriend feel about
that, Stella?

STELLA

shrug

REESE

Ohhh, Mads, he can help with the road trip!
How's that coming? Has Patrick helped at all??
It's so close. Maybe you should tell us the
plan, lol

Oh good lord. I should've kept my mouth shut.

ME

Yes, I've been picking his brain

His as in Patrick's? Or my new fake boyfriend's? Joke's on me, they are one and the same. Lie and truth mixed in together.

ME

The road trip planning is almost done! I'll give
you the details ASAP

ME

Gotta run, sisters!

STELLA

We expect another beach picture immediately

I quickly send an image of a can of beer nestled in sand with turquoise waters in the background. I grabbed it online the other day, but wince when I notice the leftover sliver of a watermark in the bottom corner of the image. I must've missed that when cropping it. I don't think they'll notice as it blends in with the sand, but I gotta be more careful.

This morning, when we finished with some sexy shenanigans, Patrick asked when I was going to come clean to my sisters. I mumbled something noncommittal and stuck my tongue in his mouth to avoid the question.

But it's a good one. When will I tell them the truth? The whole truth?

I pull the chairs from on top of the tables. It's gotta be before the road trip. In two weeks, I'm supposed to head back to New Jersey—at least according to my plane ticket and the story I've told them.

So I guess it'll be when I get back to Jersey.

But to leave this place in two weeks? I scrunch my face at the thought. It's too soon. Two weeks until the little life I've made for myself here disappears.

By the time I'm done with the chairs, the door swings open and Saoirse steps in for a quick chat before work. After she leaves, I pause for a moment, appreciating how I fit in here. I should feel out of place. A tourist in Dingle managing a pub with an American accent that everyone comments on. Someone who's always inappropriately dressed.

But as much as I don't fit in, I still feel like I belong. Like I'm needed. And wanted.

The buzz of my phone pulls me out of my daydream. It's from a bartender I trained a few days ago who's supposed to show up later this afternoon.

JAX

Sorry to do this to you, Maddie, but I'm not coming back to O'Brien's

ME

Oh no, why?

JAX

Going traveling with my girlfriend instead

ME

Text Patrick, please. He's your actual boss, not me

JAX

Can you do it

Shit.

I screenshot the message and send it to Patrick, cringing. He responds with a single expletive.

I've been trying so hard to keep the pub stuff off his plate as I know he wants to focus on the brewery. The other managers have stepped up as well, but we're still short-staffed. I had a feeling that Jax might not stick around. After working in restaurants for years, I've gotten a sense for when workers are a flight risk.

It's not until O'Brien's is officially open that I realize there's an inventory problem. We're short on everything in cans and bottles besides New Dingle and Slea Head.

As in there's nothing else in the cases, and nothing in the basement. *Oh, crap.*

There should be Magners Irish Cider, Heineken, Budweiser, Porterhouse Temple Lager, and Harp.

How did I not notice us running so low? I had the last two days off, but still. I rack my brain and remember grabbing a case from the basement and writing a message to Patrick on a Post-it note. Did I not put it in the office?

I text him again.

ME

> Sorry to do this to you, but it looks like we're short a ton of can and bottle inventory

I snap a picture of the mostly empty refrigerators and send it to him.

ME

> Is a shipment coming in today? There's nothing downstairs or out back

PATRICK

> I'm checking

A moment later he's back.

PATRICK

Damn. Nothing's scheduled

ME

Oh no

PATRICK

How did this happen?

ME

I don't know, I'm sorry

PATRICK

I'll be in after I finish up at the brewery

I lay my phone on the bar, an uncomfortable feeling settling in me. He's direct, and even himself admits he's often misunderstood. It hasn't bothered me before. But those words—*how did this happen*—seem pretty clear.

They're an accusation.

The first customers walk in, and I serve Conor and Colin, the old brothers, and let myself worry.

Things are so good between us right now. In my past life, I'd soon find out he's married, or obsessed, or hooking up with other people. My stomach twists. Is that what's happening here?

No.

Everything is great, and it's going to stay that way. It'll only end when I leave town.

I serve a new group of patrons, grabbing tea and toasties instead of pints. The door swings open again, and my head spins in that direction, anticipating Patrick.

But he doesn't show up until my shift is almost over.

———

"Fuck."

Feck is his preferred swear word, so I know he's upset.

Patrick's perched on a barstool, scrolling through something on his laptop, a folder with delivery and order paperwork in a pile next to him. The pub's starting to fill up, and he really needs to move so he doesn't get a drink spilled on his things. I glance at my phone. Ronan should be here soon. I'm already planning on staying and working a double to cover Jax's absence.

"So what happened?"

Patrick sighs and buries his hands in his dark hair, leaving it ruffled. I almost reach out to smooth it down when he looks up, but I hold back. He doesn't look like he's in a playful mood.

"Beth didn't take care of it. But it's my fault, not hers. She was just starting to deal with all the inventory and re-orders, but it all slipped through the cracks when she left."

"The same day I showed up and made you hire me?" I mean it in a light way, and I tilt my head and lean toward him, hoping he smiles.

He doesn't. It was the wrong tone for the situation.

"It's not your fault."

But it kind of is, isn't it? I saw that the inventory was going down. I'd taken over from Beth. I'm supposed to know how to run a restaurant.

It's just like when I was dating Jacob while at The Bank. My manager said I was missing things. Getting distracted.

But this time, I'm the one doing the distracting.

I'd checked in the pub office, and the note I wrote earlier in the week about the inventory levels was nowhere to be found. I should have told him verbally as well. Kept telling him. Asked about shipments. I swallow and stand up straight, crossing my arms.

But I didn't do any of that.

"It's my fault," he says gently, the softness I was missing before finally evident.

"No. It's mine, and you know it."

He rakes a hand over his face, not disagreeing.

Here I was, thinking I was doing a great job running the pub.

Helping out Patrick, but also using my brain, my past experience. Instead, I fucked it up.

"You should go."

"What?" I say, the edge in my voice contrasting with his calm tone. He's telling me to leave?

"I just mean that you've been here all day. Go home. Ronan and I can take care of tonight."

"But you've been working at the brewery. And I want to help. I can stay and you can fix the inventory problem."

"It's too late." He shakes his head. "It's a Friday night. I can reach out to the distributor in the morning for an emergency shipment."

"Let me stay."

"Madison. Come on. Leave." He sits back and looks up at the ceiling, as if I'm the most frustrating person he's dealt with all day.

I flinch. How could he want me to leave? He's hardly been able to stay away from me. Even when I'm working, he'll come in and sneak a kiss or pin me in the dark hallway.

Leave.

That's a pretty clear directive. My face heats and a spark of anger ignites in me. And beneath it, a raw rejection that I don't even want to acknowledge.

"Fine. Good luck tonight."

I bend to grab my purse from under the bar and stomp out without another word. He doesn't follow me.

"What a dick," I mumble as I welcome the evening air, pausing outside the entrance. Shit, the sun is behind gray clouds and it's much colder than it was earlier. Thankfully, due to slacking on laundry, I'm wearing leggings—not one of my stupid sleeveless summer dresses—but also a skimpy tank top.

I look up toward my flat, but don't move my feet in that direction. I can't go home now. No way. Not when I feel like this. What would I do all night in there?

Instead, I stride in the other direction without any destination in mind, the anger and hurt rolling around in my belly and mixing together into an unhappy cocktail.

I wrap my arms around my body, clinging to my bare skin.

O'Brien's is job number eleven. Patrick is guy number eleven. How humiliating.

"Maddie?"

I jerk my head up. Noreen is stopped in front of me, holding hands with Gray, the guy I met at the table my first night in Dingle.

"Oh, hey."

"You alright?" Her forehead crinkles, and she looks at me intensely.

"Yeah, I'm fine." I work on plastering some kind of smile on my face.

"You must be freezing!" Noreen's in a winter coat, her brown curls tumbling over her jacket. "Not working tonight?"

"No. Well yes, I was."

"Everything working out at the flat?" Noreen is examining my face. "I know you'd planned to head back to the States, but let me know if you want to extend the lease."

"Come on Nor, I'm desperate for a pint." Gray tugs on her hand.

"Flat's great. Go on to the pub," I say, seeing my out. "Have a good night."

I slip past them and head toward the pink neon sign of Ian's tattoo parlor, like it was my destination all along. I dart inside. Everything about me is impulsive, and I have the urge to prove it.

It's quiet and empty inside and I appreciate the warmth. My shivering slowly fades, and a moment later, Ian peeks his head out from the back room.

"Hello, lass, how can I help you?"

"I'm pissed at Patrick."

He studies me for a moment, then chuckles.

"Come on in to chat. I have whisky."

"I don't really drink whisky."

Ian ignores my protest and I follow him to the back room, where there are three empty tattoo stations and a round, black table. A thick binder sits in the middle.

"I'll be right back."

I settle into the comfortable chair and Ian ducks through a doorway, emerging a moment later with two glasses of amber liquid. He sits across from me and slides a glass my way.

"Thank you." I take a sip and wince at the heat in my throat. "Does it always taste like this?"

Ian nods. "Well, this is the good stuff, so it can burn a lot worse going down."

I sip again and appreciate it the second time, knowing what to expect.

"How's the road trip planning going? I've been thinking about it since you told me last Saturday night."

"Good." I nod. "I'm almost done. I'm gonna call it Quirks, Brews, and Views, since we'll stop at a few breweries."

"You'll be in Dingle, right? I'd love to see Oliver."

"Yeah. So you and Oliver are old friends?" I study Ian's freckled face.

"We became close while he was in Dingle. He's a talented artist. Here—" He opens the binder and flips through to a section in the back. "These are some of the designs he left behind."

I flip through the pages of my sister's fiancé's drawings. There are flowers, soccer balls, mountains, trees, rivers. A shamrock. Celtic designs. A series of hearts. Even before he touched a tattoo needle, Oliver had an eye for ink.

"Oh." I look up at Ian. The red-haired man raises his eyebrows at me.

"Oh what?"

"I just had an idea on how to make the road trip even better."

"How is that?"

My brain whirls. I loved the idea of adding brewery stops to the road trip plus quirky little side trips to make it more unique than the average driving tour of Ireland. What if we also add an official stop at Ian's tattoo parlor?

"We'll plan to stop here when we're in Dingle. I have a feeling I can convince my sisters that we need to get matching tattoos."

"Sounds grand."

"And I'll rename the road trip Quirks, Tats, Brews, and Views."

He grins. "A mouthful, but I like it."

"Thanks for your help." I throw back the rest of the whisky. "While I'm here, can I get a tattoo? That's what I actually came in for."

The corners of Ian's eyes crinkle and he nods. "What were you thinking?"

I head back to the pub a short while later, my ankle stinging where I had Ian ink three small hearts. It represents me and my sisters. My anchors. My squad.

It was impulsive, but I love it. Impulsive is who I am, and fuck anyone who doesn't like it.

I'm going to force Patrick to accept my help tonight at the pub. I have a job. Something went wrong there, and I feel terrible about it, but him telling me to go home isn't going to help the situation.

I'm not running from this job like I have from so many others.

19

PATRICK

"I just saw Maddie practically running down the street," Noreen says while I pour her second pint. "She looked upset."

I don't look up or acknowledge her words, but my whole body tenses.

Shite.

I'm such a fecking arse. Of course she's upset. I did what I always do. Sound like an arsehole. *How did this happen,* I texted her. *It's not your fault,* I said but obviously, she didn't believe me.

Leave.

I saw the look on her face before she bolted out of here. She wasn't just mad. She was hurt. I hurt her. I knew I would do it eventually, but this soon?

"Everything okay?" Concern etches Noreen's face as I slide the full pint of Guinness to her. She leans forward on the bar, her curls falling over her shoulders. "I guess the rumor that you two have a thing going on is true, then?"

Anger flares inside me and I rest my palms on the bar.

It is none of Noreen's business that I have something going on with Maddie. Noreen's kindness is annoying as hell, especially after —no. Feck that.

"Everything's fine."

Noreen takes the hint and retreats with the pair of pints, a worried look thrown back over her shoulder as she hands her boyfriend his drink.

It was Noreen who hammered the last nail in the coffin that held my heart.

She was the one I dated after getting back to Dingle. I tried with her. Tried letting her in. She was so sweet and pretty. She wanted to be my friend, and then she wanted more. *Why not*, I'd thought.

But I couldn't open myself up to her.

Her words from when she broke it off echo in my head and my empty heart: *It's like there's nothing there*, she'd said. *Maybe you'd be better off alone.*

I didn't try to fight back. It was almost a relief that she ended it before I could make more of a mess of things. I walked away.

She was right. There was nothing left beneath my surface. Cara destroyed me.

And Noreen's killed me with kindness ever since.

Feck this town and all the nosy people in it. Feck those who've found me lacking—Noreen, Cara, and the string of women I dated before who used me for my status as a professional soccer player.

But Maddie? I don't know. She doesn't find me lacking, does she? Or have I already ruined things with her by being myself?

When Maddie walks back through the door forty-five minutes later, a rush of relief washes over me.

She came back.

I step aside and let her slide back behind the bar and serve some of the crowd of people who are waiting. Ronan is here, but it's a Friday night and we could use another hand.

But I ignore the crowd, the waiting customers trying to make eye contact with me, and watch Maddie. Her cheeks are flushed and her long, dark hair hangs over her bare shoulders. She went out without a jacket, of course, because this woman does not give a feck about winter in Ireland.

While I'm furious that we lost another bartender, it's not Maddie's fault. I'm mad at myself. And the inventory issue? Also my responsibility in the end. I shouldn't have offloaded so much to her. It's not fair. She's been working here for eleven days.

But me? I'm screwing things up at the bar *and* the brewery.

Worse: I'm fecking it up with Maddie.

"Hey." She steps next to me and grabs a bottle of New Dingle from the fridge. I want to push her hair aside and nuzzle into her neck while running my hands along her waist and hips. Christ, do I want that.

"Madison . . ."

She looks at me, but I can't bring myself to apologize. I can't say the words. I was never good at saying sorry to Cara when we were together.

I didn't even know Cara in the end. I came home once and gave her a silver necklace with a small pink stone that I'd picked up at the airport at an expensive jewelry shop. Cara opened the package and stared at it. *I only wear gold,* she'd said, and then looked at me like I was a stranger.

And I was. I couldn't even figure out one gift to give her.

After that, I'd asked her to move to England with me. We'd make it work. I was committed. But she gave me another look and said Dingle was her home.

Except when she made Dublin her home.

She apologized after I found her with the American banker. Didn't try to deny it. Didn't fight for us. I didn't need that apology.

What kind of gift would I buy Maddie, anyway? I bet I can't think of a thing.

But . . . I've already done it. I bought her that bike from my neighbor. It's good quality and will keep her safe. Stupid use of my money. I'm a fecking eejit, there's no denying that.

I don't finish my sentence, so Maddie goes back to serving.

We don't say a word for the next few hours. At ten o'clock, she looks exhausted. She needs rest.

"I'll close. Go home." I lean down to say it in her ear as we stand side by side at the bar and watch a pair of women Irish dancing on the stage to lively music.

The words *go home* come out less harsh than before, but the look she gives me doesn't confirm that.

Sometimes I can't even tell when I'm being an arse.

I'll figure out a way to make up with her tomorrow morning. Or maybe I won't, because there's absolutely no point in trying to make things work between us. We're not in a relationship. This is all incredibly temporary, no matter how big it feels in the moment.

I'm no one's adventure.

Maddie turns to me, her face crumpled. She waits for a beat, during which I do absolutely nothing.

Then she's gone.

20

PATRICK

Saturday, 15 March

I lean against the counter in Mam's kitchen drying a pot, trying to ignore the uncomfortable twist in my stomach. I might've been a bit too rough in the game this morning when I aggressively blocked a shot on goal and one of the other team's midfielders got a ball to the face and a bloody nose. We have a few weeks off now, which is a relief as the weather's been absolute bollocks. And the teams in town are all sick of us winning.

Deep down I knew it unlikely, but I'd hoped that Maddie would come to watch. But she didn't.

I have the girls in a bit, so I can't show up during her shift to apologize or charm her. I'm not a charming man, anyway. I'm tempted to invite her over to the cottage when she's off. The girls would love to spend more time with Maddie. They seem to have the same goal as my sister—to force me to find a girlfriend.

But I have rules: no women at the cottage, and no women around Erin and Niamh, no matter how much they ask. It's too personal. Too close.

"You're dismissed." Mam takes the pot from my hands. "I think that's dry enough."

"Mam?"

Her eyes flick to mine briefly. I'm so lucky to have this life. To live so close to my family after a dream career in professional soccer, and now I run a bar and a brewery. What more could I want?

"Yes?" She pauses in her squat to reach the lower cabinets, and I take the pot back from her and do it myself.

"When we were little, and you and Dad went through that rough patch . . ." I close the cabinet door and stand.

Mam patiently waits for me to continue.

"How did you get through it?" I lean against the counter and keep my eyes trained on my mother.

"You've never asked that before." She picks up a dish towel and mindlessly wipes the wet counter next to the sink. "I didn't know you remembered."

"I know." I should've asked earlier. How could I not have? Maybe there's a secret here. A secret to how not to permanently break important relationships.

"I'd been unhappy, felt so swallowed up in childcare and housework." There's a faraway look in her eyes. "So your dad and I figured out a plan. I started working part-time. And when we were both home, we'd split the cleaning and the childcare. Right down the middle."

"Hmm." I do remember that. I thought it was normal for Dad to be just as involved in our lives as Mam, but eventually realized it was different for most of my mates.

"At the time, it was a big deal. Things are different now, thankfully. None of my friends could believe my husband was home cleaning the toilets. But he was."

"And that's why you started working at the travel agency?" For as long as I could remember, Mam would sit at the desk closest to the window at the one now-closed travel agency downtown and talk to people about their vacations. I always wondered why she didn't just work at the brewery with Dad.

"Exactly. I needed to have my own separate life." She drops the towel on the counter and takes one of my hands. "But it takes two committed people to make that happen. Cara was rubbish for you. She treated you terribly. She was not the one."

I blink rapidly. Mam never talks badly about Cara and Liam's family or New Dingle Brewing. It's driven me crazy for years.

"It was her fault. You were committed, *a stór*. But that's not enough. She wasn't enough for you."

I try to respond, but the words stick in my throat, and my heart squeezes at her calling me *a stór*, the term of endearment she used when I was a child.

"I did my fair share of convincing your dad not to sell Slea Head to that damn family." Her voice has a bite to it. "They can piss right off."

"Mam," I say with a laugh. "I agree, of course."

"Now this American girl? When do I get to meet her?" Mam releases my hand.

I groan. "She's only in town for a few more weeks."

And I've probably ruined that time for us.

"We'll see. Now go sit on the couch with your father. He's exhausted from cleaning the bathrooms this morning." She winks at me.

"Hey, Mam?" I pause at the door to the kitchen.

She looks over with a clean dish in her hand and raises her eyebrows.

"What's one really unique thing you've done in Ireland? For Maddie's road trip."

"Hmm." She tilts her head to one side and absentmindedly slides the dish onto a stack in the upper cabinet next to the sink. "Ah. Here's a dark one for you. There's a cave in Kilkenny. It's said that one thousand people died there in a Viking massacre. It's haunted."

"Christ, Mam. You and Saoirse with the creepy ideas."

"Like mother, like daughter. It's at least unique, no?"

I leave the kitchen with a chuckle and settle next to my snoozing father.

I could try to fix things with Maddie, short time left or not. Maybe this isn't forever, but like Mam said, I could put in the effort and commit to the time we have left. I could invite her over. Apologize. Tell her I'm broken, that none of the pub drama is her fault, except for the fact that she is completely distracting me, and I don't want that to change one bit.

I could ask her to be with me for a little while longer.

Dad makes a little snorting sound and flutters his eyes open for a second, smiling at me, then closes them again.

I unlock my mobile and stare at the quiet text chain with Maddie, then type.

ME

I'm sorry about yesterday. I shouldn't have snapped at you. None of that was your fault, and I was an arse. Forgive me?

The text changes from *delivered* to *read*, and I wait for her response. But there's no dancing dots.

ME

I've got the girls tonight

I pause. This would be the time to invite her over. My thumb lingers over the keypad.

But with a heavy sigh, I realize I'm not going to do that. I can't bring myself to. I need to protect at least a small part of myself.

ME

Can we meet up tomorrow? Breakfast? Lunch?

That's three texts in a row, the second two not even showing as read. If she doesn't respond tonight, I can show up at the pub tomorrow afternoon when she's on the schedule.

I hate the feelings inside me, crashing around like rough waves in the Irish sea. I don't do this. I've learned my lesson. And feelings like this don't last.

In the end, Cara wanted something more. I wasn't enough.

Not for her, or Noreen, or anyone.

Is Maddie different?

I push my mobile away and reach over to squeeze my father's hand before heading back into the kitchen, where Mam is making tea.

"Bye." I kiss my mother on the cheek. "Need to run to meet the girls."

"I love you, dear. Let me know if you need anything tonight."

I head home, my mind whirling.

Why would Maddie be different? I've let down my defenses with her more than I have with anyone else. It's because she's not a complete stranger. She's connected to my life by three degrees of separation. And now, she's a friend—someone I didn't know I needed in my life.

But we're also sleeping together. I've never done friends with benefits before. I know why—it's a train wreck of emotions.

Jaysus, am I confused.

The girls arrive at my cottage shortly after I do. Saoirse has a date with Ian tonight as his kids are with their mother. But when she asks me how things are with Maddie, I can't stop the scowl from my face.

"What did you do?" she asks.

"Why do you assume I did something?" I run my hand over my face, standing on the front steps with my sister, propping the door open with my body. "I didn't do anything."

"Tell me." She glares at me.

"I mean, I guess I kind of did something."

"What happened?" Saoirse crosses her arms and taps her foot on the concrete step.

"I was an arse to her." And that's all the explanation Saoirse needs.

"Don't screw this up, Pat. Maddie's good for you."

"How is she good for me?" I genuinely want to know. "And why do you even care?"

"I dunno. You've actually, like, smiled over the past few weeks? Had some fun? Been happy for the first time in years? With a decent woman who is funny and sweet and kind?"

I groan and swallow the lump in my throat.

"Yeah, well, that might all be true, but she's temporary. It doesn't matter if she's funny and sweet and kind and beautiful." My voice cracks on the last word.

"So you think she's beautiful?" A sly smile comes over Saoirse's face.

"Christ, Saoirse."

"Uncle Patrick has a girlfriend!" Erin sings from the kitchen, where I look back to see her swiping chocolate biscuits from a jar I fill just for my nieces.

"You're all insufferable."

"That's a big word for a man who's screwing things up with the woman he's dating."

"Am I dating her?"

"Bye, girls!" Erin and Niamh rush at their mother for quick hugs and dash back inside. I follow my sister a few steps away from the door, shoving my hands in my jeans pockets.

Saoirse pauses next to her car.

"You're doing *something* with her. And it's not just physical. Figure it out."

After Erin grabs another cookie and Niamh snags two, we head to the backyard. Niamh throws her arms around Kitty's head. The sheep was waiting by the back door and pushes her head against my niece, searching her sides for a hidden treat. I hand Niamh one of the bowls of oats.

"Where's Turtle?" Erin asks, peering out to the barn.

"Hiding. He'll come out eventually, probably to play soccer with us." I juggle the ball from one foot to the other, the girls cheering me on as I balance Turtle's oats in one hand.

"Let me try, Uncle Pat! I've gotten better." Erin grabs the ball and attempts to juggle, getting four touches before the ball flies off toward Niamh.

"Nice work, Erin! I can tell you've been practicing." My niece's cheeks turn pink with the compliment.

Niamh tries. She only gets one and growls in frustration.

"It's a tough skill, juggling. You have to practice every day." I place the oats onto the grass and grab two more balls, tossing one to Erin so we can all practice at the same time. "Try to get it on the top of your foot or the inside. Not your toes. You'll have more control that way."

I show them how to gently tap the soccer ball up, one foot after another, kicking it just a few inches off the tops of my feet.

"I'll never be as good as you," Niamh whines.

"Right, because I'm almost forty, and this was literally my job for fifteen years of my life."

She giggles again. "You're super old."

"That I am." I shrug.

"When are we painting the wooden sheep you made, Uncle Patrick?" Niamh asks the question, but even Erin stops what she's doing and looks for my answer.

"After dinner, loves." I love that I'm here for this part of their lives. I wouldn't change it for anything.

Five minutes later, my mobile vibrates in my pocket with a call.

"Be right back. Keep practicing." Heart racing, I stride back to the house and pull my mobile out on the way.

"Is it Maddie?" Erin calls.

It's not. It's Sean.

Damn. Disappointment smacks me across my face. I should text her again. Or maybe call.

"Sean." I slip into the kitchen. The girls give up on juggling and kick their balls into the pop-up goal.

"I'm handing in my resignation, effective immediately." Sean enunciates each word, like he's reading from a piece of paper.

"What?" Sharp panic feels like a ball to the gut.

"I'm getting too old for this nonsense."

"Wait, Sean . . ." My heart's beating so hard, I can feel it in my ears. "Let's work this out. You love this job. Or you love Slea Head, at least. And you're the best head brewer in town."

Sean and I might not always see eye to eye, or be able to stand the sight of each other, but he's damn good at his job. And Slea Head needs him.

I need him.

"Aye. But I'm just done, you hear? Cormac fucked up."

I pause and swallow. "How?" Dread creeps up from my toes to my head like a slow icy wave.

"He changed the goddamn temperature on the fermenter."

"What?" *Oh, no.*

"He said there was some handwritten note from you that he couldn't quite read, so I guess he went ahead and changed it before calling me. Or you. He turned the lager fermenter up to an ale temperature."

"Feck. When?" Lagers need to ferment at much lower temperatures than ales. This could have tainted the whole batch.

"This morning. It might be okay, but I don't think we can take the risk. We need to trash the batch."

My stomach drops out. "Both fermenters?"

"No, just one. And why would he do just one? I don't care. That kid's a fecking eejit. I'm gone."

My brain whirls. What kind of note did I leave? Damn, but I should've been there today. Yesterday. I should be checking in with

Cormac more often. He's still new, and Sean's too harsh with him to be a good boss or mentor. I'm hesitant to stand up to Sean sometimes, so I can only imagine how Cormac feels.

"Slea Head was fine just how it was before you came on board."

I massage my temples with one hand spanning my forehead. He's not right. Slea Head was not fine. It needed change. Progress. New brews. New distribution. Otherwise, we'd keep fading until we shut our doors for good.

But I keep quiet, because I have a feeling I'll only make it worse if I speak.

"I didn't need an assistant brewer. That lad's driving me bonkers. *You're* driving me bonkers. I'm gonna go home and tend to my wife and my dogs."

"Sean, can we meet tomorrow morning and talk this through?"

"No. Good luck to you."

And then he's gone.

This can't be happening.

"Fuck!" I whisper into my empty kitchen. I glance out at the girls. Erin shoots way too hard at Niamh, who takes a ball to the face. The younger girl bursts into tears. Turtle emerges from the barn and trots over to the goal, immediately nibbling on the netting, and Erin ignores her sobbing sister and casually strolls over to grab the cup of oats.

I need to get back out there, but first, I pull out my mobile. There's a text waiting from Cormac.

CORMAC

I fucked up. I'm so sorry. I thought your note
said 'raise temperature to 22 degrees Celsius,
F1 by noon Saturday'

What's he talking about?

CORMAC

It was in your office. A Post-it on the autumn brew folder. I thought it meant fermenter 1

ME

Ah. That was for the IPA. Must've been an old note from February before the IPA brew day

I bite back a retort, when I really want to ask him why I would have changed the temperature on just one of the fermenters when we have identical batches of the same brew.

CORMAC

I'm sorry. I thought maybe you were testing something out. I texted you this morning. And called you

I scroll back up and yeah, there it is, a text from ten in the morning asking to clarify the note, then a missed call, then another text confirming what he was doing after not being able to get ahold of me.

I was playing soccer and so totally distracted by my fight with Maddie that I didn't read the messages from him. Didn't even notice them, as I only had my text chain with Maddie open.

She was the only person I wanted to hear from.

ME

Sean quit. I'll be in touch tomorrow, okay?

CORMAC

I'm so sorry

I slip my mobile in my pocket and join my nieces in the backyard, plastering on a smile.

"Uncle Patrick!" Niamh jumps into my arms, the drying tears forgotten on her cheeks. "Can you teach us how to be goalkeeper again? So I don't get hit in the face all the time?"

"Of course."

What am I going to do about the brewery? About the pub? About Maddie?

Why is everything falling apart?

21

MADDIE

Sunday, March 16

It's the day before St Patrick's Day and I'm in Ireland, so I should be preparing to get shamrocks painted on my face and drink inappropriate amounts of Guinness, but instead I feel like absolute garbage.

It's raining. It's gray. And it's freaking freezing, even though it's supposed to be almost spring and the locals keep telling me the weather will break soon. I think it's a lie and that their standards are different than mine. Those sunny days tricked me. At least I finally purchased a few more pieces of clothing, and today I'm wearing thick leggings, a new hoodie, and a lined vest.

But even though I'm fitting in better with my wardrobe, I'm seriously questioning the life decisions that brought me to this miserable country.

I throw my leg over the bike Patrick gave me, pausing to look up and down Main Street while I clip the too-big helmet under my chin, my eyes lingering on the red O'Brien's awning. Last night was much busier than it's been lately as tourists are starting to descend on Dingle.

The new batch of inventory should have arrived this morning, just in time for the St Patrick's Day festivities tomorrow. Declan bartended with me last night and logged in to the system—which I don't have access to—to confirm. I'll double check the new shipments carefully when I'm in tonight.

I'm gonna work extra hard from now on to make sure there's no more mistakes. I want to help Patrick, not make his life more difficult. Despite his apologetic texts yesterday, I'm still angry at how he reacted to the inventory issue, even though I know it's at least partially my fault. Mine and the other bartenders'. All of us failed to properly notice and escalate the problem.

And the way he spoke to me . . . I haven't been bothered by how direct he is. How he doesn't sugarcoat his words. I can see how others might lean away from him, but until Friday night, I hadn't felt that way myself. His words run through my head.

How did this happen?

You should go.

Madison. Come on.

Leave.

This time, they cut deep. Theoretically, I know it's not personal. It's the way he communicates.

Still, I need a minute away from him and some fresh air. Maybe I shouldn't be out on a day this wet and rainy, given how I'm not the most confident biker. But what, I'm going to sit around all day? Wallow in the absence of Patrick? Nah.

I'd hoped he would show up during my shift yesterday. But he didn't. Ian and Saoirse stopped by the pub in the afternoon with their crew of kiddos, and Patrick's sister made it a point to tell me he had the girls that evening. Last night. They were going to paint and play soccer. She said it almost apologetically.

I pedal the bike slowly down the sidewalk, dodging people, a wheel slipping. I should be on the road, but I'm not quite brave enough amongst the parked cars, other cyclists, and vehicles driving on the wrong damn side of the street.

A few doors down, Dingle Brew is too tempting, so I park the bike. I made it a whole two hundred feet. I push my way into the warm café and order a small hot coffee, thanking Maria and grabbing a stool by the window so I can suck it down before going back out.

My sisters have been texting me nonstop the past few days. Two new ones popped up between my flat and Dingle Brew.

> **STELLA**
> Mads, I sent you money so you can start booking accommodation and whatever else
>
> **REESE**
> I did as well. Thanks so much for planning this!

I sip the coffee and enjoy the burn in my throat. Quirks, Tats, Brews, and Views—possibly the most ridiculous name for a road trip—is all coming together. It's one thing in my life that I feel like I haven't messed up, and I hope Reese and Oliver love it.

We'll have the standard Irish road trip highlights plus brewery stops, a morning at Ian's tattoo shop while in Dingle, and the seven weird little stops I've gathered so far: the Hungry Tree in Dublin, the giant salmon statue in Belfast, the hole to hell in the ground in Donegal, a waterfall, stone beehive huts, the Blarney Stone, and the Butter Museum. I crack myself up, and I'm certain it'll make the trip unique. I could use a few more of those stops, and I need to book accommodations as soon as possible. I have ideas saved in my notes app and had planned to look through them with Patrick this weekend before booking.

Harder to do when we're not speaking.

How many hotel rooms am I booking? Four or three? Reese and her fiancé. Stella and her boyfriend. Me. Patrick. It's gotta be four. Why would I even *think* of booking just three?

One thing is for sure: we're going to be an awkward group of six if Patrick and I end things on a bad note. 'Cause let's be clear:

this thing with Patrick is definitely ending. Either now or next week or next month.

This *thing* is nothing.

A holiday fling.

I shudder at the words. But I need to face reality. There's not been one singular conversation about feelings. Except for that one time he told me he liked me. But he also likes his pet sheep, so that's not saying much.

It doesn't matter. I'm just another tourist he's sleeping with, and he's a hot Irishman scratching an itch for me. We know where we stand with each other. That's why I even let myself get involved with him—it was clear what was happening and where I stood.

And that apology yesterday was probably to smooth things over ahead of the road trip so it won't be painfully awkward. It wasn't the worst apology I've ever gotten. The *Forgive me?* line made my heart warm uncomfortably.

I haven't responded.

Patrick and I are not dating. We have a weird relationship right now, a connection because his close friend and my sister are getting married. So he's not a stranger, and I'm not some random tourist.

But we're only a small step above that.

ME

> No problem. I'll start getting the rooms booked ASAP. Going on a bike ride now

STELLA

On the beach? Jealous!!!

ME

> Yeah. On the beach

REESE

Pictures, please

Oh, *for fuck's sake.*

I toss back the rest of my coffee and google bike rides on the beach. I find a picture I like on a different Caribbean island—but what does it matter which island the picture's from?—so I screenshot a bike on its side in the sand and crop it, careful to remove all of the watermark from the blog I'm blatantly stealing—borrowing —from. I gaze at the turquoise waters and clear blue sky, bright sun reflecting off the white sand.

I'd way rather be there.

Before I chicken out of today's bike ride, I wave to Maria and head back out. This time, I ride carefully on the road, which is almost easier, as I'm not constantly dodging pedestrians. Main Street turns into Goat Street, and I'm feeling pretty good about my bike riding skills.

The wind lashes my face, but it's stopped raining, so I let myself cycle faster and faster. It's blowing away all my problems: my lies to my sisters, the way I've gotten so wrapped up in my relationship with Patrick, my lack of plans for the future even though I'm supposed to be figuring everything out while I'm here.

There's the issue of my return flight, which is scheduled for less than two weeks from now. Am I getting on that plane back to New Jersey? Back to live with Reese and Oliver? Jobless? Will I have to face my oldest sister in person and tell her how I messed up everything, again?

Fuck. That sounds awful.

Dingle Bay opens up to my left, and I cross the short bridge.

I have to be in Ireland for the road trip and Scotland for the wedding. It's time I take my life seriously, like I promised I would when I got on the plane to Dublin.

A shiver runs through my body. Even with my new warm clothes, it's freezing out here, and the rain starts falling again. I'm doubting my plan to keep biking to that first spot Patrick took me to the other week. The spot where he let me nestle into his chest, protecting me from the cold and wind. It's too far.

A *baaa* jars me out of my daydream, and when I refocus on the path in front of me, there's a herd of sheep blocking the road almost completely. I'm close enough to make direct eye contact with one of them. I swear its eyes widen as I approach, going much too fast.

They're just fucking standing there, staring at me. I might be screaming, but it's hard to tell. It's much too late to stop.

I swerve away from the sheep, but my bike loses traction on the wet pavement, and I slide toward the edge of the road.

And a giant boulder.

At least I have a helmet on, but it shifts on my head, and as I approach the rock, the strap under my chin is too loose to keep it in place.

For the briefest moment, I wish so deeply that I'd taken Patrick up on the offer to find another helmet, one that fits better.

Then everything goes black.

22

PATRICK

I'm antsy as hell right now.

The smell of bacon, scrambled eggs, and fresh cinnamon rolls—I've perfected the art of making them from scratch for my nieces—wafts through my cottage, and the girls giggle at the table as they lick icing-covered fingers. This is usually one of my favorite parts of having them stay over: making an extravagant breakfast before Saoirse picks them up.

But this morning, all I can think about is Sean quitting.

It's even pushed out some of the dread around Maddie ignoring me after I was such an arsehole on Friday.

What am I gonna do about Slea Head? I'm only one person. I can't be head brewer as well as run strategy and planning and administration for the brewery, plus keep an eye on things at the pub. I need to hire more people.

It won't be easy to find someone as experienced as Sean. He knows everything about brewing and has been at Dad's side at Slea Head for decades.

If it hadn't been Cormac's screwup that was the catalyst for Sean quitting, I'd consider giving the kid more responsibilities. But I can't do that without risking even more going wrong. Not yet.

I'm gonna have to step up and step in, even though I already have so much on my plate, including the Wellington Pubs meeting this Tuesday. So much rides on that meeting. If it goes well, it could change everything for Slea Head. I can think about replacing Sean after I get through that day.

Saoirse shows up half an hour later.

"What's wrong?" The girls run to the car, but my sister's eyes are locked on me, her forehead crinkled. "You have a particularly unhappy expression on your face. Even worse than yesterday."

"Sean quit."

"No." Saoirse gasps and glances over her shoulder at her daughters, who are settled in the backseat of the car. "Why? What are you going to do?"

I shake my head. "He hates me, hates change, hates everything. You know, the expected reasons." Will I be a grumpy old man like that some day? Christ, I hope not. "I'll need to cover his role at the brewery until I can find a replacement."

"Pat, you already have, like, five jobs."

"Not sure what else to do."

"Hey." Saoirse reaches out to touch my arm. "I can cover shifts at O'Brien's if you need me to help."

"You also work too much already." The last thing I want to do is put more on my sister.

Saoirse shrugs. "Yeah. I do. But I'm getting fed up with the hotel. Maybe I'll finally accept one of your job offers."

"Anytime, Saoirse."

"Have you made up with Maddie yet?"

"Feck." I drag a hand roughly down my face. "No. She didn't respond to my texts."

"Well, she was working yesterday afternoon. Seemed disappointed when I told her you wouldn't be coming by. I made sure to tell her you had my kids."

I look up to the sky for help but find only thick gray clouds.

"Things have been shite at the pub. There's been problems.

Inventory issues. People quitting." I regret the words as soon as they leave my mouth. They are implied words of blame, and my sister recognizes that right away.

Saoirse presses her lips into a thin line.

"And is that her fault?"

"No." I sigh. "It's mine."

"You can't expect her to take over O'Brien's completely yet also call her a temporary manager. Go talk to her."

"I don't have time."

She gives me a withering glare. "It's your life to ruin."

"I'm not ruining my life." I squeeze my eyes shut. "Just because I'm spending so much time with her . . . just because I can't stop thinking of her no matter what I'm doing . . . just because I'm dying over here with her mad at me . . . all of that doesn't mean anything."

I open my eyes to Saoirse's shocked expression. Oops. Didn't mean to say all that out loud.

"Jaysus, Patrick," she huffs. "You have it even worse than I thought."

"I do not. Pretend I didn't say any of those things."

"But you did."

"Mam!" Erin yells from the backseat of the car. "Can we go?"

"One sec!" she calls to her daughters.

"I don't have time to make Maddie even more of a part of my life. I can't do it, Saoirse." I follow Saoirse to her car, and she slides into the driver's seat.

My sister does a shite job of suppressing a grin.

"What?" I throw my hands in the air.

"I should've known. I see the way you've been looking at her."

I roll my eyes so hard, I hope it offends my only sibling. It does not.

"There's nothing to know. Goodbye, Saoirse." I lean my head into the car. "Bye, girls."

Saoirse slams the door shut and backs out of my driveway, shaking her head as she goes.

Everything is a disaster.

The quiet of the cottage pushes against my eardrums. How am I going to get this all done?

My mobile buzzes, and I whip it out of my back pocket, hoping it's Maddie.

But it's Ian, and he's calling, not texting.

"Morning, Ian. Alright?" I head back to the kitchen, clicking the oven off and swiping a finger full of icing from the half-empty dish of cinnamon rolls.

"Patrick. It's Maddie."

I freeze in place and icy dread wraps itself around my heart.

"She was in a bike accident."

The air disappears from the room, leaving an eerie ringing sound in my ears.

"Is she okay?" My voice sounds distant, all garbled and muted like I'm underwater. I rake my hand into my hair and pull.

"They're on their way to the hospital. My ex called. She was one of the paramedics on the scene and made the connection because I'd told her about the American tourist last time I dropped off the kids."

"Ian. Is. She. Okay?" I repeat the question, noting that he didn't answer the first time.

He's quiet and I shove my fist against my mouth to keep the scream in my throat from escaping. I bite down on my knuckles until it stings.

"She wasn't conscious at that moment," he finally says. "Her helmet slipped, and she hit her head on a rock."

It's my fault. I should've bought her a new helmet. I knew the one she used on our bike ride was too big. Yet I still left it for her. I will never forgive myself for this. Not ever.

"She's at Dingle Regional?" I'm not sure I even ask the question out loud, but Ian answers.

"Yes."

"Call me if you hear anything more." I end the call without waiting for an answer and dash out the door, swiping my keys and nothing else, all worries about the brewery and the pub suddenly insignificant.

None of it matters because Maddie was in an accident, and she's in the hospital.

My car doesn't move fast enough. My stomach turns over and over.

What if she . . . if she was okay, wouldn't Ian's ex have told him? If she *wasn't* okay, would she have told him?

Panic threatens to take over my body and I force myself to breathe deeply as I navigate through Dingle. The hospital isn't far from the center of town, so they would've been able to get her there fast.

I scream into the empty car. I haven't felt this out of control . . . ever. Not when I found out Cara was cheating on me. Not even when I found out about Dad's stroke.

Black spots linger on the edge of my vision. Saoirse had called me that day. Dad had been at the brewery. Sean was with him and called Mam after he'd called the ambulance. They were all there when I arrived at the hospital.

That drive from O'Brien's to Dingle Regional had been torture, but at least then I knew Dad was conscious and talking to my family. I knew *something*.

I pull into the emergency room parking lot and try to dash inside, but my legs are heavy and it feels like I'm in a nightmare, trying to run but hardly moving.

All that matters is Maddie. I need to see her.

"Patrick McNulty?" a doctor calls into the waiting room. I spring up, ignoring the pulsing in my head.

"Is she okay?" I wring my hands together and rush to the doctor. He nods his head to follow him, and I do.

"She's going to be fine," he says as he ducks into a dark room, flicking on a switch and instantly blinding me with bright white lights. "She's awake and asking for you."

Profound relief washes over me, and I close my eyes for a beat to let the adrenaline in my veins slow.

It doesn't.

"She wasn't conscious when they picked her up but woke up soon after. She's got a mild concussion from hitting her head on a boulder on the side of the road. Her helmet slipped. It saved her from a worse head injury, but she still made contact. She's also got some broken skin and concrete rash from sliding on the asphalt."

Some of the relief fades away. That all sounds awful.

"What happened?"

"Apparently, she swerved to avoid a flock of sheep that was blocking the road."

My jaw drops open.

"Jaysus."

"She shouldn't have been riding a bike in these conditions, but tourists always do this. Take risks."

I flinch at him calling her a tourist.

"She really shouldn't be alone for more than a couple of hours for a few days. Are you her . . ." He leaves the question dangling.

What *am* I to her?

"She can stay with me." I'm not leaving Maddie alone in her flat. I can take care of her at the cottage. What if something happens and she doesn't have anyone to yell to? Or what if she just needs a cup of coffee? I could do that. I can at least be that to her.

"Right. Good. She can go home soon. You can see her now. Room five."

I nod and swallow the lump in my throat that won't dissipate. The doctor leaves me and I head in the direction he pointed.

With each step I take toward room five, my heart pounds

harder, louder, like a drumbeat. I clench and unclench my fists. Fear grows in me like a crescendo. Fear of what? She's fine. The doctor said so. What am I so damn afraid of?

I rest my hand against the doorframe of Maddie's room and can barely bring myself to knock on the open door.

Panic attack. I'm having a panic attack.

"Come in," Maddie calls. I step into view. "Patrick. You're here."

And she smiles at me. It's everything. She's in the hospital bed, her arm wrapped up in a bandage, looking like she got beat up.

My heart practically explodes in my chest. Words are stuck in my throat, and I stop at the bottom of the bed. I'm afraid if I open my mouth to talk, I'll cry, or scream, or melt down.

"Are you okay?" Her forehead creases. "Come sit with me?" She nods to the empty seat next to her.

There's a buzzing in my ears as I get closer to her and slip into the chair.

I knew I'd break this relationship, like I always do. I knew I'd ruin it. But I didn't think I'd be responsible for physically breaking Maddie.

She reaches for my hand. I take it and never want to let go.

"I'm sorry I never responded to your text message." Her voice is far away, that buzzing sound getting louder, the inexplicable terror seeping into every part of my body.

"What happened?" I whisper.

She looks at me with great concern. "Patrick. Are you sure you're okay? You're so pale. And you're sweating."

I nod my head, but she doesn't look convinced.

"It was so stupid." She sighs. "I got distracted, and it was wet, and a fucking herd of sheep were standing in the middle of the road."

A ghost of a smile crosses her face, but I can't even catch a breath.

What if she had . . . I gasp for air and my vision fades.

"Hey." She sits up and pulls my hand to her chest, splaying it against the bare skin above her breasts, just like I did that night I busted into the flat and scared her. "I'm okay. I'm okay, Patrick."

Her heart pounds under my hand and the steady beating slowly reassures me that she's alive. My vision begins to clear.

"Do you feel me?" Her voice is closer now. "I'm here."

She's okay. She's here.

Nothing else matters.

Only Maddie.

"Patrick?"

I nod, still unable to speak.

Feck.

Oh no.

Oh, shite.

I'm in love with this woman.

"Maddie."

She smiles. "Yes. You okay?"

And I am. My heart is slowing, the adrenaline easing off, leaving me weak.

"I'm okay now that I know you are." My voice works again, thank feck. "And my apology yesterday was shite. I should've done it in person."

"Saoirse told me you had the girls."

"I did. But this morning . . . I wish I'd called you to come over. Maybe you wouldn't have . . ." I glance at her bandaged hand.

"I feel like this sheep thing is something I'm going to get made fun of for."

"Eventually. It's too soon." My mouth quirks.

"I have a vague memory of one of them, like, nibbling on my hair. I think they felt bad and wandered over to make sure I was okay. I couldn't just barrel into them! So I swerved. Into a rock. Bad luck, really, as there was soft green grass all around it."

I stare at her face, her chocolate brown eyes, her gorgeous, plump lips. "I'm so very sorry I was an arse last week. Nothing that happened was your fault. It was my fault. All mine. I've been distracted lately, and so busy. Things keep slipping through the cracks."

"Because of me. Distracting you." She states it as fact.

I take a minute, but nod.

"You'd be better off if I weren't here."

"No. I'd be much worse off without you."

I love this woman. I tug a strand of her long hair and lean forward to kiss her gently, my hand still on her warm skin, ensuring her heart still beats.

"You're coming home with me. You can stay at my cottage."

"You're gonna take care of me?"

"Aye. Maddie."

"In your house?"

I nod, and I'm sure she understands what a big deal this is.

"You called me Maddie, so that means you're going to kiss me again."

And I do, sliding the hand I have on her chest around to the back of her neck, leaning forward and pressing my lips to hers. With that kiss, I open my whole heart to Maddie Hart.

I feel so much worse than I ever have before.

When I pull back, she's staring at me with a look I can't read. I'd give anything to know what she's thinking.

Anything except ask her.

Because the thing is, I can't tell her I love her. I don't think I could handle it if she doesn't feel the same way. Or, if she does, what the hell would we do about it? It's not worth the risk.

She's going back to New Jersey to start her new life. I'm staying here in Dingle.

There's no hope for us.

23

MADDIE

Monday, March 17

I wake up in Patrick's bed, in his cottage. Is this a dream? I stretch out my arms and wince at the sting on my right arm. Nope, that soreness is definitely real. And the pounding in my head reminds me how my skull met a giant boulder yesterday. I have a vision of a flock of sheep and moan into the pillow.

Sheep caused my bike accident.

Patrick stayed with me until the doctors said we could go, only ducking out of the room to make a few phone calls on brewery business. He wouldn't give me details, but it seemed urgent.

Then he took me to his cottage. His *home.*

We walked to the front door, his arm wrapped firmly around my waist, as if I might fall over at any moment. It was dark and I didn't even get a tour of the cottage before I collapsed on the couch, where we ate takeout and turned on a movie. I didn't watch it at all, as my head was so sore. Instead, I fell asleep wedged in the crook of his shoulder. He put me to bed in his room and woke me every three hours to ask questions like *what's your name* and *where are you from* and *what's the best amber ale you've ever tasted and why is it Slea Head Golden Amber*. Doctor's orders, he said.

We'd slept in the same bed together many times in my flat. But this was different. He'd never brought up bringing me here. It didn't seem to be something he would do. That was fine with me —it was his sacred space, his real home, where his nieces would come sleep, where he has pet sheep in the backyard.

His side of the bed is cold, but his voice carries from the other room as he talks to someone on the phone. I sit up slowly and wait for the pulsing in my head to subside, and when it does, I pull on my hoodie and shuffle out of the room.

"I'll call you later," he says as soon as I appear at the end of the hallway. He quickly pockets his phone.

I lean against the wall.

"Brewery stuff?"

He nods and presses his palms on the granite counter, his eyes locked on me, scanning for weaknesses.

"How are you feeling?" he finally says.

"Wonderful." I wince as my head pounds in response. "Mostly wonderful. But you can go to work, you know? I can go back to the flat. I hate to mess up your week. I know things are stressful right now."

Me making bad decisions—biking in the rain—is going to interfere with his life even more. But deep inside, I hope he says no. I hope he wants me to stay.

Patrick shakes his head and strides over to me, reaching for my hands. Warm and sweet, his thumbs slide over the back of my palms. Then he drops my hands and cups my face. My body heats at his touch.

"I'm not leaving you alone."

"It's a minor concussion and some scrapes." My heart squeezes.

He shakes his head. "You were in hospital."

"But it's St Patrick's Day. The pub is going to be so busy tonight."

"It's covered."

"Seriously? By who?"

Patrick ignores the question and drags his thumb along my jawline, swiping at my bottom lip.

"Did I say I'm so sorry about last week?"

I nod. "You did. I'm sorry, too."

He leans in to kiss my lips softly. "Hungry? How about left-over cinnamon rolls?"

"Sounds delicious."

"Let me show you around first."

Patrick takes my hand and leads me down the hallway, pausing at the room I just emerged from.

"My bedroom, obviously."

"Your bed is beautiful." It's wooden with a majestic head-board. Looks like the same type of wood as the coffee table at my flat.

He gives me a funny look and leads me further down the hall-way, hand still clasped around mine.

Past his bedroom, there are two closed doors. He opens one and gestures for me to step inside, letting go of my hand as I take in the pink-and-blue masterpiece.

"Niamh loves pink." There are a trio of canvas prints above her bed on one side of the room: a unicorn, a sheep, and a puppy. "But Erin will only put up with blue." Above Erin's bed on the other side there are stickers of soccer balls, a goal, and also sheep.

"It's so sweet that they have their own room at your house."

"I bought the cottage a year ago. I knew I wanted this to be a safe, fun second home for the girls. My sister needs a break once in a while, and her ex is an arse and hardly ever around." He leans against the doorframe, arms crossed, muscles bulging out of his t-shirt, while I spin slowly in a circle.

A soft throw rug tickles my toes. There's a sturdy wooden nightstand for each girl that matches the beds, with a pile of age-appropriate books. Skinny chapter books for Niamh, fatter novels for Erin.

I swallow and turn to Patrick. I'm seeing another layer of this man, one he seems to protect fiercely.

"What about the rest?" I nod my head toward the hallway.

"There's another bedroom down here. It's, uh, a bit of a workroom." He makes no move to budge from his spot.

"Do you have some dark secret hidden in there?" I close the distance between us and press myself against him, turning him toward me with my back against the doorframe. I'm deliciously trapped.

"Not quite."

"Show me." I tilt my head up and he makes a low sound as he leans down to kiss me. Too gently. I sigh. I'm not going to break, concussion or not.

Patrick leads me down the hallway and pushes the third bedroom's door open, stepping aside to let me in. It's a bright room with pieces of furniture in that same color of light wood organized randomly. A coffee table against one wall, several small bookshelves—including one set up in the middle of the room and appearing half-finished—and a worktable of carpentry supplies.

"What's this?"

He runs his hand up his neck and blushes. It's freaking adorable.

"I make furniture."

"You . . . make it? With your own two hands?" I blink a hundred times. Could this man get any hotter?

"Yes. There's a workroom attached to the shed out back where I do most of the work, but I bring some of the finished pieces in here. Plus that one bookcase that isn't quite done. I need to get a heater set up out there."

"Your bed?"

He nods.

"The girls' room?"

"I had more time before taking over Slea Head. I did a ton when I first bought the cottage. But this stuff's kind of sat here for the last three months." Patrick runs a hand through his hair.

"Understandable." I walk over to one of the bookshelves and run my hand along a smooth, thick shelf.

"One of the bookcases is for my parents and the other is for Saoirse. They're almost done. After that, I will focus on smaller pieces so I can actually complete something in a reasonable timeframe."

"These are beautiful. So sturdy. Strong. Unbreakable." Not cheaply made. Real wood, dependable, long-lasting.

That's what I want from a man. All of those things.

My gaze lands on the coffee table.

"Oh! The coffee table in my flat?"

"Yes."

"Wow." I steal a look at him. "Wait, what about that wooden wall hanging in the flat? In the shape of Ireland? Is that yours, too?"

"Yes."

"You're talented." I hug my arms across my chest, trying to douse the sweet warmth sparking inside.

He shrugs and backs up out of the room. "Want to meet the sheep?"

"As long as they're not the ones that took me down yesterday."

"Christ." His eyes widen. "Would this be triggering?"

"I'd prefer baby goats, like your neighbor has, to sheep." I step closer to him. "But it's okay. I don't blame the sheep."

"Come on, then." He half-chuckles, half-sighs, and holds out his hand. I step forward to take it.

"Wait a minute." I pull back on his hand until he turns to me.

"Hmm?"

"When you say smaller pieces, do you mean things like wooden figurines?"

"Aye. Figurines and bowls and wall decor. Just not giant pieces like the bed or bookshelves."

"The ones your nieces painted over the weekend?"

"Yes."

"Sweet. And did you happen to make a terrifying wooden sheep and leave it on the dresser in the flat?" A vision of the menacing shadow of the sheep on that first morning I woke up in Dingle flashes in my head.

"I wasn't going for terrifying." Patrick squeezes my hand.

I crack up.

"Come on. Kitty's the friendly one. Turtle hides. He's super standoffish."

I let Patrick lead me to the backyard.

"I'm gonna take a wild guess that you let your nieces name your sheep."

"Aye. I wanted to call them Brains and Holy."

"That's weird." I cock my head as we get to the sliding doors in his family room.

"You know, short for Sheep for Brains and Holy Sheep."

I cackle and follow him out the door, where Kitty stands about ten feet away. Patrick looks over his shoulder and winks at me.

My heart twitters. I'm in so much trouble with this man.

***

On Tuesday afternoon, I shove Patrick out the door to go to the brewery.

"I'll be back soon, I promise."

This morning, he filled me in on the full-blown crisis at Slea Head with Sean quitting.

And he canceled the damn Wellington Pubs meeting and didn't tell me about it until it was too late.

"You need to be at work. Go taste the IPA. Talk to your dad. Convince him to help out. And call the Wellington people!"

"I hinted at asking him to help me when I called. I'm sure he'll say yes." Patrick invited his father to join him and Cormac for the IPA tasting.

"Thank god."

"And I already emailed the Wellington people on Sunday night. They acknowledged it with *we'll get back to you with the next available date*, so I need to wait it out."

I groan. "I can't believe you did that."

"You're the most important thing right now," Patrick says, and my heart squeezes. "Not work. Are you sure you're okay with me leaving?"

I growl as he slides his phone in his pocket.

"Yeah, and if I weren't trapped here, I might head to the pub to work. Maybe I'll walk to town."

"Don't you dare." He picks up my hand and examines the healing scrapes, then touches the road rash on my forearm, which is looking so much better. "How's your head?"

"Fine. I don't have a headache today."

"Good." He moves his hand from my arm to my cheek, gently swiping a finger along my jaw.

"Think about it. You need the help, and I'm just fine. The doctor didn't say I need to sit on my ass for a week."

"You do have a very nice arse."

"Patrick."

"Absolutely not."

"Who is covering my shifts? We were already short-staffed."

"Saoirse is stepping in."

"Huh? What about her job?"

"She's cutting back on her hotel hours. I'm slowly convincing her to come work for me."

"That's great. It'd be fun to work with her." But my stomach flips, because I won't be here long enough to appreciate it.

"The girls might come over tomorrow night for a few hours, if that's okay."

"Of course, I can't wait to spend time with them."

"For now, just rest, Madison." He runs his finger under my chin. A delightful shiver shoots up my spine.

"Can I make dinner tonight?"

"You up for that?" He leans back and examines my face. "I can pick up take-away on the way home."

"Yes, I'm up for boiling water for pasta."

He laughs and hands me his credit card, telling me to order groceries online for delivery.

I accept the card and step forward, throwing my arms around his neck. I tried my best to seduce him last night, but he insisted I needed to rest.

"I'll be back soon." He peels my arms off his neck and takes a step back. "But I am very seriously reconsidering leaving you."

"Go. The brewery needs you." I gently push him out the door.

I'll make grilled chicken with rotini on the side and a home-made sauce. He has several packages of mushrooms in his fridge, so even though I'm not the biggest fan, he must love them.

After the groceries show up later that afternoon and I start dinner, I shower and put on a short blue dress, one of the things we picked up at my flat yesterday. Just because I now own more appropriate clothing for Ireland doesn't mean I can't dress up sometimes.

He gets home as delicious scents of garlic chicken and simmering sauce fill the house. Patrick drops his bag on the kitchen floor and turns to me, seeming almost surprised to find a woman in his kitchen cooking dinner.

"I missed you." I slide my hands around his waist, pulling him toward me, then run them up his chest. He smiles and encircles my waist with his hands, connecting them at the small of my back.

"I feel good." I remove one hand from his neck for a brief moment and push his hands onto my ass. "That's better."

"You look good." He presses me against him.

"Dinner's in ten, okay? Let's continue this later."

"Feck." He groans.

***

"THIS IS REALLY GOOD, Maddie, thank you for cooking."

I smile at him and bite into the chicken. I learned a few tricks working at restaurants for so long, and one of them is how to make perfectly tender and flavorful chicken.

"No problem."

"Why aren't you eating the pasta? The sauce is delicious."

"Oh, I don't like mushrooms and I'm too lazy to pick them out."

"Then why'd you put them in?" He gives me a confused look.

"Because you like them, I guessed."

Patrick blinks, then reaches over and carefully removes the mushrooms from my plate one by one. "You don't have to always do things to please other people, you know. You hate mushrooms, so don't put them in your sauce."

I freeze with my fork of mushroom-free pasta halfway to my mouth. "Hmm. This sauce might be a metaphor for my life."

"Maybe." One side of his mouth twitches up.

"So your dad approved of the IPA?"

"Yeah. He called it perfect, which is a huge compliment from him."

"Congrats."

"He actually seemed impressed with everything. He's not been to the brewery since he handed everything over to me. I think he misses it."

"Think he'd come back to work?"

"I don't think so. But he agreed to help while I'm down a head brewer. I asked him if he could give me any advice on the Sean situation, and all he said was to give him time."

"Not super helpful."

"Nope. Oh, I have two more quirky stops for you."

"Yeah? What are they?"

"Mam suggested this creepy Viking cave in Kilkenny where a thousand people died. It's haunted, or something."

"Nice, that'll go well with the gateway to hell in Donegal that your sister suggested."

He snorts. "Why is my family like this? Anyway, I found another one online."

"What is it?" He's finally embraced road trip planning and I couldn't love it more.

"In Galway, we can play footgolf."

"Footgolf?"

"Yeah, it's golf with soccer balls."

"No way. That's perfect. Now I'm at nine. Just need one more."

We clean up side by side, and the second the kitchen is done, I pull his hips against mine, my ass against the counter.

"Are you sure you feel good?" Patrick murmurs, his eyes sliding to the swell of my breasts above the scoop neck of the dress.

I move my hands from his neck down his chest and under his t-shirt, sliding my thumb along the hem of his jeans.

"Yes."

"I'll be gentle with you, Maddie." His eyes darken and he tugs up my dress, moving his hands until they're tucked in my under-wear. I breathe out at the pressure already building.

"When do I ever want gentle?" I whisper.

He tugs down my underwear and I step free. I fumble with his jeans and breathe out when I take him in my hand, savoring his hardness.

"Feck, Maddie." He moans into my mouth and buries his fingers between my legs, sliding on the slick center of me before pulling one leg up around his waist, rubbing himself against me.

"Patrick . . ." I lean back against the counter with one hand for stability as he pulls a condom out of his back pocket and slides it on.

"You're so ready for me already, Maddie," he says with his lips against my neck.

"I might have been thinking about this all day."

He pushes himself in with a thrust that wasn't as gentle as he'd promised, then pauses.

I wiggle, trying to get him to move, to ease the ache.

He smiles against my neck and moves me so my back is against a cabinet instead of the counter and I can wrap both legs around his waist, allowing him to take me against the wall, finally moving his length in and out of me. My eyelids flutter as he hits a spot I didn't even know was there.

Reality distorts as the pressure grows, my orgasm building, pulsing, and when it hits, right before he comes himself, Patrick whispers, "What are you doing to me?"

I can't respond. Even if I could, I wouldn't know what to say. I don't think he meant to say it out loud. Maybe he doesn't realize he did. Because the thing is, he's letting me in more each day, and I don't know what to do with that.

I'm terrified of how it will end.

Maybe I should be the one who ends it first. To get it over with.

But I can't. I won't. I could never.

The whole deal here was that I was going to let myself have a fling with Patrick, with whom a future is not possible. So it wasn't going to hurt when it ended, because I wasn't going to let myself fall, because I knew what it was all along.

I'm messing it all up.

I'm falling for him.

24

PATRICK

Thursday, 20 March

Having Maddie here this week has been everything.

Last night, Erin and Niamh came over and hung out for a few hours after school. Saoirse needed my help with the girls while she covered a shift at O'Brien's.

My nieces taught Maddie how to make the scones Mam showed them a few weeks ago, and there was so much giggling and squealing from the kitchen that my heart practically exploded in my chest. Then Mam stopped by to check out the finished product and not-subtly meet Maddie. They all laughed and talked and bonded. It was like she's part of the family.

And that thought terrifies me.

Look at us right now.

She's naked in my giant claw-footed tub, white bubbles all around her. Steam rises from the hot water, and I'm kneeling behind her on the bathroom floor, gently digging my fingers into her scalp to work the shampoo through dark strands of hair. Her feet peek out from the bubbles at the bottom of the tub, showing off the new three-heart tattoo she got on her left ankle after our fight on Friday night. I found it while kissing every centimeter of her body on Tuesday.

I'm washing a woman's hair. And loving it.

I'm also begging the bubbles to shift so I can see more than the peak of her nipples.

"Sit up so I can rinse." My voice cracks as I shift my legs to make room for the raging hard-on beneath my joggers. My shirt's already off so it didn't get soaked. There are so many feelings swirling inside me. Desire, affection, confusion. Love.

Christ, I love her.

"You're spoiling me." She leans forward, and I turn the handheld showerhead on and start rinsing the sides of her hair. "I don't think someone's washed my hair for me since I was a kid. Besides the hairdresser. And that's not the same vibe."

"It's my pleasure, love." I swallow hard and run my hands down her soft strands, letting my knuckles trail along her bare back. When the water's clear, I turn it off and stand.

"All done?" She looks up at me and shifts her body, and now her breasts are fully above the water.

I nod.

"Are you going to join me in here before it gets cold?" Maddie holds her hand out.

"If you insist." I practically leap out of my pants and splash into the water, making her laugh as I roll onto my back and pull her on top of me, kissing her lips, her neck, her collarbone.

It's so easy to be with her in every way.

An hour later, we're on the couch pretending to watch another movie. I'm braiding her damp hair as she sits between my legs. Her eyes are closed, and little happy whimpers keep coming out of her throat.

"I can't believe you know how to French braid."

I pull another section of hair into the thick plait, careful to smooth out the strand and link it securely around my finger so it lies flat.

"I learned so I could get the girls to school or soccer." I pause. "Erin is very picky about her hair, so I watched about one hundred YouTube videos to learn to her satisfaction."

"You're an incredible uncle. And brother. And son."

Normally, that's one of my main goals in life. But this week, I've felt like I'm in some kind of alternate universe. Being with Maddie is all that's mattered.

I've only gone to the brewery for a few hours a day even though there's so much to get done. I can't believe I delayed the Wellington Pubs meeting. It was a stupid decision. I was ready. I could've been gone on Tuesday just for the day. Saoirse or my parents would've happily checked on Maddie.

I could've requested a video call instead.

There were any number of solutions besides canceling the most important meeting of my post-soccer career.

And now Wellington's not responding to my messages asking for new dates. I might've lost the biggest chance I had to change the future of Slea Head Brewery.

But I couldn't bring myself to leave Maddie.

I cross another length of hair and carefully thread a new chunk in. Maddie opens her eyes and watches the movie, where the couple is screwing up their fake relationship by kissing for real in front of their friends at a party.

"You sure you don't have a headache?" I finish the plait and secure it with one of Niamh's stray hair ties.

She shakes her head. "Not for a few days now. You've taken good care of me."

"Come here." I gently tug her up to the couch. She complies and snuggles in next to me. The feel of her is heaven.

"This is nice." She lays her legs across my lap and leans her head on my shoulder.

I've never met anyone like her. Maybe I've just never let myself fall into someone like this before. But somehow, this woman's slipped through to me.

I'm hopelessly in love with her.

"It is." I kiss the top of her head and rub her legs.

"I feel different with you than I have with any other man."

I breathe out. So it's not just me feeling this way. But the thought of her with another man is nauseating.

"I'm lucky that your ex fecked up enough that you are here with me now."

"Blue was nothing." Maddie huffs and shakes her head.

"Have you had a lot of boyfriends before him?"

She blinks up at me. "Kinda."

"Tell me more." I don't know why I ask.

"You really want to know?"

No, I don't, but I nod my head anyway. For a few seconds I don't think she's going to say anything more.

"I have a bad habit of dating people I work with."

I raise my eyebrows and try to ignore the acceleration of my heartbeat. She and I are working together. It's no big deal though. I've been engaged. Surely that's more baggage than—

"There were ten jobs. Ten boyfriends."

"Ten?" My hands freeze on her thighs.

"Including Blue and the volunteer project." Maddie stares at me intently. "A lot of them were no big deal. Everyone makes stupid mistakes in their love life in their twenties, right?"

I nod, doing my best to keep my expression clear.

"What about the other ones? Besides the ones who were no big deal? Were they serious?"

She shrugs and watches my hands, which I start moving again. "Maybe."

I don't push for more. I'm imagining her thinking about ten other men, and it's not a good feeling. I'm imagining that I'm number eleven. I don't like that either.

"I'm sick of my bad decisions with men ruining jobs for me."

"How did they ruin jobs?"

She pulls her long plait over her shoulder, playing with the hair tie at the bottom, staring down at Niamh's pink elastic. "When things inevitably go wrong with the guy, I quit."

A cold feeling settles inside me. Every time something goes wrong with a boyfriend, she flees? That idea is terrifying.

"Do you want to hear about them? It might be good therapy for me."

"I'm not sure I can handle that, love." I'm morbidly curious, but my heart couldn't stand to hear it.

Maddie lets out a short, humorless laugh. "I get it."

She's leaving anyway, but the idea that she might do it even if she didn't have to preemptively hurts me.

Maddie stomped out of O'Brien's the other night. Sure, I told her to go, but she fled. She came back, though. That's something, right?

Loving this woman is dangerous.

"You're sure you want to go back to work tomorrow?"

She nods and looks up at me, her eyes close to my own.

"Of course. I'm completely fine. I'll take it easy, I promise."

I'm too chicken to ask if she's moving back to the flat, but I know she is. This was only while she recovered.

Besides, I didn't invite her to stay.

She doesn't actually live in Ireland.

She doesn't live here, with me, in my cottage, in Dingle.

She's not *with me* at all. Not really.

Maddie might be feeling better, but I'm far from recovered. I'm out of control. I love her. So why doesn't it feel good? I feel like I'm drowning, I can't get a full breath, my heart's always racing, like that panic attack I had at the hospital after she got hurt.

Maddie's breathing softly and her eyes are shut. I pull the fleece blanket over our legs and pause the movie.

Soon, she'll leave me. No matter what spell we're under right now, it'll break, and she'll realize who I really am.

Maybe I'm a good brother, uncle, son, but I'm no one's boyfriend.

It'll end, whether it's because she gets on a plane or leaves me before then.

One way or another, I should prepare myself for it.

25

___

MADDIE

Tuesday, March 25

Boyfriend Disaster #7: Cody the Fuckboy
Job Location & Length: Chipotle, 1 month
My Age: 26

I spent one singular month working at Chipotle. It was miserable. Maybe I hooked up with Cody—the hot twenty-three-year-old cashier who was obviously a total player—on purpose, to intentionally give myself an out. Anyway. Good riddance.

Breakup Reason: all the reasons
My Distress Level: -1 billion
Lesson Learned: Hooking up with the resident fuckboy will definitely not make you feel better, at least not for more than a minute.

My sisters' video call pops up on my screen again. This past weekend I made the mistake of telling them about my bike accident, and they freaked out. They're still freaking out, even though I've been trying to convince them for days I'm okay.

Shit. I can't answer the call. I'm working at O'Brien's in Ireland, not at a resort in Saint Lucia.

I click ignore then tap out a text.

ME

Sorry, I'm working! Once again, I feel great, I promise. No headache, scrapes all healed

REESE

Proof of life, sister, right away, or I book a flight

She sends a screenshot of a round-trip flight to Saint Lucia from Newark. In reality, Stella is much closer, just across the channel in England.

I immediately take a selfie with the same nondescript wall of the bar in the background, like Patrick suggested weeks ago.

ME

This is from yesterday afternoon at the pub with some coworkers. See? I look healthy as a horse

REESE

Should you be drinking with a concussion? And shouldn't you be tanner? Or are you pale because you feel awful?

ME

1) I was being social and I drank tea, 2) I'm offended, I use sunscreen like a good thirty-something, and 3) how many times can I tell you I feel fine??

REESE

> Ha, okay. Take care of yourself. I worry about you! Congrats on your extended internship. I'm assuming it's a good thing that they want you to stay longer. Will you have to make up any classes? When is your flight home?

I groan at her barrage of mini-mom questions.

My original flight back across the Atlantic is supposed to be this Friday. I should get on that plane and go back home for a few weeks before the road trip, then fly back to Ireland with Reese once I've come clean about everything.

That's not what I'm doing.

Instead, I told my sisters that the resort extended my internship for another few weeks.

There's no logical reason for me to stay here. I'm almost done planning the road trip. I've gotten a break from my life and had time to think about my past and what I want for the future.

A fresh start back in Jersey. Avoid the same mistakes I've made previously.

The fact that I'm dating someone I work with right now and letting my feelings rage out of control? Inconsequential. I can do whatever I want in this little interlude. Real life starts back home.

I'm not going to leave yet.

Last night, I changed my return flight to after the road trip. Including the trip, I'll get to spend almost six more weeks with Patrick. My chest warms at the thought of all that time to be with each other.

I'm waiting to tell Patrick that little nugget of information. We haven't talked about my exact departure date, anyway. I'm off tomorrow night, so I might make him dinner and tell him then.

Hopefully he'll be excited.

Hopefully he won't be able to tell I'm falling in love with him.

There's a warm twist in my stomach at the thought of it. But it's not a mere thought. So I'm staying. And working at O'Brien's. I belong here.

For now.

Two men order pints of Guinness—and by now I'm used to patrons calling it *the black stuff*—and I smile at them as I pour. The pub is quiet in the middle of the week. Patrick should try to get some groups to host recurring events here, like book clubs, or girls' night out, or even a hiking or running club. I'll have to suggest it to him.

After I push the perfect pints of Guinness—light tan foam sitting on top of the deep brown liquid—I pick up my phone to answer Reese's texts. I should tell them something more. It's time they at least know that I'm not coming back to New Jersey before the road trip.

ME

So many questions. :)

ME

Can you trust me to manage my life? Please?

REESE

I suppose I could try, lol

ME

I'll likely meet you all in Ireland directly from Saint Lucia

REESE

Really? You must need a new set of clothing??

Oh, sister. I cackle to myself, looking up quickly to see if the two men noticed. They didn't.

Reese might be surprised at how one could make a Caribbean wardrobe work in Ireland with the addition of a few key items of warm clothing. I'm basically a local now.

STELLA

Want to swing by London and travel together? I
checked and there are direct flights to London
from Saint Lucia, but none from Saint Lucia to
Dublin

REESE

I'm so proud of you, Mads. Doing so awesome
in school after all these years!

Great. A reminder how much of a disappointment my past
is. Reese's pride in me stings. Pride in something that I'm not
doing.

And Stella . . . She will be hurt when she finds out I was so
close to her all this time.

ME

That would be awesome, Stella! But let me
finalize my travel plans first. Gotta run!!

Too many exclamation points. Does that make it look like I'm
lying? But they have no reason to suspect, which almost makes it
worse. I slide my phone back under the bar, since this dress doesn't
have pockets.

"Maddie!" A whoosh of cool air sweeps into the bar, Noreen
in the center of it.

"Hey. Glad you stopped in." I have a bunch of unanswered
texts from the estate agent about whether or not I'm renewing my
lease.

"What's the decision? No one is waiting to book the flat, but
your lease is technically up this weekend, and with tourist season
approaching, we'll certainly have some short-term tenants."

She slides onto a barstool.

"I'll stay for another month."

"Oh, lovely."

"I already changed my flight." I practically whisper to her, my
co-conspirator.

Noreen grins, brown curls falling out of her messy bun and against her neck.

"Does this have anything to do with a tall, dark, handsome bartender?"

A blush heats my cheeks. It makes sense everyone in town knows there's something going on between me and Patrick. We haven't tried to hide it.

"Maybe."

"He seems so happy these days."

I bite my lip, suppressing my schoolgirl smile. "We're just hanging out. I haven't even told him I'm staying longer, so don't say anything yet."

"Of course. Whatever it is between you two, it's doing him good. Patrick's had a tough go of it. He hasn't dated anyone for years."

My curiosity is piqued. I know he got back to Dingle five years ago, but when was the last time he was with someone besides a passing tourist? If ever? I told him about my exes—at least that the ten of them exist—but he hadn't offered any information in return. I already know about Cara, and I guess she's the most important one. The only one, maybe.

"You've lived here the whole time?" I shouldn't ask her about Patrick's past. I know that. If I have questions, I should ask him, not someone else.

But didn't she bring it up?

"My whole life." Noreen smiles at me. "I could never leave Dingle."

"You said it's been years, but has Patrick dated *anyone* since he's been back?"

Ah, fuck, I can't help myself.

She blinks at me and her smile fades.

"He . . . didn't tell you?"

"Tell me what?" *Uh-oh.*

Noreen makes a low humming sound. "I don't think I should

be the one." She glances over her shoulder at the door and subtly slides off the barstool.

Now I'm starting to freak out. What's she talking about that's making her so uncomfortable?

"Noreen." I have to know. I can't let her leave without finding out. "Tell me."

So many potential situations fly through my mind. Did he knock someone up? Is he divorced?

"Well . . . " Noreen sighs deeply, surely regretting stopping by the pub. "A year after Patrick got back into town . . . he and I dated."

"What?" That is the last thing I expected her to say. And what the fuck? Patrick dated Noreen? His estate agent? And didn't tell me?

"I'm sorry if that's awkward. I just thought he'd have mentioned it."

"No, he didn't. But it's not awkward, it's totally fine, of course. It's not like he and I are *together* together, you know?" A high-pitched squeak escapes my mouth. "We're just . . . hanging out. So not awkward at all. Not even a little bit."

Of course it is. So much so.

I've been interacting with Noreen this whole time and he didn't think to let me know that she's his ex? It's close enough to a lie that it stings.

A tiny little betrayal.

I search for something else to say, and Noreen studies me with wide eyes.

"We weren't very serious. It only lasted about six months." Noreen rubs her hands together, like she's cold or nervous, and darts another look at the exit.

Six *months*? That's longer than my longest relationship. I nod my head, unsure of what the appropriate response is here.

Silence falls between us. Deeply uncomfortable silence. I search for something to say.

"What's the quirkiest thing you've done in Ireland?" I blurt out. "For the road trip I'm planning."

Her eyes widen even further. A *what the fuck* look.

"Um . . ." She squints. "Are you going to Northern Ireland?"

"Yup." I nod, thrilled we've moved off the topic of her and Patrick.

"There's a spot called the Madman's Window. It's two large limestone boulders along the sea that form a natural rocky window to the ocean. Long ago, a grieving man visited the spot every day to try to spot his love, who had drowned. It's said he went mad."

I blink about a billion times.

"Cool. Thanks."

Noreen gives me a funny look and excuses herself.

What was I just saying about fitting in? That interaction clearly says otherwise. Obviously, I don't know everything about Patrick. Or anything, really. In a normal relationship, there would be time for that. In this one? Not so much.

It's all a reminder that the man I'm sharing a bed with and opening up my heart to is basically a stranger.

26

PATRICK

Cormac and I are at one of the big tables back in the brew room, reviewing the updated brewing schedule on my laptop.

"Looks good, nice work." I study the spreadsheet outlining the next six months.

"Your da helped me check it over."

"I'm glad you're taking the initiative, Cormac. And my dad knows just about everything about brewing, so he's a good person to ask for help."

Cormac's been a model employee since his screwup with the autumn brew. He's got potential but needs the right coaching, someone kind and patient. My dad's the perfect person for that. Sean wasn't—he needs coaching on how to coach. But since it's unlikely he'll ever work here or talk to me again, that's irrelevant.

The door to the front entrance clicks open, and we both turn to look.

No fecking way.

Cara stands in front of us, like something from my bloody nightmares. We need to start locking the damn doors.

"Hello." She stares at me.

I can't get words out. My cheek twitches below my right eye.

Cormac looks at her, then turns to me.

"Can we help you?" he asks.

"This is Liam Smith's sister," I say, once my vocal chords agree to work. "Of New Dingle Brewing."

She flinches subtly, and I enjoy the idea that she's offended I've boiled her down to just a member of the competition's family.

"Are you here to steal our brewing secrets?" Cormac chuckles, then trails off as Cara and I remain silent.

"Give us a minute." I look at Cormac and nod my head to the brewery office.

"Right, of course." He gets up from the metal chair that makes an offensive screeching sound as it pushes against the floor, then scurries into the tiny brewery office and shuts the door. Leaving me alone with my ex-fiancée.

"What are you doing here, Cara?" I at least *sound* calm.

"I need to talk to you." Her voice causes a surge of emotion, which I try to mask. We haven't talked in years. Why now?

I don't answer verbally but flick my hands in the air.

She steps toward the table until she's right next to it and shimmies off her winter coat.

"Damn, it smells awful back here." She slides into the seat across from me. "I hate hanging out in breweries."

I blink at her. Like Saoirse, Cara never had any interest in taking over the family business. She'd rather waitress in Dublin. I wonder if it drives Liam crazy? Or if he tries to get her to come work with him, like I do with my sister?

"Guess you're not going to make small talk, huh." She laughs lightly, then sighs when I don't let my stony face crack. "Alright. I saw you kissing that woman at O'Brien's the other night."

I raise my eyebrows. Maddie's plan worked.

"And it made me realize I needed to make things right with you before . . . my wedding. I'm getting married."

Oh, she can feck right off. Any satisfied feelings disappear. I swallow hard, and her eyes flit to my throat, noticing. A lightning-fast memory reel goes through my mind: me proposing over white Christmas lights, her saying yes, then the excitement fading as time ticked by and we didn't move forward with wedding plans.

"Congratulations."

"That's all you have to say?"

I feel my face twist. "It's been five years since we split. We're not friends. What would you like me to say?"

I hate how bitter I sound. I thought I was over feeling that way about her. When Maddie kissed me in front of Cara, I only cared about Maddie. But now negative emotions assault me from all directions.

She doesn't say anything for a moment.

"How's it going? At Slea Head? I know it was always your dream to take over. Must feel good."

I cross my arms and keep my mouth shut. How dare she show up here and act like she belongs in this place. Like she cares about me. Like she knows me.

"You're not making this easy." She crumples her nose and squints her eyes shut for a beat. "When we were together, I know I messed up. A lot."

"You think so?" Sarcasm drips off every syllable, but she doesn't acknowledge it.

Cara looks around. "Can I get a drink?"

"No."

She looks up at me and nods.

"I'm sorry. For all of it."

"What are you sorry for?" I have a morbid curiosity to know what she's thinking.

"For dragging you to Dublin when I knew you wanted to be in Dingle. For wasting your time when I knew . . ."

I intake air sharply. "Knew what? When?"

"I knew we would never get married. I knew it shortly after we got to Dublin."

"I spent two years there," I say, mostly to myself. "Wasted two years."

"I'm sorry for not being faithful to you," she whispers. "That's not who I am."

Maybe I just proposed that Christmas because I knew, deep down, that I was losing her, that what we had had already slipped through my fingers.

Maybe she said yes only because she was caught in the moment.

I don't forgive her. I can't. I can let it go, but I can't accept her apology.

Cara searches my face for something and sighs deeply.

"There's more you don't know."

"What more could there be?" *Jaysus.*

"I told Liam you cheated on me." She scrunches her face, as if bracing herself for my reaction.

"What?"

All at once, everything becomes clear. How much Liam hated me after Cara and I broke up. How he wouldn't talk to me. I'd assumed it was because of the breakup in general, but never imagined it was because he thought I'd fecked around on his little sister.

With that lie, Cara took away our future together, my friend, and created a business enemy for me.

"Why would you do that?" I was so confused by Liam's rejection. And hurt. I hadn't understood what I did wrong.

"Because I felt like a terrible person, and I couldn't bear for my brother to think that about me, too."

I wish she'd leave this place, but I can't stop myself from asking another question.

"How did you know we wouldn't make it?" I sound pathetic, but I need to know this. I need to know because I'm on the edge of something with Maddie, and I'm terrified. Maybe similar to how Cara's feeling right now.

She studies my face, and I can almost see the thoughts swirling in her head as she decides what to say.

"You were always questioning where I was going, who I was with, what I was doing. You were so rigid. I felt like you pushed me away. You didn't get me at all. We weren't a fit, Patrick. So I found someone who was."

I harden my jaw and keep my teeth clenched together. Her words scorch my heart. I did it. I chased her away.

"I don't think I knew about us for sure until we lived in the same place. But it was obvious right away." She fiddles with the sleeve of her sweater. "Our personalities didn't work together. I'd get so offended by things you'd say . . . I think you meant well. I know I ruined it in the end, but we were broken long before then."

I want to bang on the table and scream. I want to throw my laptop against the wall.

Most of all, I want Cara to go.

"Please leave."

"Patrick . . ."

"I don't owe you my time. Or an apology. And I'm not about to accept yours."

She sighs and stands, clutching her jacket in her hand, and pauses for a beat before spinning around and disappearing through the door.

I wait for feelings to wash over me—sadness, despair, joy, anything. But I feel dead inside.

Maddie's face crystallizes in my mind. Every day I'm with her, I fall more and more in love. But I know I'll ruin it eventually. She likes me now . . . but eventually, I'll just be number eleven to her. She'll walk out on me. She'll give up on us.

Like Cara did. And Noreen.

I'd forgotten for a minute. When I'm with Maddie, anything seems possible.

But Cara reminded me of the truth.

I won't forget it again.

27

MADDIE

Wednesday, March 26

Boyfriend Disaster #8: Paul, the Friend Who Looked Like Clark Kent
Job Location & Length: Carlo's Steakhouse, 3 years
My Age: 30

Working at Carlo's Steakhouse was the longest job I'd ever had. I hit my stride as an assistant manager and knew the promotion to manager was within reach.

Paul started work as a bartender halfway through my time there. Mid-thirties, wide shoulders, chiseled jaw; he legit looked like Clark Kent. We were friends—just friends—and god knows I wanted to keep it that way. He was a good dude. A good friend.

It worked until the last month. We'd shared a bottle of wine after a shift and ended up at my apartment. How could I resist a guy who looked like Superman? He was gone before dawn, and we pretended nothing had happened.

He did, anyway.

But my feelings had changed, and I wanted more. I thought maybe it was possible, but then he started dating the hot blond hostess, acting like nothing at all had happened between us. I couldn't handle it. I told him I was leaving for better career opportunities, and he didn't push me on it. Deep down, I think he knew why. We didn't keep in touch.

I was thirty when I left.

Breakup Reason: We were just friends.
My Distress Level: 8, this one cut deep
Lesson Learned: Two lessons. First, sometimes friendships need to stay as friendships. Second, never trust a guy who is hotter than Superman.

At four o'clock, Patrick walks through the door to O'Brien's and looks at me with an intense gaze. What's going on in his head? He was so quiet last night on the couch in my flat, which is fine as I can babble for hours on my own. When I asked him about it, he shook his head and said *nothing*. He made an excuse to sleep at his cottage without inviting me back.

I tried not to make anything of it, but it's been bothering me ever since.

"Hey," I say when he gets to the bar. I wish he'd kiss me. But there's a lot of people here, including Ronan, so I get why he doesn't.

Not that it's stopped him before.

"Hello."

"Did you have a chance to look through the hotel list I sent last night after you left?"

"Yes. Can you sit for a second?"

For a minute he looks so serious that nerves swarm my stomach like angry bees. I glance at Ronan, who gives me a nod.

I sit first, and Patrick settles in the chair across from me at the usual table. He offers me a strained smile, but my insides don't untwist.

"So. Quirks, Tats, Brews, and Views. You're really going to make us do all that weird shite you found?"

"Yup."

He chuckles, but there's strain on his face.

"I can't wait." I attempt a smile.

"I had a different suggestion for the Dublin hotel. It's closer to Temple Bar area, but just far enough away that it shouldn't be too expensive. Here, I'll text you the link now." He taps on his phone and mine buzzes. "I also sent you a link to a different one for Donegal. It's in a more central area. They both had availability when I checked."

"Whatever you suggest, sure. How about the rest?"

"Agree on Saoirse's hotel for when we're in Dingle. I wish we could all fit comfortably in the cottage, but it'd be tight and then we'd have to drive to get to the city center. We can walk everywhere from the hotel. The Belfast hotel looked good. And everything else was fine."

"Thank you." I smile at him. "See? It wasn't so hard to help me."

"You're welcome." He doesn't smile back.

"I'll be so relieved to finally get it all booked. I'm going to do it after my shift."

He nods and looks around like he's ready to get up. I don't want him to leave the table yet.

"I love Dingle," I say before he can stand. "But I'm excited to get out there and go on an adventure around Ireland, you know?"

"Mmm." Patrick's response is noncommittal, but a surge of excitement jets through me. There's so much more to Ireland. I didn't even see Dublin when I first arrived. I just got on a bus straightaway.

"I can't wait to go to Temple Bar." With my sisters and Oliver and Ethan and Patrick? It's going to be an amazing trip.

Patrick just blinks at me.

"The more I research Northern Ireland, the more it tempts me. It's so wild and incredible up there. Have you been?" I'm babbling, and I know it. But he's looking at me like I'm a stranger.

"Yes. I have." His face goes pale.

"Are you okay?" I scoot my chair, but he's across the table, too far away. Something happened here and I have no idea what.

He shakes his head.

"Did I say something wrong?" I rewind to my babbles about traveling and adventuring around Ireland. Is that what he's freaking out about? Maybe me acknowledging the fact that I'll be leaving Dingle soon? I could tell him I'm staying longer. Now might be the right time. And I should wait for him to answer instead of just filling the air with my nonsense. But I can't help myself.

"I'm most excited to see Ireland with you, though. My personal tour guide. And to have you meet my sisters." I reach over for his hands, but he leaves them in his lap.

"And then you'll go back to New Jersey."

I blink about a hundred times and nod slowly. "I mean, yes, I guess that will happen." My gut twists at the thought of leaving Dingle for good. Of leaving Patrick and this little life.

"And we'll not see each other again." He swallows and I watch his Adam's apple bob in his throat. He clenches his teeth so hard; I can see his jaw working, grinding.

"Well, there's the wedding in June . . ." My head is spinning. "Hey." I wish he'd take my hands, which are still lying palms up on the table, waiting. He doesn't budge. "What's wrong? Is this about me leaving?"

Maybe he's thinking about how much he'll miss me. Miss us. I wish it didn't have to be this way.

Maybe it doesn't?

"It's exactly how it should be." His eyes are cold, exacting.

"Huh?" Adrenaline spikes in my blood. I have flashes of ten boyfriends.

Of Paul, dating the blond hostess.

Todd, the married manager.

Franco, the barista poet.

Desperate Vinny.

Jacob, Brent, Jonathan, Cody.

Number nine, telling me he'd fallen for someone else.

Number ten and his new girlfriend's Instagram feed.

The pain is in ten distinct layers just below the surface.

"You're a tourist, here for an adventure. I gave you that adventure."

"Don't be like that." I shake my head so hard it hurts. "I'm not just here for adventure. I was here . . . I don't know . . . to figure things out."

"And to lie to your family about where you are and who you're with, right?"

I'm dumbfounded. What's happening here?

"Why are you picking a fight with me?" My voice is soft and shaky. Since my bike accident, things with Patrick have been amazing. Perfect.

But now he sounds like he did that night of the inventory problem at O'Brien's.

Patrick runs his hands roughly over his face.

"Madison."

Go home.

Come on.

Leave.

He doesn't want me here. Panic builds at my center. I don't

want to hear whatever he's going to say. I don't want him to continue.

"Why didn't you tell me you dated Noreen?" It's the first thing that pops in my head, but the instant the words are out of my mouth, I regret them.

He furrows his brow, temporarily disarmed. "Where did that come from?"

"I found out and thought it was weird you hadn't told me."

He shakes his head, his face draining of all remaining color.

"We should stop this." Patrick gnaws on his bottom lip, an uncharacteristic nervous movement.

"Stop what?" But I don't want to know. Because I do know.

He lifts a hand and slowly moves it back and forth between us. "Whatever is happening. You're going to leave, and you *should* leave, because you don't belong here. You belong in the US. In New Jersey."

His words are harsh, yet calm. They don't match his demeanor, which is closer to how I feel. Shoulders lifted protectively, back rigid, jaw ticking, his cold eyes the only part of him committed to his speech.

"Saoirse gave her official notice at the hotel. She's going to come work at O'Brien's full-time. As head manager."

I have whiplash from the change in topic.

"Oh, okay, great. But let's get back to . . ."

"And I hired another bartender this week."

Realization dawns on me. He's telling me I'm no longer needed.

"I can still help. I like it. I like . . . working here. Being here. With you."

He pauses, assessing me, his body settling. He's a stranger with a thin line for a mouth and heartless hazel eyes.

"You don't want me to stay? After this week, and last week?"

"It's been . . ." he starts in a low voice, the hand on his knee twitching as if he wants to reach out to me.

"It's been what?"

But he doesn't finish the sentence.

"We don't know each other. Not really."

"We know enough."

He shakes his head. "I'm not interested in a relationship." His voice is low, and he glances around, making sure no one is within earshot. "Not with you. Not with anyone."

I flinch. *Ouch.*

"You want me to go?" I look pointedly at the entrance to the pub. "You don't want to be with me?"

Patrick doesn't respond. Just stares.

I push back my chair. Shame fills me, boiling out from my center and scalding every crevice of my body.

"So I should leave. I'm done at O'Brien's? Done with you?" My voice is too loud, too shaky. I stand, waiting for him to reach out, to say something, *anything.* "If I leave now, I'm not coming back."

Why did I say that? I don't mean it. Won't he stop me? He won't let me walk out of O'Brien's and out of his life. *Will he?*

Patrick moves his head in a slight nod. A humiliating sob escapes my throat, and that spot under his right eye twitches again.

"Well fuck you, Patrick McNulty. Just fuck you."

I spin and walk away, grabbing my purse from behind the bar and ignoring Ronan's wide eyes as I stomp out the door. My heart shatters in a million pieces as I emerge onto Main Street, pivoting to my flat and sprinting up the stairs.

My chest squeezes and my breath is short as I slam the door behind me and rest my back against it.

I can't believe that just happened.

"This is bullshit," I say to the empty, hot flat. Flaming hot. I hate this place.

I gotta get out of Dingle.

I told him if I walked out, I wasn't coming back. I *did* mean it.

I pull my giant suitcase from the second bedroom into the

bigger one and yank open all the drawers, tossing my clothes in haphazardly. I empty the closet, swipe all my toiletries into a plastic bag. Shove my books and odds and ends into my backpack. Open the fridge, pour the creamer down the drain, fill the trash.

When the flat is completely packed up, I crack open my laptop and book a flight to London.

Then I leave Dingle.

28

MADDIE

Thursday, March 27

Boyfriend Disaster #9: Noah the Heartbreaker
Job Location & Length: Terra Toscana, 2 years
My Age: 32

After one year at Terra Toscana, I was finally promoted to manager.

Noah started shortly after my promotion. He was getting his master's degree in global sports management and working on the side to help pay bills. He had the most delicious Australian accent. He'd traveled to thirty countries, was six foot four inches, and looked at me with light green eyes like I was the only person in the room. We became close friends. I had it under control. I was a manager now. I hadn't forgotten the way things went down with Paul. Surely, in my ninth job since dropping out of college, I wouldn't fall for this hot Australian?

I knew it was a mistake the first time we kissed after meeting up at a bar on our night off. He told me he wasn't looking for anything serious. That we were friends. He made sure I understood—I nodded like I agreed.

But my heart was already gone.

A month later, he told me he'd been hanging out with a girl in his program. I was devastated. Noah talked about her while he and I were together, like what we were doing was only making dinner and not also hooking up.

She was tall, well-traveled, and so smart. Successful. The exact opposite of me.

I finally made a good decision and told him we couldn't hook up anymore. I stuck it out for a few more months, determined not to let another man force me to quit a job. But when Aunt Evelyn passed away and I had the bucket list excuse to leave, I took it so fast. It was time to reimagine my life.

Noah still texts me occasionally, checking in. He now lives in Geneva with that same girl.

Breakup Reason: he found a real girlfriend
My Distress Level: 10
Lesson Learned: I can't trust myself to tell the difference between a hookup, a friendship, and a boyfriend.

***

"You know Reese is going to lose her shit over this, right?" Stella says from across the kitchen table in her flat in North London, through a mouthful of green chicken curry from her favorite Thai food place.

"What part of it?" I moan and appreciate the burning of my red curry as it scorches the taste buds on my tongue. "And also, this is the best Thai food I've ever had." I wipe a tear from below my watering eyes.

"Yup. Welcome to London." Stella stands and grabs the half-full bottle of red wine from the counter. "More wine?"

"Yes. Definitely more wine." I'm mostly a beer person, but when I'm around my sisters, the bottles of red come out.

"It's hard to pinpoint which lie she'll be most angry about. There are several to choose from." She pauses, bottle in hand.

"Don't remind me." I hold out my glass and Stella pours both of us a generous refill and settles back in her chair.

"It could be the part where you dropped out of your hospitality program because you were upset over a boy named Blue—a guy she warned you against."

"Ouch."

"Blue, Maddie. His name was Blue."

"His name was actually Brian. He's from Ohio." I can't help the smile on my face as I remember Patrick making fun of my latest ex.

"Exactly." She crinkles her nose.

I laugh at the look on her face. "Sorry we can't all be blissfully happy with a hot English rugby player."

"Whatever." Stella waves her hand around. "Ethan's alright."

I stare at her with my jaw open, and when she finally makes eye contact, we crack up.

"Fine, he's amazing. So?"

I sigh. "And I didn't quit the program because of Blue. Well, the breakup was the push I needed, but it wasn't the wrong decision."

Stella narrows her eyes at me. "Let's put a pin in that for a minute and finish talking about hot ex-pro athletes." She swirls her wine, leaving pretty red rings on the sides of the glass. "The other part that might be a bit troublesome to Reese is how you secretly flew to Ireland instead of Saint Lucia and unabashedly stalked Oliver's best friend."

I groan. "No, that's not how it went down at all, I swear. I went to Dingle because . . ." *Wait. Why did I go there?*

"Because . . ." Stella waits patiently for me to continue.

"I needed an escape. A place where I could regroup without being under Reese's magnifying glass. I couldn't stay at her house while I figured this all out."

"It actually makes sense." My sister scoops a generous mound of curry onto her spoon and shoves it in her mouth.

"But I swear it was a coincidence that I rented the flat above his pub . . . and happened to kiss him that first night. I had no idea it was him. I just wanted to make out with a sexy Irish dude."

"It's a story for the grandkids, that's for sure." She waves her spoon at me.

"There will be no grandkids. It's totally over."

Stella drops her utensil in the mostly empty bowl. "Do you really think so?"

"Yeah, I do." I showed up in London this morning with my giant suitcase and stuffed backpack. I left nothing behind. "It's no big deal. This was definitely just a holiday fling." I choke out those last words, my heart screaming at me for lying to Stella.

My sister stares at me, assessing. "Why don't I invite some of Ethan's rugby buddies to hang out with us this weekend?"

I can't help the wince.

"You don't want to meet hot rugby players."

"It's too soon." Standing, I stack our bowls and head to the kitchen, running water over the dishes. "Patrick is so cute, Stella, you have no idea," I say over my shoulder.

"Uh-huh."

I don't have to look at her to know she's waiting expectantly for more information. I turn and wipe my hands on a dish towel, nodding toward her comfy couch. She follows me over with the wine glasses. I grab the dwindling bottle and we settle down next to each other.

"I'm just not ready to go make out with some other guy, okay?"

After a pause, she says, "Sure."

But the look Stella gives me tells me she has a lot more to say on the topic. I'm thankful she bites her tongue. For now.

"You think Reese'll forgive me?"

"Forgive you?" Stella downs the rest of her wine and refills her own glass, then mine, finishing the bottle. "Girl, you are a thirty-three-year-old woman. You should not be concerned if your older sisters approve of the life choices you are making. Choices that aren't hurting a soul in this world."

"I guess."

"And what about Mom? Are you worried about what she'll think?"

"Nah. She always just wants me to be happy."

"And this is making you happy?"

"More like the hospitality program was making me *un*happy." I sip my wine, appreciating how it's relaxing my body inch by inch.

Being in Ireland was something I didn't know my soul needed. The rain and the cold and the gray clouds were so far from the expectations and perceived judgments I've been so afraid of. But now . . . *not* being there is what I need.

I think.

"Say more on that, Mads."

"I'm not meant for school." I pull my hair over a shoulder with one of my hands. "Or getting a degree. Reese worked her ass off to finish her bachelor's when Chelsea was a baby. And you have a fancy MBA. But that's just not me."

"And that is okay."

"Is it?"

"Yes! Come on, Maddie. You can make your own decisions. Fuck everyone else. Including me and Reese." Stella tucks one of her legs underneath her and turns to me, brow furrowed earnestly, wine still in hand.

"I've supported myself with all my restaurant jobs," I say.

"You have. You've paid your bills, bought a car—which is presumably parked in Reese's driveway?—and created a life. It's not the life that Reese or I have chosen, but look how different she and I are. And no one's criticizing *our* choices. Not really, anyway."

"Hmm," I murmur, mostly in agreement.

"And if they are, fuck 'em."

"Fuck them." I nod.

"That being said . . . you should probably tell Reese at some point." Stella slides her wine glass onto the coffee table.

"You sound like Patrick. He kept pushing me to tell you guys."

"He sounds smart."

"He is. I'll tell her. Soon." I'm not ready for that conversation with my oldest sister. I lean my head back on the couch and close my eyes.

"Those freaking pictures." Stella shakes her head at me. "They were a little off. When you sent the one with the beer can stuck in the sand at a pure-white beach, I kind of wondered if it was a stock photo. There was a spot in the bottom corner that looked like a watermark."

"It was." A hysterical giggle bubbles out of my mouth, and I turn to look at Stella. "I found a bunch of pictures of Saint Lucia online and borrowed them for our text chain. I realized I cropped that one badly as soon as I sent it."

"Maddie. You're a hot mess."

"Right?" I cover my face with one hand. "I should've known the advertising executive would know a stock image."

"And all this time you were a quick flight away. I could've come after your sheep incident." Stella holds out her hand for mine, and I let her examine the faint scar.

"Yeah. It was *baaaa*d."

"You did not just say that."

"I did."

We burst into laughter, and I shake my head.

"It's not really a quick journey. Sure, it's a short flight from Dublin, but Dingle is kind of in the middle of nowhere." Doing it the second time was much easier, actually. Bus to Tralee, another bus to Killarney, a train to Dublin Heuston station, then a shuttle to the Dublin airport.

Stella suppresses a smile. "It does look like it's . . ."

"The edge of the earth?"

A vision appears in my head of standing with Patrick at that breathtaking viewpoint during our Slea Head Drive bike ride, where we could see across the ocean to the Blasket Islands.

That was the edge of the earth.

My stomach twists at the memory, not because it was bad, but because it was amazing. That was when things were growing between us, when I wanted him so badly already. When he let me snuggle into him as the wind ripped around the rocky cliffs. When he pretended to be annoyed by my presence, but really wanted to make sure I was safe.

Turns out, he was right to be worried about me on a bike.

"Why are you smiling, girly?" Stella pokes me with her finger.

"He took such good care of me after my fall, Stella." I sigh softly and take another drink of wine. My glass is almost empty. "He washed and braided my hair." I can still feel his fingers massaging my head so gently.

We're quiet for a minute. I'm lost in the sweet memories of those days.

"Do you love him?"

"What?" I practically gasp hearing it out loud.

"Are you in love with him?" She pins me with her gaze.

"No. No?" I force a laugh, but Stella's staring at me with her eyebrows raised so high, they might fly off her forehead. I know that look. She does not believe me.

"You. Love. Him."

I knew I was falling for him when he took care of me at his cottage. Even farther back when we first slept together. I knew I shouldn't. I fought it. Falling in love is the last thing I went to Ireland to do.

But with Stella's words, I know. I sit up straight.

I'm in love with Patrick McNulty.

And—oh, crap—it's so much more than what I've felt for any other man, including Paul and Noah and Blue.

Oh, for fuck's sake.

"I love him." I groan loudly.

My sister has the absolute nerve to laugh at me. I throw back the rest of my wine, focusing on the liquid warming my throat and my belly.

The laugh falls off her face when she sees my grimace.

I'm not with Patrick anymore. Was I ever really with him? Realizing I'm in love with the person I'm with would be a beautiful thing. Realizing I'm in love with a person who dumped me and fired me in the same breath? Who's now in another country?

Awful. Painful. Pointless.

"Aw, Maddie. What a mess. I'm sorry I laughed."

"It's okay. It's so ridiculous, it's kind of funny."

"Are you going to go back to Dingle and tell him?"

"No. There would be no point in that."

"Are you sure—"

"Yes, I'm sure," I say, cutting her off. Never in a million years will I tell him.

"But you'll have to face him in a few weeks."

"I know." That's a problem for future me.

"What do you want to do until then? You are welcome to sleep on our couch."

"Are you sure?"

"One hundred percent sure. You can hang out here, explore London, and totally get lost in your own thoughts." She smirks at me.

I snort. "That's exactly what I'll do."

"I'll try to bring you back to reality each night."

"Did I do what I always do somehow? Mess this thing up with him? Hook up with someone at a job I like and then have to leave?" I push my empty glass next to hers on the coffee table and squint my eyes shut.

Stella makes a noncommittal sound.

"I didn't think I was doing that this time. I knew it was going to end—the job and the man. I thought I had it under control. I didn't."

I open my eyes and stare at Stella's stark white ceiling. Patrick doesn't know I left Dingle, but Saoirse texted me to say hi last night. I haven't responded. As soon as I tell her I'm in London, Patrick will find out.

Something tells me he won't get in touch. He was dead serious about ending things with me.

But it feels like there's a magnet pulling me back to Ireland. That cold, gray country managed to worm its way into my heart. I miss it. I miss coffee at Dingle Brew, chatting with Saoirse, opening the pub.

Kissing Patrick. Laughing with him.

The thought of not spending any more time there is heartbreaking. At least I'll see it once more during the road trip.

Stella tilts her head at me. "Another bottle of wine? I'm going to take off tomorrow so I can show you around."

Tomorrow. My original return flight date. I shake the thought out of my head.

"Then, yes, sister, we should obviously open another bottle of wine."

I'm staying in London.

29

PATRICK

Thursday, 10 April
(two weeks later)

S aoirse and Ian sit on barstools, waiting expectantly for me to fill their glasses with the new IPA from one of the half dozen growlers in the fridges.

"Come on, what are you waiting for, Pat?"

"Right. Here we go."

I pour a few fingers of the IPA into three pint glasses—one for me—and toss it back with them.

"Oh, mate, that's so good." Ian nods his head in approval.

"You've finally done it." Saoirse smiles widely. "The right balance of bitter and citrus."

"Exactly." I nod. "Besides this batch, we've got a few more fermenting so we can start distributing over the coming months."

"Fill them up, Patrick, then we'll get out of your way." Ian gestures to their empty glasses.

On Saturday, we'll do a limited bottle release at O'Brien's. We're also going to celebrate this week's successful meeting with Wellington Pubs. They got back to me with a last-minute opening in their calendar, so I drove to their headquarters in Dublin and pitched Slea Head Brewery. Lola came along and helped seal the deal by bonding with their distribution lead about both of them growing up on cattle farms in County Cork.

Wellington agreed to carry our lineup in a ten-door test this fall, including the IPA and the autumn brew, which we've still not got quite right.

If the test goes well, they'll consider full distribution.

It would change everything for Slea Head Brewery.

Dad's still helping out at the brewery and Saoirse starts this week as full-time head manager at O'Brien's.

Everything is finally coming together.

Once I'm done pouring, Ian takes the full glasses and retreats to an open table.

Saoirse sticks around.

"You missed dinner with Mam and Dad last weekend."

"I know. I was exhausted and needed some down time." I lean my palms on the counter and pray for customers to interrupt us.

My sister assesses me with narrowed eyes. I silently beg her not to ask me about Maddie. Not to push things more than she already has since Maddie left town.

"Have you talked to—"

"Saoirse." I cut her off. I don't need to hear Maddie's name out loud. "No. I haven't."

After she left Dingle, I found out from my sister that Maddie had changed her flight to stay in Ireland until after the road trip.

Except I scared her away. Ruined it.

I've written texts and never sent them. I've almost called but couldn't tap the button. I opened that original email chain and considered replying.

But there's nothing I can say that would make things better. I know I'd just make it worse. Best leave it as it is.

"You'll see her in a week. Why don't you call and talk things out ahead of time?"

The idea of seeing her for the first time in Dublin nauseates me. Then again, having Oliver, Reese, Stella, and Ethan around will be a buffer.

We won't have to be alone.

We won't have to talk.

We won't even have to look at each other.

"There's nothing to talk about. I'll be friendly. I promise."

Saoirse's face crumples with clear pity. I hate that she feels so bad for me. That she can sense the pain I'm in. That she probably knows I'm avoiding my family because it's too painful to be around people who can feel my unhappiness as only those who truly love me can.

Everything might be coming together, but I've never felt worse.

30

MADDIE

Friday, April 11

My phone vibrates in my pocket as I walk along the Thames, past the super-touristy bit near Parliament and the London Eye, the art museum and Shakespeare's Globe Theatre, almost to London Bridge. I'm getting my daily long walk in while I wait for Stella and Ethan to get off work and hang out with me.

I've been doing everything in my power to not think about Patrick, but I have too much damn time on my hands. There are only so many walks to take, museums to visit, coffees to drink, landmarks to view.

It's Reese calling.

I stop abruptly and someone brushes past me, grumbling.

My eyes widen and I start to panic a bit, which is my normal reaction to Reese these days. I've managed to avoid the video calls she keeps requesting. Stella's been pushing me really hard to come clean to our sister. I get why.

Because now Stella's in on the lie.

There's only one week until the road trip. Maybe I can hold off telling Reese everything until then.

The phone stills, then immediately rings again. I step out of the walkway to the edge of the path overlooking the river.

My heartbeat accelerates. Is something wrong? Why'd she call me twice in a row? She never calls without ensuring I'm available first.

Now my phone buzzes with a text.

REESE

Maddie—why are you in London? Did I miss a message chain about you heading there from Saint Lucia?

REESE

Stella? Is Maddie with you? I just tried calling you both and no one answered

Oh no. How the hell did she figure this out? Maybe Patrick told Oliver and he told her? But I can't believe Patrick would do that, at least not intentionally.

A separate text from Stella pops up.

STELLA

Mads, now's the time to deal with this. I'm going to be in trouble too, but you need to come clean. I'm in a meeting. Talk to Reese

More texts from my oldest sister roll in.

REESE

I don't understand what's going on. I'm kind of freaking out

REESE

I happened to click on your contact and realized location tracking was still on. When I checked, it showed you in England

"Oh. My. God." I press the screen of my phone to my chest.

That's what got me caught? I'd shared my location indefinitely with Reese when I moved in with her and Oliver. As a single woman, it's a good idea to let someone know where you are at all times.

I guess I never turned it off. Oops.

I cross the walkway and find a bench beneath a tree. It's cool and cloudy but at least it's dry today. I've confirmed in my two weeks here that it's just as wet in London as it is in Dingle. I take a few deep breaths and remind myself that I can make my own decisions about my life, and I don't need approval from my older sister.

"Maddie!" She answers the phone before I even hear it ring.

"Hi, Reese."

"I'm so glad to hear your voice. You're in England? What's going on?" Reese has panic in her voice, and a pang of guilt stabs my heart.

"I don't know where to start."

"How about with where you are?"

"London."

"Oh." She pauses. "Did you finish your internship early?"

"Not exactly."

"Maddie?" Reese lets out a noisy breath. "Can you fill me in? Please?"

"I'm going to give you the sixty second—maybe slightly longer—summary. Just let me get through it, okay?"

"Go ahead."

I fill my lungs with air. Here we go.

"Blue dumped me. He was cheating on me with some new girl in Saint Lucia."

Reese growls into the phone. "What a jerk. I'm so sorry, Mads."

"You were right about him. About it being just a holiday fling."

"Oh, honey, I didn't want to be right. I shouldn't have pushed so hard."

"I went to cancel the flight but couldn't get my money back, so I paid extra and changed it to Dublin. I needed to plan the road trip anyway and was looking for inspiration. I thought I'd go to Dingle. Meet Patrick. He was supposed to be helping me plan, and I needed to get away."

"Wait—you were in Ireland? With Patrick? As in Oliver's Patrick?"

I murmur an agreement and watch a twenty-something man and woman walk by. They're holding hands and moving as one, occasionally glancing at each other fondly. It makes me yearn. For Patrick, I guess. That connection we had.

"Oh my god. What about school?"

"I thought you were going to let me get through this?"

"Fine, fine, go ahead."

"I left the program."

Reese gasps. "No, Maddie, really?"

"It wasn't for me. I was much happier working in restaurants. Well, mostly."

For a few seconds, ten jobs and ten men flash through my mind. Eleven. Now it's eleven. I shake my head to get the thoughts out.

Reese is quiet, so I continue.

"I met up with Patrick . . ."

Here we go. This part might be harder than the rest to share. How I seem to be repeating my mistakes over and over again.

Even though it was different with Patrick.

". . . and ended up working at his pub for a while. I loved it. And Patrick was amazing." My voice has a dreamy, wispy sound to it.

Reese doesn't say anything for at least thirty seconds. Absorbing, I guess.

"Madison Elizabeth Hart," she finally says.

"What?" I sit up straight on the bench. She's got her mini-mom voice on.

"You hooked up with Patrick, didn't you? And then it went wrong, like it always does at your jobs."

I flinch, but that's a solid summary.

"Yeah." I wish I could argue with her. Convince her it was different this time. I know it was. I think it was. But what evidence do I have of that?

From the outside, it looks exactly the same.

Like I've learned nothing.

Reese sighs. The bone deep, exhausted sigh of a mother, or at least a sister who acts like a mother. "I wish you'd have been honest with me."

"I'm sorry. I really am. I shouldn't have lied. But I was so afraid of what you'd think."

She's quiet.

"What about school, Maddie?" Her voice is softer, kinder. "Was that another impulsive decision?"

Ouch.

"At the time, yes, but it was the right one. Because what I've learned over the past month is that I love working in pubs. Restaurants. Whatever. And school isn't for me."

I feel more confident talking about this part. This is something I did figure out while in Dingle. What I want to be doing with my career.

"Hmm."

"Also . . . it was more than just a hookup with Patrick." I might not have evidence, but as my sister, maybe she'll understand.

She breathes in loudly through the phone. "Yeah?"

"Yeah." I nod my head even though she can't see me, and she pauses a beat before responding.

"So what happened? Are you still with him?"

"No. It ended. He pushed me away. It was too much, too fast. *I'm* too much. As always."

"Maddie. You are never too much."

"Always a bridesmaid."

"I mean, technically, you are a bridesmaid this time," Reese says.

I let out a giggle, and she joins me for a beat. Then tears spring to my eyes.

I give her some details, including the story about the first night we kissed. She laughs and groans at the right spots. Then lets out an appropriate *aww* when I tell her about how he took care of me after the bike accident, his cottage, his pet sheep, his nieces.

As we talk, relief slowly seeps through my body, releasing the tension and stress from not only today, but the past few weeks. Months.

Why have I been so afraid to tell her what's going on?

"You know I'll support you through whatever, Maddie. I'm sorry you didn't think you could talk to me."

"I don't want to disappoint you."

"Oh, little sister. I just want you to be happy. To find your way, your place in the world. That's no easy thing."

I can't help but think how happy and settled she and Stella both are. Careers, significant others, where they live. They're so confident in their choices.

"I can't believe you found me through location tracking." I sigh. "I didn't even think to turn it off."

"What about all those freaking pictures? Sunsets, sand, surf?"

"Screenshots from the internet. Oh, except for the pub. That is actually O'Brien's. I was afraid you'd show it to Oliver and he'd recognize the background."

"You are such an asshole."

We both burst into laughter.

"Wait. how long have you been in London with Stella?" She gasps, as if she's figuring it all out. "She's been lying to me, too?"

Oh, shit.

31

PATRICK

Saturday, 19 April

I'm hyperaware of my proximity to Maddie.

It's Saturday night in Dublin at Temple Bar and I'm waiting at the bar with Oliver and Ethan, Stella's boyfriend and a giant ex-rugby player, for two glasses of red wine and four pints of Guinness. I glance over my shoulder at Maddie and her two sisters, smiling and laughing at a table together.

I can't stop sneaking looks. It's been three weeks since I've seen her. Three weeks without that smile, the easy laugh, her sweet words.

Maddie looks so happy and relaxed with her sisters. Not that she doesn't always look happy—except when I'm firing her, or breaking up with her, or being an overall fecking eejit.

We've not spoke directly since I arrived, just a few awkward glances. My plan was to avoid her completely, but I'm not sure how that's possible.

I won't survive this road trip.

"I'll get these back to Reese and Stella." Ethan takes the two glasses of red wine from the bartender.

"Shame they dinna have Slea Head here," Oliver says, his Scottish accent a comforting sound to my ears.

I nod. "Maybe one day." The bartender expertly fills Guinness pint glasses with deep brown liquid, creamy foam swirled on top. "If it works out in the test pubs, maybe I'll get to Dublin. That's the dream."

"Congratulations, Patrick. I'm proud of you."

"Congratulate me when we can have a pint of Slea Head Irish Oktoberfest in Temple Bar."

"Aye."

Oliver looks from me to the table of Hart sisters, where I can't stop myself from stealing glances.

"So you and Maddie, huh?"

"Reese told you."

"Of course she did. Was it serious?" Oliver studies me. He knows me. He knows how I don't date, don't do relationships. Not after Cara and Noreen.

I shrug. "It doesn't matter. It's over now, and after this road trip and your wedding, we'll never see each other again."

"Well, that's a clean break then, aye?" Oliver continues to watch me.

"Yes it is."

"But maybe have a quick chat with her? So you don't keep looking at each other like that."

"Like what?"

"Like that." Oliver rolls his eyes and nods back to the women.

At that moment, Maddie looks over. Her expression is filled with sadness and something else I can't identify, and she attempts to wipe it clear as soon as our eyes meet.

Oliver chuckles. "Come on, mate."

I shake my head and look down at my pint, swirling the dark liquid gently. My mobile vibrates with a text from my sister, and Oliver returns to the table with two of the pints.

SAOIRSE

How are things in Dublin?

ME

Fine

SAOIRSE

How's Maddie?

ME

Why don't you ask Maddie as I'm sure you're texting her too

SAOIRSE

Talk to her. Like for real talk to her

But why, when I can just pretend nothing's wrong?

Noreen stopped by the pub on Thursday afternoon. She apologized for telling Maddie about our history. I shrugged it off, but then she kept talking. *I shouldn't have been so hard on you back then,* she said. *I remember saying really awful things, even though I didn't mean to. You are full of life and heart, Patrick. I hope you know that.*

It's remarkable that in the past few weeks, both Cara and Noreen have given me their sides of our relationships. Cara's confessions made me spiral, a precursor to the final fight I had with Maddie.

All because Maddie used the word *adventure.*

But wasn't that what *she* was to *me*? When I got to know her in Dingle? Kissed her? Loved her, even if she didn't know?

Maddie was my adventure.

I wasted it. I lost her.

I groan and shut my eyes. I cannot bear to feel this way for the next twelve days.

ME

I'd rather just come home

My mobile rings in my hand. The bartender is staring at me expectantly, so I pass her my credit card.

"Yeah?" I answer the call.

"You are not coming home. Don't be a baby."

"Saoirse . . ."

"You helped Maddie plan this road trip, and you have the chance to not only hang out with your best friend, but also make things right with Maddie. Even if you don't end up together—"

"We're not going to end up together." Frustration laces my voice. It's impossible. Everyone knows that.

"Okay. Sure. But stop being awkward. Leave things on a good note. Be Irish and have some craic, if you can possibly manage to let yourself. Then, when you see her at the wedding this summer, it won't be so painful."

I look across the bar and watch Maddie throw her head back and laugh at something Stella says, then return her gaze back to her sister with interest and affection.

To have her look at me like that. Laugh at something I say. I laughed more with her in that month she was in Dingle than I have in years. I had her in my life. Then I chased her away. On purpose.

"Pat? Are you there?"

"Yeah, I'm here." I sign an iPad with my finger and accept my credit card from the bartender.

"Pull it together. Everything is fine here. I'll stop by the brewery tomorrow, like I promised. Take some time to sort out what's inside your soul. Talk to Maddie. Figure out how you really feel. Tell her. Please, for all our sakes. You're driving me crazy."

I nod, but she can't see me. My sister clicks off.

I already know how I really feel. I'm in love with Maddie.

But there's no way I'll tell Saoirse or anyone else that.

Especially not Maddie.

I make eye contact with Oliver, and he makes a drinking motion. I head back to the table with the last two pints. As I settle into my seat, Oliver kicks off a story about a weekend when he and I came up to Dublin while he was in Ireland.

"We drank the whole of Temple Bar, I think, right, Patrick?" Oliver says.

I nod. "It was not pretty."

"We stumbled back to our hotel room and passed out till noon the next day, then got back in the car to return to Dingle."

"That was a fecking rough drive."

"Aye."

Ethan laughs and tells us about playing rugby outside of Dublin back when he was pro. Rugby's big here, although Gaelic football—a mashup of rugby and soccer—is popular as well and mainly played in Ireland.

My mind wanders and I pull my mobile back out to text Cormac, who is covering the brewery with my dad and Saoirse on standby. There's a speck of hope that Sean will come back. The old man stopped by O'Brien's yesterday and casually asked how things were going at Slea Head. I answered, but he cut the conversation short. I fully intend to stop by his cottage once I'm back in Dingle.

My dad was right. It was best to be patient and wait for him to come to me.

The bar gets more crowded. Stella moves to chat close to Ethan, and Oliver drags me to the bar for shots while Reese and Maddie lean in to whisper and laugh together.

"To Winchester Football Club?" Oliver says.

"To Winchester." I toss back the clear liquid and suppress a gag. "Feck, did you buy us vodka?"

Oliver laughs. "Aye. You looked like you were falling asleep, so I needed to wake you up."

"It worked." I cringe at the aftertaste. I push the empty shot glass toward the bartender.

"You alright? You seem lost in your head."

"Nah, I'm fine," I lie and shrug.

Reese saves me by yelling for her fiancé. I'm not sure I can take another person trying to convince me to talk to Maddie. I follow him back to the table, relieved to avoid the conversation with Oliver.

My best friend swoops down and plants his lips on Reese's mouth, who immediately responds by reaching up and burying her hand in his thick blond curls.

"Aw, that's disgustingly cute," Maddie laughs, then looks up at me and stills, as if she'd forgotten I was here. There's only one chair left at the table, and it's next to Maddie.

I slowly lower myself into the seat as Oliver whispers something in Reese's ear and she smiles.

Fine. I'll talk to Maddie and get Oliver and Saoirse off my back.

"Hey," I say to Maddie softly, turning my head to look her in the eyes. Maybe if I appear to smooth things over, Oliver will back off. Because that man could get the truth out of me. I'm surprised he hasn't done so already.

"Hi." She's wearing a short dress, the black one she'd wear to work sometimes with a swooping neckline and no sleeves, showing off smooth shoulders. Her dark hair is curtained over her bare arms, and I have the almost irresistible urge to push it back.

Being this close to her is torture. My fingers ache to touch her.

"Since we're here," I start, unsure how to continue.

"Since we're here . . ." A shadow of a smile crosses her face, and she drinks from her dark pint.

"I don't want this to be awkward." Feck, I sound like an arse. "This road trip. Or the wedding."

"Me neither."

I nod. "I thought we could be, I don't know, friendly."

"I don't mean not to be friendly, Patrick." Her brow furrows and she stares intently into my eyes, those deep brown ones threatening to swallow me whole. Hearing my name on her lips, something stirs inside me.

"I know." I shift in my chair and turn my body toward her.

"You're the friendliest person I've ever known. Like sunshine personified."

Maddie laughs and her eyes light up, then the smile fades. She puts her pint down and slides it away from her, showing off the pink scar on the back of her hand.

I reach out and touch it gently with my finger, lingering on the ridges.

"Does it hurt?"

"Nah." Our knees are touching, our thighs making a V in between us.

"Maybe you should get a tattoo to cover it up."

"I already have one, and I might get another on this trip with my sisters. Are you suggesting a third?"

A corner of my mouth twitches.

"I forgot about your ankle tattoo." Like hell I forgot about it. My mind immediately goes back to the bathtub event at my cottage, where her ankles were peeking out of the bubbly water, along with other parts of her body.

She turns her chair fully toward me and swings her leg up and onto my knee in a graceful movement, displaying the three tiny hearts grouped on her ankle. "I did that the night of our first fight."

Yeah, I remember.

I lay my hand on her ankle and rub my thumb on the ink. The physical contact is shocking. It's everything. Warmth flows from where our bodies are connected. *Jaysus, the feel of her skin.* The memories of our touches flood me, and I swallow roughly and look up at her, ripping my eyes from her ankle.

"I need to apologize about that." I keep my hand on her leg and slowly move it up and down the bottom half of her calf. The movement is too much, and yet completely natural. She shivers beneath my hand. "It was all my fault, that inventory shite."

"No, it was mine, too," she says firmly.

"And Beth's."

"Huh?"

"She stopped by O'Brien's a few weeks ago. Apologized for leaving so abruptly and said she'd been thinking about the inventory since she left but was too embarrassed to come by and explain."

"Wow."

"And she told me she went to New Dingle for hours that would work better with her kid." Maddie's leg is still lying across my knees, and I stare down at my still hand.

"She should've talked to you. I bet you would've worked with her."

I nod. Of course, Maddie sees the best in me, even now.

"Maddie." I look at her, and she's already staring at me. "I found a Post-it note about the inventory buried under other paperwork on my desk. It must have stuck to something else when you put it in the inbox."

"Oh. Good, I guess."

The silence stretches, and I look away. I want to tell her more. Everything. I've missed her.

"Cara stopped by Slea Head two weeks ago."

"What?" Maddie touches my hand with hers.

"She's getting married and wanted to make peace with me."

"And did she?"

"No. I didn't let her." But why was I so harsh with her? It's been five years. I should've given her what she needed. Forgiven her. Let it all go. "She told Liam that I cheated on her. At the end. In Dublin."

Maddie gasps softly. "No, really?"

"Which explains so much." I move my hand, running my thumb over her sharp ankle bone. Her eyes dart down. She blinks, color rushing into her cheeks, then pulls her leg off me and sits up straight.

"Sorry. You okay? What are you thinking?" Probably that I crossed a line touching her like that. That she doesn't need to be my sounding board anymore. I don't have the right to any of that.

She moves her head back and forth and looks away, reaching for her pint.

I've lost the privilege of asking what's going on in her gorgeous head.

I should've told her I loved her when I had the chance. Instead, I was an arsehole. Saoirse's words echo in my head—*tell her how you feel*—but I won't do that. It'd just screw with her more. It might break her. I've already broken us, how could I break her, too?

I could've spent the last few weeks being with Maddie. Instead, I self-destructed. Regret hits me like a bus.

I'm in love with her.

But it's too late.

32

MADDIE

Monday, April 21

Boyfriend Disaster #10: Blue the Holiday Fling
Job Location & Length: Saint Lucia, 1 month
My Age: 33

I met Blue on the beach. I think why I clung so hard to the
idea of him is because of how he made me feel that first
night on the island. With the background soundtrack of
crashing waves, salty sea air, and soft white sand under our
toes, Blue looked into my eyes and really listened to me
talk.
But we were just acting out parts in a holiday fling.
Now I see it for what it was. It should've ended when I left.
But at the time, I really thought it was more.
My mistake.

Breakup Reason: delusion (mine)
My Distress Level: 10, not because I loved him so much,

but because of how clearly the ending highlighted my relationship failures

Lesson Learned: I need to make some serious changes in
my life.

We spent two nights in Dublin, stopping at the Guinness Brewery and walking around the city center for touristy stuff like visiting the Book of Kells in the stately old Trinity College Library. We also visited the Hungry Tree, Patrick's suggestion of that tree in Dublin that is slowly consuming a bench. My sisters giggled for hours when I handed out the printed itinerary titled Quirks, Tats, Brews, and Views with the ten quirky stops sprinkled throughout the trip.

I managed to avoid being one-on-one with Patrick again for the rest of the Dublin stay. That first night at the pub was too much. Him touching my leg, us talking about Cara and New Dingle and clearing the air about the inventory drama. There's no point. He doesn't want to be with me. We have no future. It hurt too much.

Then we picked up the rental car. Since there are six of us, we needed two vehicles: Patrick's plus a rental.

I nearly ended up in his car alone with him.

Reese and Oliver were in the rental already, and when Ethan turned toward Patrick, my traitorous sister grabbed his hand and tried to pull him to Oliver's. I was faster. I darted over to the rental car and gave her a victorious look.

But then I realized Patrick saw the whole thing, and the look on his face showed he understood what I just did.

I'm such an asshole.

This morning, after an afternoon and gentle evening in Belfast, which included visiting the giant fish statue—thanks, Ian—we're going through some of the sights in Northern Ireland. Noreen's suggestion for visiting the Madman's Window, those window-shaped rocks looking out to the sea, was eerie and cool.

Now we're at the Dark Hedges, a remote avenue of two-hundred-year-old beech trees that are interconnected at the top and were filmed in a popular fantasy series.

Thick fog sits on the road, making visibility low and giving the tall trees a horror-film type feel. My sisters and I are standing together, watching the spot in the fog where the men disappeared a moment ago.

"This is so creepy," Stella says.

"So creepy," Reese agrees.

We stand in silence for a moment and then Reese grabs my hand.

"You okay, Mads?" She squeezes.

"What do you mean?" I turn to her.

"There is so much tension between you and Patrick."

"Is there? I hadn't noticed."

Both of my sisters turn to stare at me, and we all burst into laughter. The giggles taper down, and they watch me expectantly.

I sigh deeply.

"I love him. I can't be normal around him. Not even close."

Reese's jaw drops. "Mads. I didn't know. I mean, I knew what you told me . . . but not that you love him." She drops my hand and drapes her arm around my shoulder, which is at the same exact height as hers, and pulls me closer.

"Yeah. I was hoping if I didn't say it out loud again, it would no longer be true."

"Did that work?" Reese leans her head against mine.

"Nope."

"Sorry, Maddie." Stella wraps her arms around me and Reese.

"Thank you so much for planning this whole trip," Reese whispers into my ear. "Even the weird shit you added on."

I bite back a smile and lean back to search Reese's face. We all drop our arms but stay close.

"I'm just glad you're not still mad at me."

Stella groans. "Maddie, what did we talk about?"

"Something about how I shouldn't live to impress my older sisters? That I'm an adult who can make my own life choices?"

"You got it!" Stella sings.

Reese wraps me into a second full body hug, and I melt in her arms.

"I'm so sorry if I made you feel that way. Like what you're doing is not good enough." She pulls back and glances at Stella.

"It's okay." My throat tightens.

"And I'm glad you talked to Stella. Thank goodness she was so close. I worry about you."

I'm so relieved everything is out in the open with them now, but it was all part of the process. I figured out a few things about myself in the three weeks since Patrick and I broke up.

Maybe it was the endless days wandering around London in and out of pubs, restaurants, and cafés, where I had to hold myself back from asking if they were hiring or making suggestions on ways to improve their businesses.

I'm a hard worker. I'm good at food retail. And I have even more to offer my next job.

"Have you talked to Patrick since our first night?" Reese asks.

I groan and shift from one foot to the other. "Can we not talk about that?"

"No," my sisters say in unison.

"Ugh." I groan. "Reese, I hate that I might be making things awkward on your big trip."

"This is *our* trip, not just mine. And while I wouldn't be super excited if you guys hated each other, we'll find a way to make it work. We'll keep you separated at the wedding somehow."

"We don't hate each other." I'd kinda hoped we could turn things into a friendship during this trip, but there's too much baggage between us.

"And after the wedding, you never have to see each other again," Reese says.

"Which makes you feel how, Maddie?" Stella tilts her head.

Fucking awful.

"Things are over with me and Patrick. He doesn't want me in his life, for one reason or another." I hate how my voice catches at the end. The regret that's simmering inside my chest overflows and burns my heart.

"Stella," Ethan calls from through the fog. A few feet from him, Oliver emerges and holds his hand out for Reese.

"I'll make sure the mist doesn't consume the car," I call as my sisters walk into the thick ground cloud to join their partners.

It's then that Patrick steps into visibility, hands in his pockets, watching me from ten feet away.

A lump forms in my throat. I love what I've figured out about myself in London. But I wish I could've done it earlier. In Saint Lucia. At one of the nine jobs I had before that.

But mostly while I was with Patrick in Dingle.

For that short period of time, he made me feel so good. He looked at me like I was a magical creature, not scared away by his grumbling or stony looks. He didn't judge my decisions. He invited me into his home, took care of me, picked the mushrooms off my plate, and washed my damn hair.

And when he pushed me away, I let him. I ran.

Now it's too late. We wasted the little time we had together. It's truly over.

Warmth fills my chest as I remember the feel of his arms around me, the way his hazel eyes would bore into my very soul. He was really into me.

I've been in love with him for a long time.

But I've ruined it.

He's ruined it.

I will him to wave me over, hold out a hand, smile . . . anything.

But he just turns and disappears into the fog.

33

PATRICK

Wednesday, 23 April

I follow Oliver onto the swaying Carrick-a-Rede rope bridge, which connects the small island to the mainland. Threatening clouds stretch across the sky, and I'm shocked we're not soaked already.

I don't normally have a fear of heights, but we're thirty meters above the rocky shoreline and the bridge is swaying back and forth in the strong wind. But it's not exactly a solitary experience, as there's people ahead of us following the path to the tiny fisherman's cottage on the island, and there's a line behind us to cross the bridge once we're over. Reese and Maddie are next, and Ethan and Stella are behind them.

There's a small child with their granny ahead of us, laughing.

Still, terrifying.

I'm relieved to get across onto solid ground, and Oliver waves me to walk slowly on with him instead of waiting for the women.

"So . . ." Oliver says the word like a sentence.

"So what?" I focus on the rocks beneath my feet.

"Tell me what's happening with Maddie. For real. Because I've had a chance to observe you over the past five days, and I have opinions."

We walk side by side up the meandering path. I roll my neck and stare out into the Atlantic Ocean, where on a clear day you can see Scottish islands in the distance. Today is not that day.

"What do you mean?" I say, to buy myself time. How many details does he know? How much did Maddie tell her sisters?

"You said you and Maddie had a thing, but I was under the assumption it was actually over."

"It is."

Oliver looks over at me and cocks his head. "I get it, I really do."

"Get what?" The wind whips around us and I'm dreading the inevitable trek back across the rope bridge.

"The absolute fucking denial you're in."

"Oh, feck off. I'm not in denial." But my insides twist and my protest is weak.

"Remember when I called you after Reese had left Scotland to go back to America?"

"Yeah, I do."

"How you called my bullshit and told me I'm obviously in love with her?"

"Mmm. I'm not sure it went down quite like that."

"Aye, it did."

Should I just tell him? Say it out loud, even though I swore to myself I wouldn't?

It might feel good to get it off my chest. Maybe if I speak the words, then I can somehow move on, even though I'd rather hide behind the thick stony walls surrounding my heart.

But hiding's getting really fecking old.

Two summers ago when we talked, it was so obvious to me what was happening with him and Reese. I knew it from the texts he wrote me and the way he talked about her. He was in love but hadn't accepted it yet.

This is different. I know I'm in love with Maddie.

I feel it in every bit of my being. In the sharp wind that whips around my ears, the ocean spray flying up from the jagged shoreline, the angry gray clouds. They're all reminding me, pushing me, furious at me for screwing everything up.

"I'm not in denial. I'm in love with her."

Oliver screeches to a halt.

"Shite, I didna ken you were in that deep."

I stop next to him.

"But, you just—"

He laughs. "I was testing you. I'm not nearly as perceptive as you are." Oliver glances behind us and I have a terrible feeling Maddie's right there.

"Is she behind me?" I practically whisper.

"No, sheep for brains. Come on."

"No need to bring my sheep into this." I continue to follow Oliver, and soon we're at the edge of the viewing area, the ocean crashing against the jagged rocks below us, a view of the bridge behind us.

"What are you going to do about it?" Oliver asks.

"Nothing." But I don't feel as certain about that as I did a few minutes ago.

"Wrong answer. She's right here. She's not gone back to America yet. Dinna wait until it's too late to tell her how you feel."

The bottom falls out of my stomach. Tell her? How can I tell her how I feel?

"I can't."

"Why not?"

"I don't know." The rain starts spitting down, and I pull up the hood of my sweatshirt.

"Well, think about it. Figure it out. Talk to her before it's too late."

"You sound like my sister," I grumble.

Stella and Ethan are halfway across the bridge, and the other women are almost at the island, Maddie ahead of Reese, laughing with her hair blowing around her, crazy in the wind. At least she's wearing leggings today instead of a dress.

That woman is wild and gorgeous.

I wish she were mine.

"Feck."

"She's still right in front of you. Don't lose your chance."

I close my eyes for a second and picture it. Telling her how I really feel. Opening up the part of my heart that's been closed off for a long time.

I want to feel vulnerable with her again. I was there . . . and then I self-destructed. Chased her away.

I'm ready now.

"Alright."

"Alright?" Oliver looks at me with wide eyes.

"Yeah. I'll do it. I'll tell her."

It's selfish. It's too late. She'll reject me.

But I'm going to tell her how I feel anyway.

34

MADDIE

Donegal Town is a delightful town in County Donegal, Ireland, and we're all enjoying pints at McKinney's, a lively bar in the city center. The pub has low ceilings, cozy brick walls, a wooden bar, and mismatched, quirky tables. Most of all, it's warm and dry and not swaying a hundred feet above rough ocean waters.

Nor is it a super creepy hole in the ground that's rumored to be a gateway to hell. We found out we couldn't actually go to the island it's on and visit the monastery built above the hole, so we skipped Saoirse's suggestion for a stop in Donegal.

The lively band of fiddlers is loud and we can barely talk above them. I sip my pint of Guinness and enjoy the lilting music. If I close my eyes, I could be back at O'Brien's on that first Friday night, the one where I asked Patrick to kiss me in the dark hallway.

The band breaks and much softer music sounds out of the speakers. Patrick and Oliver return with another round of pints and glasses of red wine, and as soon as they're settled, Reese clears her throat.

"Hey, so Oliver and I have something to tell you guys."

The rest of us perk up.

"You can't be pregnant," Stella says. "Because I've seen you drink about a dozen glasses of wine on this trip."

I laugh at Stella's joke, but note Reese barely chuckles before biting her lip.

"What, Reese?" I glance quickly at Oliver, then back to my oldest sister.

"This summer, after the wedding, we're going to move to Scotland to be near Oliver's son."

Stella and I both gasp and everyone is quiet for a beat.

"You'll be so close." Stella breaks the silence and reaches over to grab Reese's hand. "A train ride away."

My insides twist and an array of emotions bleed from my heart. Good for them, just being a train ride away. *But where does that leave me?* I hate how selfish I feel. I should be supportive. Happy for her.

"Lucas is twelve, and I want to be closer to my son. I've been gone for near two years," Oliver explains.

Patrick is nodding. How dare he be understanding to his friend while my life feels upended once again?

"And Chelsea's off to college in the fall, so she's not going to be living at home." Reese takes Oliver's hand and squeezes.

I press my lips together and attempt to swallow, but there's a giant fucking rock in my throat. Everything is changing, and I'm still just me. Maybe I feel like I figured things out, but what if I've learned nothing?

"I'm keeping my house as a home base." Reese turns to me. "And I was hoping you'd live there, Maddie, when you go back to Jersey."

"Oh," I say, my stomach dropping at the idea of living in Reese's house all by myself. "Okay."

"We'll come back a lot," Reese continues, the words pouring out of her, her eyes on me. "To see Mom. And during Chelsea's school breaks. You'll have her as a roommate then. We'll also try to get her to Scotland as much as possible."

"My old coach from when I was a kid runs a professional women's football club. He's been bugging me to get Chelsea to come try out."

That sounds just perfect for Chelsea. For Reese. And Oliver.

Oliver goes on to tell us about his charming hometown of Stirling, a small city northwest of Edinburgh where Lucas lives with his mother, but I tune them out. I've heard him talk about this a hundred times.

For all her talk of me not telling her about breaking up with Blue, going to Ireland, and dropping out of the hospitality program, Reese hadn't told me or Stella about this huge decision.

Everyone has their own lives, their own plans for the future. Everyone except me. As good as I was feeling earlier, all I have to show for my time here are a few flimsy revelations.

I should've been living my life on my terms all along. Not caring what anyone else thinks. Not leaving good jobs because of men.

I make the mistake of looking across the table, and my eyes meet Patrick's. We stare at each other, as if connected by an unbreakable but hopeless connection, terrifying and impossible, like the swaying bridge earlier today.

The band starts up again and the music is too loud, the pub too crowded, and I need a minute.

I love him. I want him. But I can't have him.

I stand and head to the restroom, but a hand on my shoulder stops me.

"Mads. The offer to live at the house is real." It's Reese, and she wraps her fingers around my biceps and looks right in my eyes.

"You didn't tell us. Over the last few days, all the time we spent together, all the things we talked about, but you kept this a secret." It's a statement of fact.

And I'm kind of mad.

"I'm sorry—"

Stella appears next to her, hands on her hips, shaking her head. "Really, Reese? You couldn't have given us a heads up?"

Yes. I'm thankful Stella agrees.

"After all your speeches about me being honest with you," I say. "And you hid this?"

Reese drops her arms and sighs deeply, fluttering her eyes shut.

"I kept chickening out. I feel like I'm abandoning our family. Leaving Mom behind, and Chelsea, even though she'll be at college. And you, Maddie. What are we going to do about you?"

A tornado of feelings whips up inside me. It's jarring to see my confident, settled sister so uncertain.

"I'll figure it out." I shrug, doing my best to project nonchalance.

"But—"

"I'm happy for you, Reese." I cut her off. "For you and Oliver and Chelsea."

It's my life, and I gotta figure it out on my own. Without the help of my sisters.

She opens her arms and we all hug in a tight circle, heads down, sniffling. When we finally pull away, they're both smiling, but I don't feel like it. Nothing changes for Stella except having a sister on the same continent. And Reese is making all the exciting changes. The right ones for her family. She's got her daughter and Oliver and Lucas to guide her decisions.

I've got no one.

"I need a minute." I force a smile and duck into the bathroom, leaving my sisters in the hallway.

I lean against the cold, tiled wall and close my eyes.

Why does everyone else get to rewrite the rules of love and life, but I feel all this pressure to conform? Reese and Oliver were an impossible situation. More so even than me and Patrick. They both had children to think about, one on each side of the Atlantic Ocean. Yet here they are, planning their wedding and a huge move, so fucking happy and in love. They're making it work.

Why is this thing between me and Patrick so impossible, then?

I want him more than I did when I was staying at his cottage, when he rubbed suds of soap into my skin, snuggled with me on his couch, introduced me to Turtle and Kitty, kissed me like I was the only woman on the planet.

I don't want to run away. I don't want to get on a plane and only see him once more at the wedding.

I wish I were more like Patrick. He's got such deep-set roots in Dingle. His parents, Saoirse and Niamh and Erin, his cozy cottage, O'Brien's, and Slea Head. His sheep.

He belongs to Dingle. He's not mine to have.

But maybe I owe it to myself to talk to him about everything, before the road trip and wedding are over and we never see each other again.

35

PATRICK

Thursday, 24 April

My heart pounds as I stand on the edge of the Cliffs of Moher, staring out into the endless sea all the way to the Aran Islands off the western coast of Ireland, the dramatic cliffs in front of me dropping off into the Atlantic Ocean. While the Cliffs of Moher attract many tourists with its admission fees, paved pathways, stone safety fencing, and huge visitor center, it is truly breathtaking.

Oliver and Reese are wrapped around each other a few meters away, and Ethan and Stella are taking a selfie with the background of the sun beginning to set. Maddie's somewhere on the other side of them, the two of us sad slices of bread to a sandwich of happiness.

This is possibly the most romantic spot on earth. A marked contrast to footgolf, our activity in Galway earlier today. And this time, my heart's not pounding because of a competitive game of golf with soccer balls, but because of what I'm about to do.

This is the place where I will tell Maddie I'm in love with her.

It's the perfect location, wild and beautiful, just like she is. I told Oliver my plan, and he's going to make sure I get her alone.

Is confessing my love for her now the best idea, since there's no escaping each other for another three days?

No, probably not.

But I can't wait any longer. I can't risk time slipping away and not getting to tell Maddie how I feel. I can't make the same mistake Oliver did and assume it'll work out, like it did for him.

My best friend steps next to me, gripping Reese's hand. Stella and Ethan disappear into the visitor's center.

"We'll meet you inside," he says quietly. Oliver reaches out and briefly touches my forearm. "Good luck."

Then they're gone, and I'm alone with Maddie.

She's gazing out at the fiery sunset, the colors orange and yellow and red. There are a few other small groups around, but the crowds are thinning, since it's almost dark. We still have an hour drive to our hotel in Limerick, so I better do this so we can all move on with our lives.

I swallow and stride toward her, my feet feeling light as air. I don't have many expectations for how she will react to this conversation. But she needs to understand how she makes me feel.

"Madison."

Maddie turns to me and offers a surprised smile, her hair streaming out toward the sea with the chilly evening wind, her dress pressing against the back of her legs, also seeking the water with billowing fabric.

"Are we back to that again?" She crosses her arms on her chest, only a thin sweater on her shoulders.

"Maddie."

"Better." She looks around, seeming to just now notice that we're alone. "They all go inside?"

"Yes." I keep my eyes trained on her. "You must be freezing."

Maddie tilts her head. "I think we've established I'm not great at dressing for Irish weather."

"You got here in the literal winter and mostly brought short dresses." I slip off my lined windbreaker, stepping closer to wrap it around her shoulders.

"Hey, I bought some appropriate clothing eventually." She shrugs her arms in the sleeves without argument. "Thank you."

Now's the moment, and a wave of terror hits me in the chest, making it hard to breathe. What were the words I was going to say? I forget every single one.

Except I love you.

"Should we find the others so we can get on the road?"

"No." I shake my head firmly. "I want to talk to you first."

Maddie blinks at me. After a beat, she says, "Okay."

"I have something to say." I run my hand along my chin, letting the stubble prickle my palm. "When you got to town, I thought you were just another tourist."

"I kinda was."

"You were never just another tourist, Maddie." I don't know what to do with my hands, so I clasp them together. "And when I found out who you really were, it scared the shite out of me."

She opens her mouth but doesn't speak, so I keep talking.

"I've been avoiding women for years. Since Cara and I broke up and I moved back to Dingle. Since I tried dating Noreen and it was clear I would destroy every relationship I was in."

"No, Patrick, it wasn't—"

"Wait. Please. Let me get through this."

She nods.

"I swore there would be no more." I separate my hands and clench my fists at my sides. "No more serious relationships. It was safer that way."

"You deserve more than that." Maddie steps forward and grabs my balled hands, entwining her fingers with mine.

The warmth of her hands. The electricity running between our bodies. I missed this. I missed her.

Miss her.

"But you. You were dangerous." My voice is raspy. I clear my throat. "Deep down I knew it right away. I fought it. When you kissed me that night at the pub—"

"Which time?" Her mouth quirks.

I squeeze her hands. "Both times, really, but definitely the second time. When Cara was there. That was the beginning of me truly healing. And when Cara came to talk to me at the brewery? That was the closure I needed. It took me a while to realize it. And by then, you were already gone."

"I shouldn't have run like that." Her forehead creases, and she bites her bottom lip before continuing. "I proved that I'm too impulsive, that I don't give things a chance to work out. I should've stayed and talked to you."

"Luckily, you're here now. You've made me realize that I could miss out on someone like you by continuing to hold on to the hurt from my past."

"When did you realize that?"

"Just now, actually."

She laughs.

"Maddie." I drop one of her hands and touch her cheek with the back of my finger, caressing her soft skin, letting my touch slide down along her hair, the orange light of the sunset reflecting on the dark strands. "You make me feel like I'm worth . . . something."

I almost said loving. But I can't imagine she loves me.

"You've changed everything in me since you showed up and pulled me against the wall in that dark hallway."

She laughs, a light, airy sound, and her eyes are wide and bright.

"Maddie, you're perfect as you are."

She shakes her head. "Definitely not perfect."

"To me, you are." I push her hair back from where it flies in front of her face. "For me. You brought the light back into my life. You made me understand that I can't only live for my parents, my sister, my nieces, the business. I need joy for myself."

There's a bursting inside of me as I understand all the truths I'm voicing.

"I feel like I just mess things up for you, Patrick. Things have gone better since I left. You got that deal with Wellington, right? And released the IPA? I heard you talking to Oliver and Ethan about it. I'm happy for you." The spot between her eyebrows crinkles and I want to wipe the worry from her face. From her life.

"Never better without you." I catch her hair again and she huffs out a laugh, smiling. I love seeing her like this. Wild and free and happy.

"Really?"

I let her hair go and cup her jaw with my hand. It's so personal, so intimate, but she leans into my palm and sighs.

"I could've used not having to speed to the hospital after you almost took down a flock of sheep, that's true."

"Sorry about that." She barely suppresses a smile.

"I know you came here for a break from your life. So you could heal from your breakup with the arsehole from Ohio before starting over back home."

"Yeah. All true." Her face is now serious, following my words carefully.

"And dropping out of the program made you feel like you were letting your family down. But I bet they weren't mad when you told them."

"No. They weren't."

"You bring joy and light wherever you go. Whoever you are around will be so very lucky."

"Whoever, huh." Her shoulders sag and she closes her eyes.

"Maddie, I don't want this to be goodbye." My voice catches in my throat. I must be clear.

"You don't?" Her eyes fly open.

"I love you. I'm in love with you. I think I was from that first kiss, and definitely by the second one."

She breathes in deeply, the pain falling off her face.

"You love me?"

"Yes, Madison Elizabeth Hart. And it's okay that you don't love me back. I'm not telling you for any kind of reciprocation—"

Maddie leaps at me with her full body and throws her arms around my neck, her legs wrapped tightly around my waist, stealing the air from my lungs. She buries her face in my neck and her hot breath warms my entire body.

"Jaysus, Maddie," I say once I can breathe. But I'm laughing through the words. She feels so right in my arms.

Maddie leans back to look at me, her brown eyes sparking with flames from the setting sun.

"I love you too, Patrick McNulty. I figured it out for sure in London, but I think it happened before I fell off that damn bike. The week I spent at your cottage was the best of my life. It was everything. I fell even more in love with you and your family and your sheep, even though I'll forever be a tiny bit terrified of them."

My heart explodes with love. Our lips are mere centimeters apart. I cup my hands on her arse to keep her firmly against me.

"When we were together, you made me feel like the only woman in the world. Like I was the most important thing, no matter how giggly and cheerful and annoying I was. You made me feel like I was doing a great job at O'Brien's."

"Why else do you love me?" I know I'm being greedy, but I'm intoxicated by her words and don't want them to stop.

"Well, you look pretty hot in a soccer uniform. That's basically it. Thick thighs and killer abs. That's all I need to fall in love."

"You're quite shallow." But I smile and squeeze her arse until she squeals. "But I'm happy to wear my soccer kit for you whenever you want."

She grins and it reaches her eyes, but I need to know what she thinks *whenever* means. I can't bear the thought of her going back to New Jersey.

"Patrick, you're my adventure."

I don't even flinch at the word.

"And you're mine," I say back.

Her intense gaze flits from my eyes to my lips.

She moves one of her hands onto the back of my head, burying it in my hair. "You deserve so much love. Your nieces, your parents, your sister . . . I love you, and I love Dingle, and your life there."

Is it possible? Can this work? Fragile hope springs from my center.

"I want you to come back to Dingle with me, Maddie. Will you? I will beg, if needed."

What will I do if she says no? I'd have to follow her wherever she goes. I'll follow her to the ends of the earth, if she lets me, family and business in Dingle or not.

"Yes. I'll come back to Dingle with you. I can't imagine going anywhere else."

"What about your family?" The words come out as a whisper. That fragile hope strengthens.

"Reese is moving to Scotland, remember? Stella lives in London. I'll go back to see my mom. And honestly? You're thinking too far ahead. Just kiss me."

And I do, our lips joining gently at first, then pressing harder together. I can't believe I get this. Forever? It better be forever.

"You can move in with me at the cottage," I say against her mouth, pulling away slightly. "There's plenty of room . . ."

"I think we should take it slow." She looks at me thoughtfully. "Think your flat is available?"

"Aye. I'll make it available for you if you want it. We can take it slow."

"As slow as moving to another country for a man is, anyway."

"But for the record, I don't want to take it slow."

She kisses me again and I feel her smile against my lips.

"One question." She pauses and kisses me again, sweetly, gently. "Do you think I can have a job?"

"Of course. O'Brien's would love to have you back."

"I was actually thinking about Slea Head, although I'm happy to help at the pub. I have more ideas. Marketing, events, promotions . . ."

"Like your Dingle passport idea? Or book club nights at the pub?"

"Yup. Those. And more."

"I could use a marketing person to work with Lola. We can start there."

"That's perfect."

"You're hired. Now I have one more question." I adjust her body, still wrapped around mine. I never want to set her down.

"What's that?" Maddie glances down at my lips then up into my eyes.

"Can we share a room tonight?"

She laughs and kisses me again.

36

MADDIE

Saturday, April 26

Boyfriend ~~Disaster~~ #11: Patrick
Job Location & Length: Slea Head Brewery, presently
employed
My Age: 33

I met Patrick at an Irish pub in Dingle, Ireland. I asked
him to kiss me to help me get over my ex, and he complied.
The next day I figured out that he is my sister's fiancé's best
friend.
We made a mess of things for a while, but it all worked out
when he told me he loved me on the Cliffs of Moher.
He's my eleventh relationship at my eleventh job since
dropping out of college.
And he's going to be the last one.

Breakup Reason: n/a
My Distress Level: no distress, just love

Lesson Learned: Follow your heart, no matter how scary it is.

The group got to Dingle yesterday, and I've never been so happy to show my sisters around. I know this remarkable place as well as if it's my home.

Which it is.

Patrick rushed off to important brewery business, and the rest of us stopped at Ian's tattoo parlor. Ian and Oliver caught up, Ethan showed off his sleeve tattoos, and Reese, Stella, and I picked out matching shamrock designs—drawn by Oliver when he lived in Dingle—and made an appointment to get inked.

I wake up with Patrick wrapped around me in the hotel room. I sit and wiggle to the edge of the bed so I can get ready to meet my sisters downstairs for our appointment.

"Get your cute arse back over here, Maddie."

Patrick sits up and hooks me around the waist, collapsing back on the bed and pressing his front—his very naked front—against my backside. Also naked.

"That's better." He cements me in place with his arm.

"Patrick. I am meeting my sisters in thirty minutes. I need to shower and not look like I just had sex."

He presses his hand against my stomach and slowly moves his fingers lower and lower, caressing the sensitive skin just above where I want him to be.

I let out a low moan and relax back against him, arching my back and lifting my hand to his head to bury my fingers in his hair.

"Okay," I say breathlessly. "Gotta make it quick."

Patrick growls and flips me around. "I can do that."

I laugh as he buries his head in my neck.

TWO HOURS LATER, my sisters and I are at the park with steaming coffees from Dingle Brew in our hands, watching the boys casually kick a ball around. We all got small tattoos on the inside of our wrists. Is it cheesy to get a shamrock tattoo while in Ireland? Perhaps. But we don't care.

It's Reese's second ink. The shamrock is on the opposite wrist from her compass tattoo, which she got last summer to represent how she found her true north with Oliver after her divorce.

Stella has a butterfly on one of her wrists. It stands for both her independence as well as her transformation from someone who'd been closed off since our father died when we were kids, to a woman happy and in love, while also keeping who she is close.

For me? It's also my second, along with the three hearts on my left ankle.

I run my thumb along the sensitive inside of my wrist, slightly irritated from the needles, not taking my eyes off my boyfriend as he dribbles the ball down the field.

"He's so good at that," I say wistfully.

"He is." Reese watches Oliver.

"I wouldn't want to be going up against Ethan, though." Stella sips her hot coffee. Ethan approaches Oliver, his bulky frame making both soccer players—each well over six feet tall—look slight.

"He'll be okay," Reese says. Oliver darts around Ethan and dribbles away from the rugby player's colorful expletives.

After the Cliffs of Moher, we spent the night in Limerick. The next morning, we visited a magically pretty waterfall, which was Patrick's suggestion. Today we'll drive the Ring of Kerry and spot the beehive huts along Slea Head Drive. We all agreed to skip the Blarney Stone—Patrick was thrilled—and Maria's suggestion of the Butter Museum in Cork so we could spend another day in Dingle. Then we'll head back to Dublin with stops at the creepy Viking massacre cave in Kilkenny and Glendalough, an old monastery set in the Wicklow Mountains National Park.

After that, everyone heads to the airport for their flights.

Except me, of course.

"Will we be passing the scene of the sheep crime on today's drive?" Stella tears her eyes away from Ethan and looks over at me.

"Haha." I attempt sarcasm. "But . . . yes. Yes we will."

Stella giggles. "I can't believe you crashed into a flock of sheep."

"*Almost* crashed into a flock of sheep. I didn't crash into them. I saved them by swerving off the road into an inconveniently located boulder."

"Maddie." Reese shakes her head.

"What?"

"I hope in the future you'll be more careful. I don't want to spend my life worrying about you on a bike in Ireland."

"Listen, you don't have to worry—wait, hmm, maybe you *should* worry, but only about me biking." I look over at Patrick and smile.

Stella laughs and Reese sighs.

Patrick catches my eye and winks, turning to trot in my direction, letting Ethan and Oliver battle it out for the ball.

"Hi." He leans over and kisses me on the lips. Butterflies take flight in my belly.

"Awwww," Reese and Stella say in unison.

"Hey." I smile, and heat rises in my cheeks.

"Oliver and Ethan are going back to the hotel, but I thought maybe you and I could go on a quick errand before we leave for the Ring of Kerry."

"Yeah, sure." I furrow my brow. "What errand?"

"You'll see."

"See you in a few," I say to my sisters. Patrick holds out his hand and I take it, letting him entwine our fingers together.

He leads me all the way back past my flat and stops in front of his car, parked a few doors down.

"Where are we going?" I slip into the passenger seat when Patrick holds open the door for me.

"I need to show you something at the cottage." He slams the door shut and strides around the car to the driver's side.

"Ohhhhkay. A good something?"

"A good three somethings." He clicks his seatbelt in place and turns to me. "At least I hope it's good."

"So mysterious. Can I have a clue?"

"No. Be patient."

"Not sure if you've noticed, but I'm not the most patient person."

Patrick snorts and reaches over to put his hand on my thigh. He pulls into traffic with a grin on his face.

A few minutes later, I follow Patrick into his cottage. *This will be my home one day.* I can't wait.

"I have three gifts for you." He stops in the kitchen and nods to his table, where a brand-new bike helmet sits.

I chuckle. "Ha. Thank you. Think it fits?"

"Aye. There's no way I'm letting you on a bike again without a properly fitted helmet. Not that I could stop you."

"Exactly." I pick up the helmet and pull it onto my head. It's snug and comfortable. "Perfect. Thank you."

He nods. "Wait right here for gift number two." Patrick disappears down the hallway and turns into the last bedroom—not his bedroom, not the girls' room, but the woodworking room.

"Did you make me a bookcase?" I call. "Because that would mean I need to buy a bunch of books. I could do that."

He emerges holding something smaller, about the length of his forearm. I can't tell what it is.

"First of all, you can take the helmet off now." He shakes his head and sighs, but an adoring smile takes over his face.

"Oh yeah." I pull the helmet off my head and deposit it back on the table. "What do you have there?"

"Well, you'd commented on the one in the flat. I thought we could add this to the wall while you're living there."

I take the piece from him. It's a wooden carving of the state of New Jersey, just like the one of Ireland.

"This is amazing. I love it." I reach out and touch his arm. "When did you make it?"

"After you left for London. I couldn't stop thinking about you. I'm not sure what I was planning to do with it . . . but it makes sense now. It was a gift for you all along."

I throw an arm around his neck and lean into him, clutching the wooden decor against my chest with the other hand.

"Thank you. It's so thoughtful." There's a lump in my throat and a sting in the back of my eyes. I don't want to let go of him.

"One more." Patrick leans back until I release my grip on his neck, then takes the carving from my hand and puts it on the table next to the helmet. His face is flushed, and he gives me a gentle kiss before nodding his head to the sliding door. "Come on. It's out back."

"What would be in the backyard?" But I follow him outside. Kitty trots over right away, nuzzling against Patrick's pockets. He pulls out a treat and the sheep takes it from his palm.

"It's behind the barn, probably."

"Behind the barn?" I laugh. "Probably?"

"Maybe hanging out with Turtle."

"Patrick, what did you do?" But then I find out.

Out from behind the barn trots the tiniest little hooved creature I have ever seen.

"There she is."

I gasp. "Is that a baby goat?"

"Yes, sure is. And it's called a kid."

The kid comes right over to me, and I lean down and reach out to her. She sniffs at my hand and looks up at me accusingly after realizing I have nothing to offer.

Just then, she bleats loudly, startling me. I let out a giggle. The kid turns around and leaps away, bounding in the air before jumping and practically clicking her heels together.

"I love her so much!" I turn to Patrick, laughing.

"Good. She's yours. I mean, she's my responsibility. I'll take care of her. But I thought Turtle and Kitty would like to have a new friend, and I recall you saying how much you love baby goats."

"I'm not sure the conversation went quite like that, but I don't care. She is adorable." I grab Patrick by the waist and look up at him. He leans down and kisses me gently. "What's her name?"

"You get to name her."

"I don't know about that. I think Erin and Niamh will be mad if I don't let them do it."

"Fair enough." He chuckles and pulls me against him tighter. "I picked her up yesterday. My neighbor said she couldn't keep all the kids her mama goat has had. So here we are. I have two sheep and a goat in my backyard."

I crack up and kiss him again.

———

BACK IN THE Dingle city center, a light mist falls. I tug the hood of my windbreaker over my head and step closer to Patrick, loving the feel of his arm against mine as we stride down the road.

On the way back from the cottage, Patrick told me all about convincing Sean to come back to Slea Head. Yesterday, he brought the old brewer the new autumn brew—which is apparently delicious—and asked Sean to come back as head brewer. Patrick and Lola will manage all the new product development, taking the parts Sean hates off his plate completely.

"And he really said he thought it would taste like a pumpkin vomited in a bowl of nutmeg?"

"Sean's got a way with words, doesn't he?"

I laugh. "I guess so."

"He hasn't said yes yet, but I know he will. It'll all work out."

"Where is this optimism coming from? Where's the Patrick who was panicking about everything falling apart when I first got here?"

He halts and spins me toward him.

"I don't panic. I'm very level-headed and rational."

I straighten out my smile. "Of course."

"But . . . it's because of you, Maddie." He slides his hands on either side of my face and tilts my head up to him. "You've inspired me to change my life. It might look similar from the outside, but who I am inside has fundamentally shifted since I met you."

"You're not going to say something like *you complete me*, are you?"

He presses his lips to mine and pulls back.

"That's exactly what I was going to say. I haven't felt this complete ever in my life."

Tears sting my eyes, but I blink them away.

"There's one problem still."

Patrick's eyes widen slightly. "What?"

"We have a visa situation. As in, I don't have one."

"Oh, I have a plan for that, too, Maddie, but you might not be ready to hear it yet."

Now my eyes widen. Is he suggesting . . .

"I pay you under the table, for now."

I breathe out. It wouldn't have been such a bad thing if he'd been referring to marriage. I'd marry this guy tomorrow if it meant I got to stay here, with him.

"And then we get married."

I gasp. "We get married?"

"I'm not proposing to you just yet, Madison Hart, but I think that's the only logical solution to this problem in the long term."

"Clearly there's no other possible way."

"Exactly."

He leans in to kiss me. "Now let's go on a drive."

37

***

PATRICK

Sunday, 27 April

I head from our table to the bar, weaving in and out of groups of people. Today was a perfect day, and this is the perfect ending.

The six of us went on an early cycle to Slea Head this morning since yesterday's scenic drive was full of rain and fog. Maddie used her bike, which I'd kept in my barn with mine, along with the brand-new, well-fitting helmet. I borrowed the rest of the bikes from neighbors and Saoirse so we wouldn't have to rent wonky ones from that shop down the road from the pub. After lunch, I took the group to the brewery for a short tour and tasting, and now we're at O'Brien's.

It's finally tourist season, so the pub is busy. I lift a hand to Saoirse, who holds up one finger before starting another round of drinks for my group. I wait patiently, lost in my thoughts.

I'm basking in the memory of my conversation with Maddie yesterday after giving her the three gifts. Gifts which were so easy to figure out. I could easily come up with a hundred more.

We have a plan to get married. The fact that she'll even consider spending her life with me? It's everything.

Suddenly, I'm aware of someone standing next to me.

"Patrick."

It's fecking Liam. I have to remember not to hate him on sight the way I've gotten so used to for the past five years. I have to remember that Cara lied to him. That he thinks he's been a good, protective big brother.

"Hello," I say.

"Hello." Liam stares at me and I fight the urge to roll my eyes or make a dismissing motion with my hand.

"I'm not actually working, but Declan or Saoirse can sort you right out."

"Two pints for you, Pat," my sister says, sliding the glasses to me right on cue. She glances between me and Liam with raised eyebrows.

"Thank you." I nod to her as she heads back for the rest of the drinks.

"I'm not here to order drinks. I'm here to talk to you." Liam swigs from his bottle of New Dingle Amber Ale, draining it.

"Oh, Christ, why?"

Liam sighs and runs his free hand through his floppy brown hair.

"I'm going to do this once, so listen up. I owe you an apology."

I let out a surprised huff, and Liam narrows his eyes at me before breathing in deeply.

"Sorry. Go on."

"My sister recently told me that she lied to me about how things ended between you two."

Saoirse places two glasses of red wine next to the pints. I bet she wants to stand here and listen to our conversation, but she has two more to grab for me. I lift a pint to my lips and drink deeply, letting the creamy foam of Slea Head Devil's Dark sit on my tongue before swallowing. I look away from Liam.

"I also recently found that out."

"I thought—" He stops, and I give him a few seconds to continue, but he looks frozen, like a streaming movie stuck on the same scene.

"What did you think?" I need to hear the words from him. To know that the end of our friendship wasn't my fault. Not only my fault, anyway.

"I need a drink for this." Liam gestures to Declan and accepts a fresh bottle from the bartender. "She told me you cheated on her. That you'd been cheating on her the whole time you were in England, and she caught you in Dublin."

"Which is all false."

"Yes. I know that now." He swallows. "It didn't sound like you."

We lock eyes for a few beats. I remember how close we used to be. It feels like a lifetime ago.

"You could have asked for my side of the story."

He nods and shrugs at the same time. I have a feeling it's too late to start over.

"I'm sorry for being such a dick to you over the past five years. I guess you didn't completely deserve it."

Saoirse slides the last two pints over. Time to get away from this conversation.

"Thank you, I guess. So are we going to be best friends, or something?" I'm not sure what Liam's still standing around for.

He studies me. "Nah, I don't think so."

"Well. That's a relief."

After a second, he chuckles, and I do the same.

Out of the corner of my eye, I see Stella and Reese walk back to our table, and I glance over. Reese kisses Oliver on the lips and sits in the chair next to him, and Stella settles on Ethan's lap. Maddie's watching me from across the room.

"Have a good night, Liam." I carry a pint and two glasses of red wine to the table, and by the time I go back for the other pints, Liam's gone.

As I get back, Maddie's rolling her eyes at Stella and Ethan, who are kissing.

"Ugh, get a room." She turns, sliding her hand up the outside of my thigh and staring at me with her big brown eyes. She's wearing another of her dresses tonight, and even though it's fully spring in Ireland, it's still not quite warm enough to justify the short dress. But I'm damn thankful for it.

"Hey." I sit and press my lips to hers.

"Hi." She kisses me again, lingering a bit longer before pulling away. "What was that about?" Maddie nods her head to where I was with Liam at the bar.

"He apologized for hating me for the past five years."

"Wow."

"Yes. Wow." My eyes drift down to her bare legs. "You look gorgeous tonight, as usual." I settle a hand on her thigh.

"Thanks. Noreen just texted me. The flat will be ready next week after the current people check out and it gets cleaned. I have a feeling you guys canceled a few bookings for me."

I shrug. She's right.

"It'd be better if you were living with me." I squeeze her leg gently.

"Soon."

"When?"

"How about once we find out the Irish Oktoberfest is a huge hit?"

"It's a deal." I run my thumb along her soft leg, inching up to below the hem of her dress. "I was thinking, I don't know nearly enough about the woman I'm in love with."

"What do you want to know?"

"Hmm. First kiss?"

"Oh, lord. Freshman year of high school. A skinny kid who played guitar named Markus. In a dark science room after school."

"Wow."

"How about you?"

"I was sixteen. No, seventeen."

"Pretty late, huh?"

"Don't judge. I was too busy with soccer to worry about girls."

"Whatever you say." Maddie's eyes twinkle. "Tell me more."

"Her name was Elaine. I first said 'hi' to her at the corner shop and we met there every day for a week until I convinced her to let me stick my tongue down her throat. She never showed up again."

Maddie laughs and I savor the sight of her happiness and her smooth throat, begging for my lips.

"You must've improved dramatically since then," she says when she stops chuckling.

"You're so mean." I move my hand under her dress until it's borderline inappropriate and she inhales sharply.

"Next question?"

"When did you first leave the States?"

She tilts her head. "I visited Stella in London once a few years ago. That's it, though. I'd like to travel more now that I'm living here."

"We can make that happen."

"How about you? When did you start your international travels?"

"Mam and Dad took us to Paris when I was five. But I've traveled pretty much everywhere in Europe, and a handful of other places as well."

"Show off." Maddie rolls her eyes.

I lean forward to kiss her. "Hey, come with me. I have to show you something."

"What? Another gift?"

"Don't be greedy."

The side of her mouth turns up, and she lets me drag her through the crowded bar, past my sister serving drinks, and toward our dark hallway, the one that leads to the pub office, restrooms, stairs to the basement storage, and the locked door to the flat.

"Oh, are we going to have fun in the office again?"

I grin, remembering laying her out on the desk. "Not quite."

"Aw, shame."

"Another time, although Saoirse might have something to say about us defiling her office." I stop in the dark hallway and press my back against the wall, pulling her against me.

"Hey, tourist." Even in the dim light, I see her smiling, her eyes sparking.

She wraps her arms around my waist. I layer mine on top of hers.

"Hey, hot bartender."

"When we first met in this hallway, you told me you were getting over someone and needed a kiss to help you forget him."

"Did I say that? Pretty forward of me."

"It was. I'm so glad you took that chance."

"Me too."

"Have you done it? Forgotten him?"

She laughs. "I don't even remember his name."

"Good."

And I kiss her.

EPILOGUE
MADDIE

Saturday, June 7
(six weeks later)

Reese is wearing a stunning gray gown that sweeps the stone steps of Eilean Donan Castle as she descends to her bridal party, the backdrop of the Scottish Highlands breathtaking behind her. The dress has a neckline that dips down in a deep V with a simple A-line cut at the waist. The dark gray silk is covered in a lighter gray lace.

It's the perfect wedding dress for my big sister. I grip Stella's hand on one side, and my mom's hand on the other. Chelsea stands next to Mom, her hands clasped together. A local photographer snaps pictures.

"I feel ridiculous being the center of attention like this," Reese says, smiling at us and blushing prettily as she joins our group.

"You deserve to be the center of attention," Stella says. "And we need to document this day. It's important." She envelops Reese into a hug.

"Says the woman who doesn't believe in marriage." Reese pulls away and looks at Stella, reaching for Chelsea's hand.

298

"Just because I don't personally plan to get married doesn't mean I don't believe in love."

"Congratulations, Reese, you look perfect." I wrap my arms around my oldest sister, careful not to mess up her curled dark hair, so much like mine but stopping just below her shoulders and generally more styled and tamed. Mine is slightly less wild than usual today, thanks to the stylist.

"You really do look great, Mom," Chelsea says.

"You too, sweetheart." Reese touches Chelsea's blond waves, which look similar to her Aunt Stella's. "It means everything that you're here with me. That you're all here."

Tears spring to my eyes. Stella bites her lip, and tears drip down our mom's cheeks.

"Grandma, no! Your makeup!" Chelsea looks horrified.

Reese didn't go overboard on the intimate wedding, but she did spring on a professional makeup artist and hair stylist. I'm particularly enjoying the fake eyelashes that make us all look like we're using some kind of real-life filter.

We all laugh together, and the photographer clicks away, capturing the moment.

"What am I going to do with my three daughters living over here? And all in different countries?" Mom opens her arms and waves us into a group hug.

"I'll be in the US for most of the year, Grandma." Chelsea pulls away and poses with her hands on her hips. Over the last two days, she's peppered Oliver and Patrick with questions about their time playing pro soccer, as if she hadn't talked about it nonstop with Oliver back in Jersey. And she's desperate to come play in Europe, even though we all think she'll have a chance at playing in the US after college, which is the best for women's soccer.

I glance at my mom. Her remaining in New Jersey while I stay in Ireland has weighed on me. I feel like I'm abandoning her. And especially because I didn't expect Reese to move to Scotland. I thought she and Oliver would stay in her home in New Jersey forever, but then again, I didn't really think through the fact that they'd want to spend time with Oliver's son in Scotland after Chelsea graduated high school.

It's complicated, as is everything with love and family.

"Chelsea will be at college, but we will come back in the fall so we can see some of her games," says Reese when the hug breaks apart.

"Everyone understands, Mom," Chelsea says, a slight roll to her eyes confirming she is still a teenager, even if she's off to college soon. "Lucas needs you guys, too."

"Well . . ." Mom nods, but her eyes continue to fill with tears, threatening to overflow again. "Your stepfather and I decided we'll be spending every summer somewhere over here. We'll split our time between Scotland, England, and Ireland. We won't move here completely because of his kids and grandkids. But I can't bear to be apart from all of you."

I politely push those familiar feelings of doubt and guilt away. I have to live my life for me, not make decisions based on keeping my sisters or my mother happy. That's something I've learned since arriving in Ireland on a cold, rainy February day.

"Apologies for the interruption, but it's time." A man dressed in a kilt peeks around the corner, his thick Scottish accent absolutely glorious.

Mom's going to walk Reese into the outside courtyard of the castle and down the short aisle. Stella, Chelsea, and I leave them to take our seats first, weaving through the old stone castle walls and into the open area, down the aisle covered in a rolled-out white carpet, and toward the small group of people seated in silver folding chairs decorated with wide gray-and-white ribbon.

The Scottish weather came through for us today. Apparently, the default plan is to have the wedding ceremony in the Banqueting Hall—the biggest and prettiest room in the castle—as the weather is usually crappy.

But today, it's glorious. There's a scattering of dark clouds in the sky, but the sun is shining through the gloomy puffs. The mountains of the Isle of Skye tower a short way across the sea. I can't imagine a more romantic place for a wedding ceremony.

Oliver, dressed in a formal kilt, stands in the middle of the stone courtyard next to the wedding officiant, waiting for Reese.

"Our sister's marrying a seriously hot Scottish dude today," Stella whispers as we walk up the aisle.

I laugh and nod, but I'm really staring at my hot Irish dude, who's turned in his seat in the front row, waiting patiently for me to join him, an expression on his face that is heated and intense. There are about a dozen other people seated in the rows of white chairs. Oliver's parents and son are in the front row across the aisle from Patrick, next to Lucas's mother and her husband. Behind them are a handful of friends from Oliver's soccer life, including his old coach, who we met last night.

Stella settles between Patrick and Ethan, kissing her boyfriend on the mouth and then lifting a hand to Mom's husband, who is on the other side of Ethan. I slip into the empty seat next to Patrick. Reese had three friends from the US fly in to see her get married—her boss and two longtime friends from Chelsea's school years—and they are seated in the rows behind us, two of them with significant others and another on her own.

"You are beautiful." Patrick examines my face like I'm a detailed text to memorize before an exam, and lets his eyes wander down my body.

I can't help but blush under his heated assessment. Reese let her three bridesmaids—me, Stella, and Chelsea—pick out our own dresses. She suggested a dark color that would go with her gray dress, so Stella and I chose a mid-length dark blue silk dress from a shop in London. We video called with Chelsea to make sure she was happy with it as well.

My heart grows with warm joy at his words.

"Thank you. You clean up pretty well, too," I whisper. And it's true—he's smoking hot in a tuxedo. "But maybe you should consider wearing a kilt sometime." I nod my head toward Oliver.

"You offend me." Patrick gives me an unimpressed glare.

I bite back a smile. "A tuxedo works, I guess."

"I thought you just wanted me in a soccer kit?"

"Sure. That too." I shrug.

"Tourist. Behave." He leans down and presses our lips together, letting the kiss linger and taking my left hand in his. His fingers play with the silver Claddagh ring that's on my middle finger. He gave it to me for my birthday last month and explained that the heart represents love, the crown loyalty, and the two hands friendship. And if the tip of the heart is pointing toward my own heart, it means I'm taken. I'm definitely taken.

Everything is unbelievably perfect.

I've settled into my new role at Slea Head Brewery. Lola—the product development manager—is a delight and a match for my extroverted self. I've loved picking everyone's brains about what we can do with the brewery. There's an empty space two doors down that I want to rent and convert into a tasting room. We'll do tours of the brewery and send visitors there afterward. We'll sell merchandise and beer to go. We can make Slea Head Brewery a microbrewery destination for locals and tourists alike.

"You know I'd marry you today if I could, right?" he says as he breaks our kiss, putting a few inches between our lips.

Saoirse and Patrick's dad are watching over the brewery while we're here, and Niamh and Erin are taking care of Turtle, Kitty, and Gator.

Yup, the girls named my baby goat Alligator, Gator for short.

"I know." I nod and kiss him again.

I've been overseas for three months, and Dingle feels more like my home than anywhere else I've ever been. Saoirse and the girls are a second family to me. Lola is a new bestie, and Noreen has even been extra friendly, although it's taken me a minute to stop picturing her and Patrick together.

Liam's come into O'Brien's more frequently and occasionally he and Patrick chat about the breweries or talk shit about soccer. It's a tentative truce.

Liam still hasn't scored a goal against Patrick.

"There she is!" Stella whispers from next to me, as if we didn't just see the bride a few minutes ago.

I turn to watch Reese walk toward us, her arm linked with Mom's. My sister looks beautiful in the gray dress that matches both her eyes and the moody Scottish sky. Her gaze is locked with the man waiting for her at the end of the aisle.

"She's so bonnie!" Oliver's son loudly states from across the aisle, and everyone chuckles quietly, his mother shushing him with a smile.

"She is the *most* bonnie woman in the world," Oliver says to his son.

Patrick leans into my ear, his lips brushing against the bottom of my earlobe.

"You should know that you are the most beautiful woman in the world. I'll keep that to myself for now, given it's your sister's wedding day."

I squeeze his hand. My sister reaches Oliver, hugs my mother, then kisses her soon-to-be husband on the lips.

"Dear family and friends, we are gathered here today . . ."

Patrick brings my hand to his lips.

"I love you, Maddie."

And I know he does.

It's the beginning of forever for us, too.

The End

WANT to read one more chapter with Maddie & Patrick? Get the bonus epilogue by subscribing to Chrissy's newsletter on her website: www.ChrissyHopewell.com. Also available to Chrissy's newsletter subscribers: *One Hundred Lights*, a free novella, other bonus material, plus the latest news on upcoming releases.

Loved *Since We're Here?* Leave an honest review on Amazon or Goodreads. It helps so much!

Check out *Unless It's You*, Stella & Ethan's love story.

Check out *If We Pretend*, Reese & Oliver's love story.

Stay in touch:
Instagram: @ChrissyHopewell
Facebook: ChrissyHopewellAuthor
TikTok: @ChrissyHopewellBooks
Email: Chrissy@ChrissyHopewell.com

Free novella & bonus chapters:
www.ChrissyHopewell.com

MADDIE'S 12 DAY IRISH ROAD TRIP

Day 1—3 Dublin: Temple Bar, Guinness Brewery, Trinity College/ Book of Kells; Quirk: Hungry Tree

Day 3 Northern Ireland, Belfast: Quirk: Salmon of Knowledge statute

Day 4 Northern Ireland drive: Dark Hedges, Giant's Causeway, Carrick-a-Rede rope bridge; Quirk: Madman's Window

Day 5 Donegal; Quirk: hole in the ground at St Patrick's Purgatory that's rumored to be a gateway to hell

Day 6 Galway: Quirk: Footgolf

Day 7 Travel day: Cliffs of Moher; Limerick; Quirk: Clare Glens forest waterfall

Day 8-9 Dingle: Ring of Kerry drive, Ian's tattoo shop, Slea Head Brewery, bike ride; Quirk: old stone beehive huts that hermit monks lived in fourteen hundred years ago

Day 10 Travel day: Blarney Castle (County Cork); Rock of Cashel (County Tipperary); Quirk: Butter Museum (County Cork)

Day 11 Travel day ending in Dublin: Wicklow Mountains National Park, Glendalough (County Cork); Quirk: Viking massacre cave in Kilkenny

Day 12 Dublin

ACKNOWLEDGMENTS

I really hope you loved immersing yourself in Ireland as much as I loved writing about it. When I was nineteen, I spent a summer in Dublin with a friend. We got jobs at pubs and traveled around the country. I still question my parents' decision to approve that trip! Back then, I didn't bike Slea Head Drive in Dingle because it was raining and I was wearing glasses. Having Maddie do it in *Since We're Here* was my way of rectifying that mistake. I should probably get back over there and do it in person, but until then, this book will have to be good enough.

As always, thank you to everyone who's been there for me in this journey, including my Pitch Wars support network and all my beta readers and CPs who made this book so much better, especially Sarah and Ericka. Thanks to my high school besties, Discord writing buddies (looking at you, Cincy Authors Coven), and my husband and (mostly) delightful children for cheering me on.

Thank you to my editor, Brenda Chin, my cover designer, Stephanie Anderson at Alt 19 Creative, and Lindsey Hinkel, my proofreader.

Last but not least, thank you, dear readers, for coming along on this journey with me!

Love, Chrissy

ABOUT THE AUTHOR

Chrissy Hopewell started her love for romance novels by sneaking her mom's steamy books in middle school. She has spent varying amounts of time overseas, including working at a pub in Dublin, waitressing at a hotel in the Scottish Borders, and studying and living in London. Because of these experiences, international flair and accents often show up in her writing. Chrissy now lives in the suburbs of Cincinnati, Ohio with her family, and she no longer has to sneak what she reads.

instagram.com/chrissyhopewell

tiktok.com/@chrissyhopewellbooks

facebook.com/chrissyhopewellauthor